Dilemma

Volume Two of The Ellie Rose Series

ANGELA CAIRNS

WINDSINGER BOOKS

www.angelacairnsauthor.co.uk

For permission requests, contact the author at
angela@angelacairnsauthor.co.uk

ISBN Number: 978-1-8384074-0-7

Cover design – Shannon Kuzmich
Interior Formatting by Platform House Publishing
www.platformhousepublishing.com

To my beloved Gordon Setters, Ginny, and Wooster,
you remain beside me always.

To Mum,

With love
from
[illegible] xxx

Acknowledgements

To my Friday Friends from the Writers Company at Wivenhoe, all talented authors. Thank you for beta reading and for your continuous support.
www.thewriterscompany.co.uk

To Becky Wright at Platform House Publishing for interior artwork and formatting the text – I would be lost without you. www.platformhousepublishing.co.uk

To Kay at Full Proof Editing for doing an amazing copy editing job. www.fullproofediting.com

To Susan Yearwood from the Susan Yearwood Literary Agency for your editorial advice.
www.susanyearwoodagency.com

To Shannon Kuzmitch for the beautiful cover design
www.shannonkuzmitch.com

To my social media writing family, it would be hard to find a more supportive group anywhere. Thank you for sharing all the ups and downs, and literally for sharing.

Prologue

My name is Ellie Rose. I'm a physiotherapist, I'm in love, and my life is fine.

Well, it is now. If you'd seen me five years ago, I was falling apart, standing in the middle of my shattered dreams. My boyfriend and soulmate, Brett, died. He was thirty, talented, and I loved him. We had plans to marry, work together and travel, but those plans died with him.

Brett and I started as flatmates when I was in Australia, taking a post-graduate physiotherapy course. He was a physio too, but also a semi-professional photographer. We fell in love one evening quite by accident. If I hadn't stopped to smell the frangipani, hadn't worn that red dress and the glance that became the look, that became the kiss hadn't happened, my heart would not have been broken. But it's too late to think like that. What happened, happened, and we had one idyllic Summer together that was perfect in every way.

The one tiny flaw? He ought never to have died. He should have been with me.

When my course ended, Brett promised that he'd come to England to meet my family so they'd understand why I was emigrating. But he got an exciting job offer, a photography contract to capture sunrise photographs over the Australian outback for Nature magazine, and he chose to do that instead. We argued for the first time about his decision, and I felt hurt and angry. In the end, we compromised, and I left for England alone.

We thought we had all the time in the world to work things out when I got back, except there was the accident. Brett's plane went down, exploded on impact, and he died. I will never forget that phone call, my flatmate Annie's voice on the phone, choked by tears whispering, "He's gone, Ellie. Brett's gone."

A free spirit and maverick, Brett brought out a side to me that I hadn't realised existed. I grieved for him and that sense of adventure for long after he was gone but found a new way to survive. I worked hard, cared for others, and built a thriving career.

Time blunts the knife-like pain of loss, and I began to look back less. Eventually, I realised that I was in danger of being blind to a second chance for happiness. Mark is my new partner. I love him in a quiet, steady way, less impulsive and breathless. He was wounded from a sham relationship when we first knew each other. We've felt our way together and tried to trust and love again.

Chapter One

Pen's Baby

Mark waved his piece of toast cheerily as he headed for the door, planting a buttery, Marmite kiss on my lips. "See you tonight, Gorgeous."

"I'm calling in on Pen on my way home. I think it's today Angus goes up to Scotland with his dad. I'll check she's OK and maybe bring her up for dinner. She probably won't eat otherwise."

He nodded, still chewing. "Good plan, gotta' run, Babe or I'll be late."

"Go, GO!" I almost shouted. I watched Mark fold his tall slim body into the front seat of his car, his mop of curly brown hair lifting slightly in the breeze. He owed his olive skin to the Italian side of his family, and the long-lidded, almond-shaped, brown eyes were almost the same as his Mother Alessandra's. I felt that familiar tug of attraction to him that made me feel warm inside. I glimpsed the brown skin above his white shirt collar. It was a favourite spot of mine to plant a trail of kisses, but that wouldn't happen today. Mark was always finessed in the morning, leaving no margin for error on time. I was used to it now after living together for a year and had ceased to let it stress me or to make comparison.

My own pale skin, dotted with freckles and russet-coloured hair, spoke of a Celtic background, but as far as we knew from the family tree, I was English on both sides. Of medium height with an hourglass figure, my childhood dream of being tall and willowy had not been granted by my fairy godmother.

I sighed as I watched Mark go, if only our relationship was always this easy. I thought back to our conversation of the night before.

"You know you said you'd like a family 'some time'?" Mark said.

"Yes?" I'd cosily thought that my previous answer had been enough to put the matter to bed for a while. In my mind, some time was in the hazy future.

He smiled and took my hands. "Well, what about soon, like now?"

"It takes nine months minimum! Even I can't change that," I prevaricated.

He looked at his watch. "We'd better get started then!" He was joking, but the thought intruded on my currently perfectly happy consciousness that somehow he was serious.

I felt a flutter of anxiety start to gnaw at the pit of my stomach. I wasn't sure I was ready to have a baby yet. Running my business was a full-time occupation, and adding a baby to an already hectic schedule seemed daunting. For one thing, I couldn't begin to imagine how much reorganisation would be needed at the clinic. It seemed very unfair that the baby clock ticks faster for women than men. At thirty-two, I'd already had numerous remarks suggesting I needed to make up my mind about a baby quickly. No one was plaguing Mark like this about biological clocks. They were still talking to him about normal things like work and football.

Mark had let the subject drop, and he seemed fine this morning, but I'd lain awake last night thinking of all the reasons why this wasn't a good idea right now.

As his car disappeared around the bend in the drive, I turned back to the house.

The barn sat on the edge of our friends' Angus and Pen's farm on the Maldon Road. It belonged to Mark, and I had moved in with him just over a year ago.

Robin, my colleague at the clinic, was currently renting my cottage. A pretty doll's house of a place that I'd bought before I met Mark.

Work on the barn conversion we currently live in had been Mark's salvation after he discovered the truth about his relationship with his fiancée Katrina. We'd been new friends, little more than acquaintances when I'd first seen the barn. I watched it turn from a semi-ruin into the beautiful home it was now, and during the process, our friendship turned to love.

Mark had done most of the work himself, which had helped him piece his life back together. During the time he was renovating, Mark also decided to turn his back on a corporate career in favour of quality of life and his sanity. He had begun to work with small businesses as a consultant.

People are generally more important to me than places, but the barn had always had a warm, positive energy, and it was a special place for us. I particularly loved the open beams that arced over the interior. Mark had restored them by hand with hours of painstaking work. Their surface scars belied their strength, and warmth radiated from their rich, golden colour. I looked at them lovingly as I crossed towards the study and decided to ring Pen to check if it was convenient to pop in this afternoon. My best friend, confidante and dog training partner had already taken the plunge. She was eight months pregnant and far from blooming. If I felt like her when I was pregnant, I'd struggle to work, that was certain.

I dialled Pen's number at the farm and waited for her to pick up. I imagined her late pregnancy rolling gait as she moved towards the phone. "Hi Hun, how are you today?"

She huffed, "What, apart from the vomiting, the backache, and the stretch marks? Everything's peachy!"

I sympathised with the note of bitterness and desperation, she had been through hell. "Is the sickness bad today?"

"Every day, Ellie. I thought this would be over at three months. How did I get this stupid Hyperemesis Gravidarium crap? I was supposed to bounce through pregnancy with a wonderful glow, looking queenly and fecund. I look terrible."

I remembered how dreadful Pen had looked the last time we met. Pen's normally thick, bouncy hair was dry and brittle, her beautiful rosy cheeks were pale, and her skin seemed slightly grey. She was also way too thin, apart from her neat, round bump.

Never fat, Pen usually looked curvy and fit, oozing good health from every pore, but somehow she'd shrunk and seemed listless and frail. We had all been worried about her, Angus, her husband, most of all.

I tapped a pen that was lying by the phone on the notepad "You aren't a great advert for this pregnancy lark, Pen."

"I know, sorry. Not many people get extreme sickness like this, though, no one I know has ever had it. Don't let me put you off, Ellie. You'll probably sail through the whole nine months."

I began to doodle a border on the top page. "Maybe, but what if I don't?"

I could almost see the silent shrug. "Well, you'll cope, I suppose; it's not like you get a choice."

"I'm not sure I'm ready anyway." I punctuated my speech with question marks and exclamations on the page. "I've always thought I'd have kids sometime – as in the future nebulous, but Mark is getting really serious about us trying for a family now. It's alright for him. Whatever would I do at the clinic if I was ill like you've been or had complications?"

Pen sounded slightly impatient. "I can see your point, but you can't make all your decisions based around work, Ellie. Putting it off won't change those issues anyway, they'll be there whenever you go for it. It would be lovely if our kids were close in age, too."

I rolled my eyes. "Don't you start, Pen Drayton, you sound like Mark."

I didn't want to point out to her that she and I weren't in quite the same boat. I had a business loan to repay, and I'd worked so hard to get Touch, my physiotherapy clinic, up and running.

I knew Pen worked hard, too, she was always busy, but hers wasn't a formal nine-to-five job. She had married into a lifestyle; she helped her husband Angus on their farm, did heaps of important community work and ran her home.

To me, Touch wasn't just a business either. I had been through so much after Brett's death and had stumbled through the first years, longing to turn back the clock and have him with me still. Touch was a symbol that I had come through the worst of it and had learned to survive by keeping Brett's memory in my heart as I moved on, one day at a time. I wasn't sure Pen fully understood, so I changed the subject.

"Did Angus go to Scotland today?"

"Yes, his dad was desperate to see his brother. He's quite elderly now and has been so unwell. Angus wanted to see his uncle too. This week was the last opportunity for Angus to go for a while, partly because of me and the baby but also because the wheat harvest will start soon. Just waiting for a good Hagberg."

I frowned, "What on earth is that?"

"Angus could tell you better, but it's a test which shows when the wheat is ready to harvest so that you get flour-grade wheat."

I began to doodle ears of wheat on the phone pad. "Does Angus have to do the testing?"

"No, the co-operative we sell to, send their scientific officer round. Angus is hoping to get the harvest done before the baby is born, so he'll have more free time with us."

I nodded, "Angus told me he felt he had to go otherwise, his dad would have gone off on his own, and he didn't want him to."

"Yes, his dad would, that's the problem, but he oughtn't drive all that way alone. It's not that long since his heart attack, and with all the stress of his brother being so ill…"

I felt deflated at the mention of Angus's uncle close to death. The grief of this finality came back for a moment as if Brett's death were yesterday, and I caught my breath. Completely over his loss, I wasn't sure why Brett had been intruding into my thoughts more recently. I was glad that Angus and his family would have time to say their goodbyes. Brett and I had not been that lucky.

I turned my ears of wheat into a wreath, then scribbled over it and ripped off the page. I screwed it up and launched it into the bin. "He seemed a bit torn when I spoke to him."

"He was, even though he's decided to go. Angus is fretting that the baby may come early and he'll miss the birth. I told him to stop fussing. First babies are always late."

Angus had been to see me before he left, and we'd had a long chat. He was an interesting guy. Before I knew him, he'd come back to the farm temporarily because of his dad's illness but was now in charge and staying permanently. I kept forgetting he'd been in human resources in the city before that. He sometimes surprised me with his quiet observation of people and situations. His lazy eyes under slightly hooded lids didn't miss a trick.

He felt between a rock and a hard place because he was so worried about Pen. I'd promised to keep an eye on her and help with the dog walking while he took his father to Scotland.

Daisy and Belle were Pen's Pointers and were great pals with my Gordon Setters, Jeeves and Bird. As Mark and I neighboured Pen and Angus's farm, it was no hardship to help. Pen and I often walked together. It was nice to return the favour as well. Pen had looked after my dogs often enough when I was setting up the clinic.

"Shall I bring my acupuncture needles around after work, and we'll do a session for your nausea again? It helped for a while last time…"

She sighed, "Anything, Ellie, anything would be great."

I glanced at the clock as I rang off. It was time to head for Touch.

Just a short drive away, I reached work in under ten minutes and thanked my lucky stars for the umpteenth time that I didn't have to commute like so many people in the town did. The dogs hopped out of the car on their leads and, as we went inside, headed happily to their beds in the office – they knew the drill. Robin, my colleague, was already working. He was an early bird and happily treated people before they went into work from six onwards. I felt more human if I came to gently, walked the dogs and then faced the day sometime after eight.

I heard the hum of his Kiwi accent and a muffled laugh as I walked past his treatment room. I smiled. When he came to the clinic in an emergency last year, he had been a godsend for me. Persuaded to stay, he already had a large group of devotees who loved his no-nonsense kindness and can-do attitude. Robin looked like the clean-cut boy-next-door and had something about him which invited confidences. He had fallen for one of my patients, Louise, and they looked like a long-term item. I was glad he had fallen for a local girl, in part out of self-interest. I had built the practice from scratch, working alone. Now, I didn't know what I would do without him.

With her head deep in the stationery cupboard, I made Sarah, my practice manager, jump out of her skin with my cheery 'Good Morning!'

She put a hand over her heart. "Ellie, I almost had a heart attack. You're early."

I grimaced, "I need to get a couple of letters done before I start. I want to get away promptly this afternoon to see Pen."

Sarah immediately looked worried. "Is everything alright?"

I made a so-so gesture with my hand. "She is still sick all the time and a bit down. I know Angus needed to go away, but I don't like to think of her on her own. I'll try to persuade her to come and stay with us at the barn, but she's as stubborn as a mule!"

"Takes one to know one," Sarah retorted, raising her eyebrows. "You gave us plenty of trouble when you injured your knee last year, being Miss Independent."

I laughed, "Touché! I shall grab a coffee and make myself scarce. Are you here all day? Or is Lizzie in as well?"

"Lizzie takes over at lunchtime because I came in early to cover Robin's early start."

I had several progress reports to write for my patients, so I started on my first letter. Walt Newman, the orthopaedic surgeon who had fixed my knee last year, had been as good as his word and sent us a steady stream of post-operative patients to rehab. I was worried about one of them, Maureen.

She had been attending physiotherapy on and off for many years with a gradually worsening knee. Despite her predilection for cream cakes and sweets, her total aversion to exercise and her steadily expanding waistline, we had managed to stave off the surgery for nearly five years. Six weeks ago, she had finally had a routine knee replacement. Initially, her recovery had seemed standard, but this last few days, she wasn't doing well. Maureen was in a lot of pain, and her knee remained obstinately hot and swollen. Mysterious bruising kept appearing too, so I wanted some checks done.

I had made an emergency appointment for her with Walt because of a nagging doubt that she may have an infection. She had promised to collect her letter on the way to her appointment.

Letters dictated and handed to Sarah, and I was on time to welcome my first patient. Then, it was so busy that it hardly seemed five minutes until I collected the home visit box. A small, rectangular toolbox, it worked very well to house physio essentials for home visits. I headed to the farm to see Pen.

"Helloooo," I called as I kicked off my shoes and opened the side door.

"In here," came the reply.

Surprised not to find Pen in the kitchen, it was her normal lair, with its big Aga and comfy wheel-backed chairs around the refectory table. I walked through to the spacious living room, where I found her pacing restlessly in front of a fan.

"I'm so hot, I can't get comfortable," she complained.

Pen looked very pale with beads of perspiration over her top lip. "Shall I make us a cup of tea? Or a cordial or something?"

She looked at me with something akin to loathing and rushed as best she could waddle in the direction of the downstairs toilet from where the sound of retching soon emanated. When the spasm passed, she came back looking grey and exhausted. "This baby will be the death of me," she groaned. "I can barely sip water today, and my back is so achy. I'm having loads of those Braxton Hicks contraction things too. They are bloody painful."

I nodded, feeling sorry for her plight. "Can you get comfy anywhere? Then we can try acupuncture, and I can massage your back while the needles are working."

In the end, sitting on a gym ball, leaning forwards onto the table on a pile of pillows, seemed best, and Pen began to relax as we worked.

She gave a sigh of contentment. "Ellie, do me a favour, can you cancel your life and stay here to rub my back all day? That's heaven."

I laughed, "Get in the queue, Pen, I've had a few requests for full-time attendance from patients already. Have you heard from Angus?"

She nodded, "He rang from Scotch Corner. They still have about four hours to go. So, at least they'll get a night's sleep. He and his dad are staying at the farm tonight with his auntie and can visit his uncle tomorrow. They'll be in time to see him, but he hasn't got long."

"Good job they made the journey then."

Her voice wobbled as she answered. "I wish I could have gone. I won't see Angus's uncle again, and he was lovely." She promptly burst into tears, which was so unlike her. It worried me more than anything else, the poor girl was at the end of her tether. "I feel so useless," she wailed, wiping tears furiously across her face.

I held her and let her cry. In the face of her distress, I felt useless myself

Eventually, she was all cried out, and I grabbed a tissue from the home visit box. Her previously grey face was livid and blotched with tears, and I wracked my brain to think of anything else that might help.

I gave her a hand to stand up. "Why don't you put your feet up on the couch for a moment, Hun."

Her hand closed over my arm. "Ellie, you won't decide not to have a baby because I've been ill, will you? I mean, after what you said this morning, I'd be devastated." Tears were threatening to spill over again, so I hastened to reassure her.

"No, don't be silly. You're not to fret about me. Look, back in the day, Brett and I both wanted kids, and I had no doubts at all, but that was us imagining a rosy, romantic future." I paused, seeking the right words. "I've more responsibility now, and I'm older. The idea of having a baby is much more real. The truth is, I like my life the way it is, and I don't know if I'm ready to change all that."

Her face creased with concern. "Have you talked to Mark about this properly? It's just he seems to think…"

I pulled a face, "Tell me about it. We do need to talk more, but I need to get things straight in my mind first." I gave her a playful tap. "This is all your fault, putting ideas into Mark's head."

She laughed slightly doubtfully. "I'd talk to Mark first about how you'd manage a family between you. He might take on half the childcare as you're both self-employed. At least he'd see you were thinking about it seriously, and you might feel less like you're going to lose your life and more like it's a new adventure for you both to share."

I shrugged, "Maybe, I'll see. Look, shall I give the dogs a quick run? Then you could come back to the barn with me until Angus gets back from Scotland."

"Oh yes, please give the dogs a run, that'd be great, poor things, but I think I'm better off here. If I threw up all the time at your house, I'd feel mortified, and I can wander about here, even in the middle of the night, without worrying anyone. Thank you for the offer, though."

I frowned, "Think about it while I'm out. I promise we don't mind any of that. If you aren't comfortable with coming to the barn, perhaps I could come and stay with you for a couple of nights instead."

"We'll see," was all she would say. "I don't feel as sick since the acupuncture."

I left, wondering what to say to Mark once I was home, as I secured dog leads and walked out.

Chapter Two

A Long Night

When I returned to the farm, about half an hour later, all four dogs had heaving flanks and lolling tongues, having run the length of the nearby sea wall. Close to the farm, the river Crouch widened to form the start of its estuary. At the boundary of the fields, water-meadow merged into saltmarsh, and man-made flood defences made a high path along the riverbank. I loved the breeze up there as I walked along the top. The gentle palette of the Essex countryside reflected the dry climate and glowed from straw golds through to dry greens on one side of the path. On the other was the broad river channel where the water could lap menacingly pewter at the top of the sea wall at high tide. Today we'd seen a narrow, low tide flow which exposed shiny mudflats and hidden islands, a temporary hunting ground for wading birds. The dogs had careered up and down the steep banks of the flood defence, abandoned to the joy of running. I popped them in the kennels to cool off and made my way into Pen. She looked ashen as if she'd seen a ghost.

"Ellie, unless I just seriously wet myself, I think my waters broke while you were out." She groaned with pain and clutched at her back and abdomen. “Oh my God, the baby’s coming. What are we going to do? Angus is in Scotland! I can’t have the baby yet.”

Clicking into professional mode, I said, “Too late to worry about that, Pen. How many contractions have you had?”

She shook her head as if trying to marshall her thoughts. “Three or four, I think.”

I quickly did the sums in my head. That made them fairly frequent, judging by the time I’d been out. “Where’s your list of phone numbers?” I asked, maintaining a fair imitation of calm but with a thousand thoughts flashing through my mind. Pen indicated a folder on the table, which I rifled through until I found the local maternity unit’s number.

I waitcd as thc phonc rang and rang.

C’mon, c’mon, where are you? I thought frantically. Finally, someone answered. “St John’s, midwife speaking.”

“Ellie Rose, physiotherapist, I’m with my friend Pen Drayton. Her waters have broken, and she’s in labour, contractions every seven minutes. She is week thirty-five currently.” I looked at Pen to confirm, and she nodded as she paced up and down, holding her back.

“Right-Ho!” came the cheerful reply. “The main thing is to stay nice and calm. There will be plenty of time. Can you get her to us? Or do you need an ambulance? We need to do a check-up as soon as possible because the baby is early. It’s obviously in a rush to join us.”

Glad to have clear instructions and comforted by her confidence, I said, “I can get her to you. Anything we should do in the meantime?”

"Bring some towels for the car. We'll be waiting for you. Drive carefully."

The next contraction was on us, and I talked Pen through it, breathing with her. When it was over, I said, "Listen, I'll grab some essentials for you, I think we'll get going. I'm going to see if Mark is home to drive us, or if not, unfortunately, you're coming in the dog car. We can sort everything else out later."

Pen looked anxious. "What about Angus? He wanted to be here. Ellie, this is all wrong. What about Angus?" She creased her face as the next contraction came, and I could see she was close to tears again.

"We won't worry about Angus for now. I'll get Mark to contact him. I'm sure we can get him on a flight or something. Mark can sort that out. The main thing is to get you into the hospital."

Pen's face crumpled. "Ellie, please, can you stay with me, please. I don't think I can do this on my own."

"Of course, I'll stay, don't be silly. I'm not going to leave you." I gave her a smile, which I hoped exuded confidence and took in her frightened face. "Let me call Mark before the next contraction."

He picked up, he was home early for once, and I'd never been happier to hear his voice. "Pen's gone into labour early, Mark. I need you to take us to St John's. She's devastated that Angus isn't here and quite frightened."

He seemed un-phased and always a good man in a crisis said, "On my way. Have you got what you need for Pen? Get her to write down Angus's contact number in Scotland, and I'll do my level best to contact him."

Another groan from Pen. I glanced at my watch, that was a shorter gap, six minutes, and the contraction lasted longer this time. I wracked my brains for all my student maternity training. I was beginning to wonder if Pen had been in the first stage of labour earlier without realising. She might be further along than we realised. "Hun, where is the TENS machine I ordered you? We could get it set up, and it will help with the pain."

Gasping, she said, "It's by the bed. I was looking at it the other night when I couldn't sleep."

I collected up the little machine and its electrodes and ran back downstairs. With the electrodes in place and the controller in her hand, I hoped the prospect of some pain relief and something she could do to mask the contractions would make her feel less anxious.

It was a relief to hear Mark's car pull in, and I was thankful that it was not low to the ground like his best friend Dom's sporty job. Mark walked through the door, looked from my forced smile to Pen's panicked face, and immediately lied. "Ellie says you're doing great! Come on, I'll help you to the car."

"The dogs," she gasped, "what about the dogs? I can't leave them."

Mark rubbed her hand and said, "Pen, you don't need to worry about them now. I will be back to collect them just as soon as you're safely at the hospital."

She clung to his arm and looked up at him. "And Angus, can you get Angus?"

I nodded and handed Mark a paper with the number Pen had given me. He smiled reassuringly, "I'll ask Dominic, see what he can do. You're not to worry. We'll get it sorted."

I timed contractions, and we breathed through them as Mark drove towards our closest maternity unit in

Chelmsford. He kept up his flow of reassuring small talk, which seemed to soothe Pen's restless worry. Only a slight sheen of sweat on his forehead betrayed that he had any concerns.

As we drew up in front of the door to the maternity wing, we rode through another contraction, a five-minute gap this time. A midwife came to the car and took Pen's arm. She looked up at Mark and said, "Are you, Dad?"

"No, just a friend," he replied.

I turned to Mark, "Can you go rescue the dogs and see what you can do to get Angus here? I have a feeling Pen is further on than she thinks."

"OK, you'll do a great job as his stand-in. Love you," he called as I turned to follow Pen inside.

St John's was an old Victorian building, formerly a workhouse, then a mental health institution – it had been a hospital since just before the Second World War. As I sat outside Pen's room while the staff settled her in and took an initial assessment, I felt reassured by the old-fashioned gloss-painted walls and government-issue green curtains around the beds. The staff seemed lovely, and there was an air of efficiency about the place.

"You're the physio I spoke to on the phone," said another midwife, who introduced herself as Gill, as she came out of Pen's room. "That's good, someone sensible. I've been coping with fathers getting high, having sneaky drags on the gas and air all evening. Then one passed out, hit his head, and ended up in A&E." She grinned, "Anyway, Pen's coming along nicely, not quite in the second stage yet. You can go in."

In the dimmed light of the room, as the night wore on, orchestrated by the rhythm of Pen's contractions, I lost all sense of time. I did what women have done through millennia; comforted, massaged, encouraged, supported and waited, hoping that everything would be all right. Relaxed by the gas and air, Pen became less fretful, her energy and concentration absorbed in her labour.

About four a.m, something changed, the contractions deepened, and Pen, taken by surprise, said, "I need to push." She became fretful again, wanting to stand up. "Don't let it come 'til Angus gets here, Ellie. I can't do this without Angus."

The midwife had warned me that this transition could feel out of control and scary, so I did my best to comfort her. "You're doing great, Pen. I'm going to get the midwife. Then if you like, I'll pop out to the phone; Mark may have some news."

"Yes, please, Ellie, tell him to hurry up." But as I started to leave, another contraction came, and she shouted, "No, don't go!"

Gill appeared at the door; she nodded to me, "Off you go. Pen, listen to me; I'm sure Ellie needs to pee, she'll just be gone a moment, and I need to listen to baby's heartbeat anyway."

The phone at the barn had barely rung when Mark answered, "How is it all going?"

"She's doing well, Mark, but she's on the last stretch and wants Angus. Did you get hold of him?"

"Better than that, Ellie… Dominic put some calls in. A wealthy business mate of his was in Scotland playing golf with his private plane. He knows some useful people. Anyway, the guy offered to fly Angus back, and Dom should be driving him in at any time."

I grinned into the phone stupidly, "You are kidding me!"

He chuckled, "Nope, hand on heart. Dom rang about half an hour ago to say they'd landed."

"Oh, my goodness, Mark, you're amazing. Dom's amazing. I love you to bits. Let's hope Angus makes it in time. I am so going to hug that man when I see him. Look, I can't stay; I'd better get back to Pen with the good news."

"Are you alright? It's been a bit of a night."

"It has, but I'm fine, running on adrenaline."

"I've asked Sarah to move your client list from tomorrow, hope that's okay. I didn't think you'd be in any state to go in."

I blew a kiss into the phone. "I love you even more if that's possible."

I tiptoed back into the labour room as Pen seemed to be resting with her eyes closed. She opened them wearily.

I smiled, "Taking a breather? Would you like something to drink?"

Pen rolled her head to look at the bedside locker. "Can I have some cold water, please? I'm thirsty, and I'm tired, Ellie, I want this baby out now."

I passed her a glass with a straw, and she took a couple of sips. "You're amazing, Pen," I said, wiping her face with a cold flannel. "Angus is coming. He got a flight, and Dom is driving him here right now."

She looked at me, "Are you just saying that?"

I shook my head, "No, it's true, Mark told me."

She sighed. The first light of dawn was bathing the room in a soft glow. "Listen, I can hear the birds."

I held her hand, and we both listened to the dawn chorus; we were in the eye of the storm.

The next run of contractions was violent, and Pen seemed to withdraw into a world of her own, gasping for breath between contractions. It was at the end of one of these that Angus arrived, face alight with worry, apologies tumbling from his lips.

Pen looked up as the door opened. "A bit late," she said.

He gave a rueful smile. "Better late than never. I thought I wasn't going to make it. Dom broke the land speed record getting me here."

Pen gasped, "Let me up, I need to get up," the next contraction was coming. Quite naturally, as if he'd been doing this all his life, Angus supported her half squatting as her whole body contracted, pushing the baby down.

Five, twenty-seven exactly; during the last three contractions, Pen had been told to huff, hold back and not push. With the last effort, first the head, then shoulders, and finally, the whole baby arrived and was laid tenderly on Pen's stomach. After a tense moment, a thin cry broke the silence.

"Congratulations, you have a baby girl," said Gill.

The baby was tiny but perfectly formed with a crown of dark hair and ridiculously long lashes. She was pink and bruised from the epic struggle, five pounds six ounces, and not much bigger than her Daddy's hands.

Angus stared in wonder. "You did it, Pen, you did it," he kept repeating over.

Exhausted, Pen nevertheless looked at her baby with love, then turned to look at me and stretched out a weary hand, which I took. "Thank you, Ellie."

I smiled, took one last look at the baby, and turned to leave the new family to their moment. I walked outside into the morning of a new day. At that moment, overcome by a torrent of emotion, I knew everything had changed forever, again. Like the morning I took the phone call telling me that

Brett had died, five years ago now. The intense love for her baby that I'd seen in Pen's eyes irrationally made me afraid for her. I'd felt that same body and soul love for Brett, and it had only brought me pain.

I looked around the almost empty car park and realised I had no transport. I suddenly felt drained and sank onto the low wall outside the hospital, not knowing what to do next.

Chapter Three

A Star is Born

I barely registered the headlights as they entered the car park until a familiar voice said, “Taxi for Miss Rose.” I looked up.

“Mark! It’s you, oh, thank goodness.”

“Of course, it’s me,” he grinned, “who did you think it was at five in the morning? Dom came back and said he’d dropped off Angus, so I thought I’d come and wait, but here you are.”

“I am so pleased to see you,” I managed to say before the fatigue and emotion overcame me and tears ran streaming down my cheeks.

“Hey, what’s wrong? Is something wrong with Pen or the baby?”

“No, the baby is stunning, a little girl with the longest eyelashes. Pen is a bit battered and so tired but doing fine. I’m just exhausted, I think; take no notice.”

“It wasn’t a usual midweek evening, that’s for sure,” he said, turning to me, eyes full of love and with a proud smile on his face. “I think we’re a good team in an emergency. Let’s hope it isn’t this dramatic when it’s our turn.”

I faltered, "Our turn?"

He smiled, eyes alight with anticipation. "Yes, when we have a baby. I can't wait. Pen and Angus have made me feel broody."

I frowned, "We aren't quite there yet, are we?"

He shrugged, "No, but I assumed it would be soon. Before Katrina left me, she and I had planned, at least, she said she wanted kids, and you and Brett did too." He paused, and a flicker of pain showed in his eyes. "I know, as it turned out, everything Katrina and I planned was based on lies, but I genuinely wanted to have a family." He turned to face me. "I'd still like that, a steady home, a family, but with you, Ellie, based on something solid and real. We've been together a while now. This is a good time, isn't it?"

I wasn't ready to commit to the whole baby thing yet, so I fobbed him off. "This isn't the right moment to be talking to me about babies. After what's just happened, it might take me a while to feel enthusiastic about giving birth. Give me a break!"

His face fell, and his voice sounded flat. "There's never a good time though, Ellie. You're always putting me off. What's so different about me that you aren't sure about having a family. You were sure with Brett."

I was more than exhausted, and welling up from a dark place inside, I felt an old fear gnawing at me. It had been so hard to cope after Brett died, to rebuild a new life for myself, and I had done it by founding and developing Touch. Pen was a big part of that new life, too, our walks with the dogs, our long chats and laughter. Then Mark came along, and we were happy as a couple.

Suddenly all the things that had made me feel safe were changing because of the baby coming, and Mark wanting a family made me feel vulnerable again.

My insecurity made me lash out. "Don't you dare make this about Brett or try to compare. It's not about him and you or who I love the most. I'm a different person now. I have a business to consider; we have a lovely life. I want to enjoy that for a while. After everything I went through, and after what you went through with Katrina, is that so terrible?"

He looked exasperated. "Ellie, can't we move on and make our own life without looking back or being afraid?"

I shrugged, "Can't we just have some fun first? Do I have to leap straight into all the upheaval of having children the minute things are going well for me? I mean, I had that call from James the wine importer guy, who runs the Federation of Small Businesses. He wants me to do some talks around the region about how I've developed Touch. I couldn't do that if I had a baby, and he made it sound really interesting."

Mark shot me a hard glance and was about to say something, but I continued, "Look, I'm sorry, I'm wrung out. I didn't mean to sound so negative."

Mark's expression softened. He placed a hand on my knee and rocked it soothingly. "You're right, sorry. Bad timing. You're exhausted. Let's get you home."

The barn in the early morning light looked mellow and welcoming. The rising sun reflected golden through the windows but was yet to dispel the hazy mist that hung over the ground.

There was no need to knock. The dogs knew we were home. The face of my Gordon Setter, Bird, appeared at the

French windows, followed by my other Setter, Jeeves, and Pen's two pointers, Belle and Daisy. All four tails wagged in unison, and I had to smile. They came running over as I opened the door, their enthusiastic welcome engulfing me. Jeeves wouldn't leave me alone, sniffing around my trousers and polo shirt.

I wrinkled my nose. "I think I must need a shower. I've been in this uniform since seven o'clock yesterday, and heaven knows what's on it. But first, I'd love a cup of tea."

Marked looked up from stroking the dogs. "Why don't I run you a bath? Would you like a soak?"

I sighed, "That sounds like heaven, thanks."

Almost floating in the deep warm water, a haze of citrus perfume rising with the steam, and a cup of tea on the side, I let the events of the night roll away. Mark came to sit on the edge of the bath. He picked up the china jug from the vanity unit and filled it with warm water. I tipped my head back and allowed the water to flow through my hair, eyes closed, finally relaxing as he poured slowly. He began to gently massage shampoo into my hair, working his long fingers in firm circles around my scalp. He rolled my head gently as he worked, then drew his fingers along the length of my hair and back to my scalp.

"That's wonderful," I murmured.

"Shhh, relax."

More water flowed through my hair to rinse, and my head lolled heavily in his supporting hand. Gently lifting it forwards, Mark wrapped my hair in a warm towel and then took a second towel from the rail to cocoon me inside. I was half asleep as I stepped out of the bath and into the soft towel, happy to be nurtured. Two gentle strokes across my face removed the last drops of water, and then Mark kissed me lightly on the lips.

I padded through the morning-lit barn with bare feet, leaving damp footprints on the wooden floor, slipped out of my towels and snuggled into our king-size bed. I barely remember Mark closing the blinds before I succumbed to sleep.

As Mark opened the blinds and the harsh mid-day sun streamed in, I groaned.

"It's twelve-thirty, Dom and Vale are downstairs."

Dom, Mark's best friend from school and a successful entrepreneur, had always managed to have a beautiful girl on his arm. Vale was different; she came from Mississippi but was based in London with her company. Beautiful, and also very clever, with a high-flying corporate career, it turned out she was a keeper, and Dom was besotted. They'd been together for almost a year now. When we first met, I had found her a bit overwhelming, with her picture-perfect looks, amazing grooming and stellar career. I'd thought we wouldn't have a lot in common but as we got to know each other, and we both relaxed, I realised that I'd been seeing her shop front. Underneath the clothes, the poise and the make-up, she was funny and kind. Happily, because the boys were like brothers, we'd also become close, and we met often.

"We just spoke to Angus; Pen is feeling a bit better for some sleep, so he'd like us to go in and meet the baby. Visiting is at two."

I pulled on a loose summer dress, slipped my feet into sandals and made my way downstairs, drawn by the smell of grilled bacon and fresh coffee.

"Woah! You look like you had a tough night, sister," said Vale, immaculate as ever in matching coordinates, her ash blonde hair gleaming in the sun. Neither she nor Dom looked like they had driven half the night on a mercy mission to collect Angus. How did they do it?

I squinted drowsily in the kitchen mirror at my puffy eyes and my tousled locks, the fringe sticking up on one side. "I went to bed with wet hair, and yes, I did have a tough night, but nothing like poor old Pen. I hope this baby is worth it."

"Here, have some coffee and a sandwich, you'll feel better," Mark pushed a plate and a steaming mug towards me. "Angus can't stop talking about how wonderful Pen and the baby are. He's the archetypal proud father."

Dom piped up, "We're going to stop in the baby shop in town to get some prem-size baby-grows and nappies. The baby's drowned in her first-sized ones, apparently." He sounded for all the world as if this was all in a day's work for him.

"I want to get her something nice to wear for her first photos, too," said Vale.

I couldn't help laughing as I looked at them all clucking over baby clothes and nappies. "What?" said Mark looking surprised.

"Well, this isn't how our usual conversations run, is it?"

"Right, come on," said Dom, "We're dying to see this baby. Finish that sandwich, Ellie, make yourself presentable, and let's get going."

"Okay, don't rush me," I grumbled as I wandered back upstairs to wet my hair at the front and tame it into some kind of shape. I also slicked on some mascara to try to hide my puffy eyes, which was a marginal improvement.

The baby shop was an Aladdin's cave for mums and babies. After what seemed like forever, we finally left and set off for the hospital, armed with virtually every tiny baby-grow the shop possessed and an eye-wateringly expensive lacy number for the baby's first photos, that both the men loved on sight. We had also bought some baby-chic, pink dungarees and tee-shirts for her to grow into, picked by Vale's unerring eye. I had chosen a lovely rose-scented aromatherapy cream in a beautiful, midnight-blue jar that I hoped would make Pen feel special.

Pen was in a small side-ward with three other mums and their babies. As we clustered around the bed, she presented the tiny bundle in her arms and said, "Meet baby Charlotte Elizabeth. Lottie, to her friends."

Mark was the first to reach out. "Can I?" He said, and as Pen nodded, he took the tiny baby in his arms and rocked her gently. "Lottie," he said, tucking the blanket down away from her face, "You're beautiful."

Dom touched Lottie's tiny hand, and she gripped onto his finger.

"She's a monster," said Angus affectionately, gazing at her. "She's had us awake three times wanting food already. Got her mum's appetite."

All three men seemed entranced.

Pen smiled briefly at the joke. "The consultant says she probably has a headache and a massive hang-over from the birth, which is why she's a bit fretful. But she seems to like you, Mark."

"Babies do," he said, "I could always calm them down at the place Katrina worked."

"Was she a nursery nurse? Your ex?" asked Vale, then cast a worried look towards me as if she may have spoken out of turn.

"No, when she was at uni, part of her course was working with special-needs children, but there were always family babies in the centre as well and never enough hands. I've always loved kids, so I helped sometimes."

I glanced towards him. Katrina had left Mark and disappeared without a word of explanation, just as they were planning to marry. Terrified for her safety, he had tried to trace her. It turned out that Katrina was already married to an older man back in Russia. Her relationship with Mark had been a sham from start to finish. Mark had money and a car, and she had used him while she was here. He had been devastated by the deception and gone to pieces for a while. I wondered if seeing the baby might bring back sad memories.

When we first met, we had both lost partners and been hurt in different ways. Speaking about Brett and Katrina had been difficult for both of us, so our friends had skated around the subjects. Today Mark seemed to mention Katrina quite naturally. I still found it hard to talk about Brett.

Pen looked tired, and I suggested they all took Angus downstairs for a coffee.

"How are you?" I said as I put the now sleeping Charlotte into her crib. "You look tired."

"I feel really sore and so stiff. I must've been clenching my teeth yesterday because I can hardly open my mouth today."

I glanced at her sympathetically. "Are you allowed a bath yet? It might loosen you up."

"Yes, I had just lowered myself into one this morning, and it felt like heaven, when the nurse knocked, Lottie was crying, and I had to get straight back out."

I thought back to my luxurious uninterrupted bath of the night before and felt guilty.

"I guess that's motherhood for you," she continued.

"Look, it's just us for a few minutes, how about a massage?" I settled her on the bed, got out the rose body lotion I'd bought and started to massage her neck and shoulders, then gently, her face. I was about to change to her feet when a wail emanated from the crib.

"See what I mean," said Pen, "Lottie has a sixth sense. I'd better feed and change her." She levered herself off the bed gingerly and sat in the winged armchair. "Can you pass her over?"

We didn't visit for long, as Pen needed to rest. Angus needed to leave, too, to check on the farm. He offered to collect their dogs, but we agreed that they should stay with us to begin with while Pen was still in the hospital.

Dom and Vale were heading back to London, so we said our goodbyes at the barn and waved them off in a cloud of dust that rose from the chase as Dom roared off.

Mark rested his arm across my shoulder as we walked back into our house. "What a day," he said contentedly.

Chewing my lip, I looked away into the distance. "Everything has changed."

Mark frowned, taken by surprise. "What do you mean?"

"Nothing will be quite the same now. I can feel it already, Pen is different, you're different. I'm happy, but I'm a little scared too."

He laughed, “Scared? Why on earth are you scared? Change can be a good thing, and this is good for all of us. I haven’t changed anyway.”

I looked at him, he was wrong, we had all subtly changed, and he hadn’t realised yet. Although I couldn’t say anything more, I felt thrown off balance. I liked things the way they were.

Chapter Four

Wisteria Cottage

It did me good to have the prospect of normality the next day. I got up at six-thirty to walk the dogs and was thankful for work, routine and a busy day ahead.

Wisteria Cottage was on my route to work. A big house, it sat back from the road behind a large front garden and was built of stone with a decorative thatched roof. Although the roses were almost over, a few still bloomed in the garden and the wisteria that gave the cottage its name arched gracefully over the door. Delicate powder blue blooms cascaded from the branches in a waterfall of colour. Today the cottage was still. Peter Bane, its owner, was in Surrey with Mark's mum, Alessandra.

They had become friends after meeting at our village fete, and much like Mark and me, their early friendship had slowly turned to love, and now they spent their time between her home and the cottage.

I sighed. Pam, Peter's late wife, had been a very good friend. I still missed her forthright cheerfulness and great listening skills. If she'd been in the cottage, I would have popped in for a chat and a piece of her wonderful lemon drizzle cake. I used to tell her everything, and I longed to explain my current dilemma and how conflicted I felt to someone who wouldn't judge me.

"Oh well," I said to the dogs, "I'll sort it out. You both listen to my ramblings, don't you?" I glanced in the mirror. Jeeves had his head cocked on one side with a look of undivided attention, and I had to laugh despite my misgivings.

"Hi, Lizzie," I said as I pushed open the door at Touch. The small water feature burbled in the corner, and relaxation music played in the background while the ever-present smell of aromatherapy oils emanated from our massage wax. I drank in the calm, let my shoulders drop and smiled at her. "What's my day like?"

"Frantic, I'm afraid, because we moved everyone yesterday."

Good, I thought. Ever since Brett died, working 'til I dropped had always been my go-to strategy to hold demons at bay. To Lizzie, I said, "Go on then, do your worst. Show me my list."

I read through the names. That should do the trick, I thought. Wall-to-wall patients and no time to think about my own troubles.

"Sorry we've packed so much in," she said as I scanned the page, misreading my reaction completely. "Oh, and Robin knows you're busy but asked if he could have a quick word if that's alright?"

"Um, yes, but only if our lunch breaks coincide, by the look of it." A little knot of anxiety tweaked. I always had this irrational fear that Robin may leave. I suppose it's a leftover from losing Brett. Nothing seemed invulnerable anymore.

She smiled, "I can give Doorsteps a ring to bring you both a sandwich, you can meet and eat, they'll deliver."

I nodded my agreement, "Good plan."

How's the baby?" Lizzie asked.

"She's adorable, so tiny and with lots of dark hair. Charlotte Elizabeth." It was funny, I noted, before Lottie was born, everyone asked about Pen. Now they were only interested in the baby.

Bertram was my first patient; he was just what I needed to keep any anxiety at bay about why Robin needed to see me urgently. Right now, I was escalating to just short of full-blown panic.

Bertram Randolph, Bertie to his friends, was a long-time resident of the village. His family had been here long before it became a new town, they had had links here since the turn of the century.

"I see Wisteria Cottage is empty," he said casually, watching like a hawk for my reaction.

"Yes, I think Peter is still away," I replied equally casually, not wanting to be the source of any village gossip.

He shook his head, "Lovely cottage. It was sad Pam died; she was a real trooper."

I smiled warmly, "Yes, she was a lovely lady. I still miss her."

"That cottage always had good people living there," he continued, shaking his head again, "sad though, a couple of the women who lived there died young, but despite that, the cottage has always seemed to have a nice atmosphere."

I was intrigued, "Oh, who owned it before the Banes?"

"Before that, the house belonged to the Bells. Now they were lovely people, Dominic and Primrose. Dominic had green fingers. He laid out the garden so well no one has changed it since."

We chatted for a while, and as I listened to Bertie reminisce about the inhabitants of Wisteria cottage. His stories, full of permanence and happy days, made me feel silly to be so unsettled. I needed to buck up.

The lunchtime meeting with Robin still made me feel apprehensive. I chose a sandwich from the plate Lizzie had ordered and shredded it nervously, not feeling very hungry. Robin sat with me, and we talked about Pen and the baby for a short while before he changed the subject.

"Ellie, you know when I first came, we talked about me having a long break sometimes, so I could travel?"

My heart sank. "Yes, I do."

"I was wondering if we could arrange to let me get away next year, say two to three months in the Spring? I want to take Louise back to New Zealand to meet my folks, and she hasn't done a lot of travelling, so I'd like us to visit places on the way."

Anxiety made me want to gnaw my nails, but I resisted and outwardly calm, replied, "Um, yes, I suppose so. I think the clinic is too busy for me to manage on my own now, which is different to when we talked about you travelling before."

He nodded his agreement. "What about if I ask around for another Kiwi locum? My friend's sister, Maisie, was looking for work a couple of weeks ago, but there are always a few of them over. I'm sure someone would like to earn some money before they go off around Europe for the Summer."

I ran through my own commitments around that time in my head, "I go to Yorkshire in the Spring to grouse count with the dogs. If we dovetail that with your leaving date, we should be able to cover it. I can't let my friend Mike down next year because Pen still won't be able to go."

He grinned, "Don't look so worried, it'll be fine, and I promise we're coming back. The locum can sub-let my place if they want to – well, I know it's your place, so they'd be sub-sub-letting. That's if you want me back. You might prefer the next guy that comes."

"Or girl," I said, "Anyway, of course, I'll want you back. The women patients will be languishing while you're gone, not to mention Sarah and Lizzie!"

We both laughed and had to leave it at that, there were busy lists to get back to.

It was too late when I finished work to visit Pen and Lottie at the hospital. By the time I'd written up all my notes, I realised it was nearly eight o'clock.

As I drove towards the barn, I hoped Mark had walked all the dogs for me, as he was working from home today. I knew a walk would do me good but I felt like being lazy and putting my feet up. As I pulled onto the drive, I could see Mark's tall silhouette in the kitchen. With luck, he might even have made supper too.

"Hiya," I called, surprised not to have an avalanche of dogs to welcome me. "Where are the dogs?"

Mark emerged from the kitchen, slender, encased in a striped apron, and bent to kiss me. "Hello, you." He stood back and looked at me. "You've had a busy day. I began to think you were doing an all-nighter. Dogs are in the kennels at the farm. They went swimming, so Angus suggested I leave them to dry off."

I was surprised, "When did you see Angus?"

"Oh, we walked the dogs together this afternoon. Angus is going to take the Pointers back because Pen may be home tomorrow if all Lottie's checks are fine. We went into the hospital after the walk. I offered to drive Angus because he still looks shattered. I can collect our dogs while the lasagne is cooking."

"Mark Roxbury, back to visit again?" I teased, "I think you're besotted by that little girl. How is Pen today?"

"She is gorgeous – Lottie, that is. I think Pen's doing well, she's still a little quiet, but I guess it all takes a bit of getting used to."

I raised my eyebrows, "She probably feels like she has been driven over by a tank. I can't remember when the first big hormone shift happens, but I think there is a horrible baby-blues thing that happens a few days after the baby is born, so she may be feeling hormonal, not to mention shattered. She wasn't well before she went in."

"That's true, poor old Pen. Hopefully, now she's had Lottie, she'll bounce back." He checked the oven from where a mouth-watering smell issued. "How was your day? Apart from long and busy."

I told Mark about Robin's plans and tried to explain my concerns as I picked at the quick of my thumb. "I don't want to let anyone down or turn people away just as we've built everything up so nicely."

Mark put his hand over mine and sounded eminently reasonable. "You've got time to look for someone to cover, though, and Robin said he'd help. It's not like the panic last year when you injured your knee."

I began to feel a bit miffed; he didn't need to remind me about the impact of my past injury. Although we had managed, it had still been a difficult time and it was easy for him to say, 'don't panic'.

He put his arm around me. "I can see you're worrying already. You're hungry and tired. It all probably seems worse than it is."

"Maybe," I said, unconvinced.

He gave my hand a tug. "Come and get a glass of red while I pop over to fetch the dogs, and then you can have some of my Nona's special recipe lasagne. We can think about all this in the morning."

I narrowed my eyes to slits as I watched his retreating form. *Why was everyone so flipping chirpy today?*

Red wine in hand, I drifted upstairs and sat in the recliner on the mezzanine to watch the sun begin to set. Tonight, a ferocious red-blazed behind the silhouette of trees on the skyline, with wisps of horizontal grey cloud streaking the sky.

Nona Gemelli's signature lasagne did go a fair way to lifting my spirits. She was Alessandra's mother, as short and round as Alessandra was tall and sleek. Her homemade pasta recipes were to die for, and, even better, she had taught Mark to cook them.

I sighed contentedly as we stood by the sink. "That was fabulous, Mark, so creamy. Thank you for cooking tonight." I laced my arms around his neck and kissed him, snuggling into him.

Mark started to rock gently, and soon we were slow dancing to an unplayed song in the dying light of the day. Taking my hand, he led me towards the stairs. At the bottom, we stopped to kiss again, he laughed and took off his apron, hanging it on the newel post.

"Your turn," he said.

I pushed one shoe off, then the other and left them tucked under the first step.

"Disappointing, Miss Rose! I was hoping for something more tantalising."

I'd show him disappointing. I sat halfway up the stairs and extended one leg towards him with the toe provocatively pointed. "Aha," he said and bent to remove first that sock, then as I extended the other leg, the second one. Holding my foot, he kissed the inside of my ankle and then tugged at the hem of my trousers.

"Oh no, you're next," I said, backing up two more steps to get a vantage point. "Shirt off, Mr Roxbury," I said, lifting my chin as I half dared him.

He slowly peeled it off to display his enviable tan and then swooped forwards to kiss me again. His smooth skin felt delicious under my fingers, and he smelt wonderful. I was tempted to give in but pushed him away, and stood to make a run for the top of the stairs.

"Caught, Miss Rose," he laughed as he grabbed me by the bedroom door and leaned into the wall.

"My forfeit," he whispered in my ear. Leaning back, he looked me up and down, considering, and then slowly eased the scrunchie out of my hair and ran his fingers through the waves as they fell.

Too much! I kissed him in earnest, suddenly drowning in my need to make love to him. I wrapped my legs around him, and he carried me into our room and lowered me onto the bed. My trousers and top flung to the floor, Mark took more time in the removal of the rest and made love to me slowly.

I smiled as I followed the trail of garments back downstairs the next morning.

"Coffee?" he said as I got to the kitchen.

"Yes, please, a quick one and then I must run."

He cocked his head to one side, "Toast?"

I shook my head, "I'll eat something when I get there, my stomach hasn't woken up yet."

Mark frowned, "Promise?"

I playfully punched his arm, "Yes, stop nagging!"

He grinned, "Just checking. Can't have you wasting away."

Whatever problems I had, wasting away was not one of them.

I checked the clock. "Why are you still here anyway? You've usually gone to work in a cloud of dust by now."

He stretched and yawned. "First appointment's this afternoon, so I'm doing the planning from home this morning. Would you like me to keep the dogs?"

I gave him a thumbs up and grabbed my bag, ready to leave. "Brill, I'll see you tonight." As I shut the door, I sighed contentedly, what Mark and I had was so good that right now, I didn't want to alter a thing.

Chapter Five

Peter and Alessandra

Peter and Alessandra were waiting outside the barn as I got back from work.

"Hello, what a lovely surprise," I said, mentally reviewing the barn and trying to remember if I had removed all evidence of last night's striptease before leaving that morning. As far as I remembered, all clothing had been retrieved.

"Darling, we had to come back to see the baby, what a little beauty," Alessandra said. She kissed me on both cheeks and left a subtle waft of expensive perfume as she moved, then wagged a warning finger at me. "Mark will be broody, beware! He loves babies."

"Hello, Peter," I said, dodging that topic of conversation. "Are you both going to stay at Wisteria Cottage for a few days?"

He rolled his eyes heavenward. "Yes, Alessandra has baby fever. And it's time I tended the garden before it turns into a jungle."

Alessandra waved a hand. "We arranged with Mark to pop in and see you both before we go and settle back in. Having two homes is exhausting!"

Nice problem to have, as problems go, I thought, then felt mean for thinking it. They had both had their share of troubles and loneliness. It was good for them both to be together.

"We have been talking about selling one," said Alessandra.

Things are getting serious! I thought as I unlocked the door. I stood back and ushered them inside. "Let me get you a drink. Mark won't be long, I'm sure. He must've been held up in traffic or with his client."

"I have a photo of Lottie for you from Pen." I looked, it was a close-up of Lottie's face with a sweep of long lashes against her cheeks, peacefully asleep.

"Look on the back," said Alessandra, clapping her hands together in anticipation of my reaction.

The message in Pen's rounded handwriting was, "With love to my new Godparents?"

I looked at her excited face and smiled. "Gosh, how lovely. Is Pen going to entrust Mark and me with that responsibility? She must be mad."

"Nonsense, you live so close, your two families will grow up intertwined. Who better?" said Alessandra, looking to Peter for support.

"Darling, you're doing your Italian matriarch thing again," said Peter with a wry smile. "Mark and Ellie may not want children. They both have good careers."

I shot him a grateful look. Alessandra paused with an arrested look on her face, then burst out laughing. "You are teasing me, stop it."

I took my cue and headed for the kitchen. I would be having words with Pen later about all this hassle I was getting.

Mark arrived while I was pouring the drinks, looking impossibly sexy, hot and slightly dishevelled, his tie discarded and a slight five o'clock shadow around his jaw. I handed out long, cold glasses of lime and soda, relinquishing mine to him before going to fetch another and some nibbles.

Mark shook Peter's hand and then turned to Alessandra. He opened his arms, and she stepped into his bear hug. "Mamma, it's good to see you."

"You too," she said, pushing him away to look at him. She twisted a curl of hair on his collar. "You need a haircut."

"You always say that."

Peter followed me into the kitchen. "You're going to get a lot of this," he remarked, "the baby bullying."

"I know. Mum, Sarah, Alessandra, they're all at it. Alessandra's right about Mark, though. Since Pen got pregnant and had Lottie, he's been broody."

He looked at me enquiringly. "How do you feel about that?"

I shrugged and busied myself tipping olives into bowls. "I don't know, Peter. Pen was so ill when she was pregnant. I couldn't work if I was like that, and I've just got Touch off the ground, it's important to me." I arranged the bowls on a tray and opened a packet of breadsticks to dip in the houmous. "Still, there's no rush, we have plenty of time to think about it."

He nodded thoughtfully, "There would be ways around managing Touch, of course, and you may not be ill like Pen, but I understand. The business is quite dependent on you as it is. It might be worth talking to a consultant, they'd help you re-structure to remedy that."

I began to feel a bit threatened. Touch was part of my survival persona. In some ways, it was my baby. "But I'm a clinician, I like working," I said with more force than strictly necessary.

"Look, you'll work it out," said Peter, with a smile. "You're a sensible girl. When the time is right for you if ever, get your plans in place. Children aren't the be-all and end-all."

I wasn't sure Mark would see it that way, and a small feeling of dread pulled at my stomach. Would I lose Mark if I decided I didn't want a baby?

Peter continued, "Pam and I wanted kids, it just never happened. We were having such a good time, and I was working hard, so we left it a bit late before we discovered we had issues. We could have gone the IVF route, but we were very happy and decided to stay as we were."

I don't think I had ever had such a personal conversation with Peter. What was it about babies that brought out all this disclosure? Lottie seemed to have triggered a shift in our group dynamic, and she wasn't out of the hospital yet. Changes I wasn't ready for seemed to be pursuing me relentlessly.

I handed him the olives and dip to carry through and followed with another drink. At least he'd confirmed that some people did manage to live happily ever after without children.

"Show Mark the photo," said Alessandra as I sat down.

He looked at me, "What photo's this?"

I handed him the Polaroid print, and he smiled as he looked down at Lottie. "She's beautiful."

"Turn it over, look at the back," said Alessandra eagerly.

"Oh, wow," said Mark, and he turned to me with a massive grin on his face. "That's amazing, I'm delighted. It'll be great, won't it?"

"Mmmm," I said, avoiding Peter's eye. "Great."

Mark put the photo on the mantelpiece. "We'll get a frame for that unless you've got a nice one stashed away somewhere, Ellie?"

Baby photos and frames, heaven help us. "I'll have a look later."

I had a brave try at turning the conversation away from Lottie, but there was little point, so I let myself drift off as they discussed Dom's heroic rescue of Angus and the drama of the baby arriving early. Peter gave the illusion of hanging on every word, but I suspected, like me, his mind was elsewhere.

I was brought back with a snap as Alessandra said, "We've got to decide whether to sell Wisteria Cottage or the house in Surrey, haven't we Peter? It's silly living part-time in both."

Wisteria Cottage held fond memories for me, and I would be sad to see it sold. Pam had been special to me, and the cottage seemed linked to her memory. I wondered how Peter felt about possibly selling it so soon. Pam had died more recently than Mark's dad, and I wondered if the thought of selling might upset him.

"Or we could sell both places and buy something else if we saw something we liked," he replied.

Just me feeling sentimental then, clearly.

"Wisteria Cottage would be lovely when we have grandchildren," said Alessandra. "It's like the Secret Garden, they'd love it, and we'd be close enough to help you two out."

Peter glanced at me with an I told you so look. “Talking of secret gardens, come on, Alessandra, we need to get going, I want to cut the lawn while it’s dry.”

She pulled a face at me. “Gardening! See what things have come to already, Ellie? No romance in his soul.”

“You’d be welcome to stay and eat if you like,” I offered but was quite relieved when they declined. I’d had enough talk of starting a family for one day.

“Do you fancy going to the cinema tonight?” I suggested to Mark as we closed the door.

He nodded, “Sure. We could pop in and see Pen on the way into Chelmsford, as she hasn’t come home, and confirm that Lottie has her godparents.”

I nodded, “Tell you what, I’ll treat you to fish and chips in the wrapper. We can eat them while the dogs have a run and head straight off.”

“Done,” he said and bounded off up the stairs two at a time to shed his work clothes.

We sat by the river to eat our supper, looking across the water. The dogs snuffled around on the bank, played tug of war with seaweed and wallowed in the shallows. The heat of the day lessened, as in the warm evening light, we were fanned by a cool breeze. Several ducks were still swimming, and from time to time, they bobbed, beaks down, tail feathers up, searching for food. Others had settled on the bank and were preening feathers or had their heads tucked in, snoozing.

I looked at Mark, “Will you mind if Peter and your Mum decide to sell the house in Surrey? And come to that, will you mind them living so close? I’d die if my Mum moved in almost next door.”

"Mum living close, I think would be fine. She is busy with her own life, and it might be nice, we get on well. Would you mind?"

I shook my head, "No, I love your Mum, she's great. What about selling the Surrey house?"

He shrugged, "Oh, that wouldn't bother me at all. I was a teenager when they bought the house in Surrey, so it doesn't have sentimental attachments for me."

Frowning, I said, "I'd rather they didn't make the decision based on the prospect of us having kids, though," then smiled, "I'm glad it isn't my folks. I could cope with my dad, but Mum and I are better when we wish we saw each other more."

Mark looked serious for a moment. "We will try for kids, though, won't we?"

"Yes, at some stage," I said airily and started to bundle up the fish and chip wrappers. "Your mum was right, you are broody."

The atmosphere felt slightly strained during the drive to Chelmsford. I had a sinking feeling that this particular elephant had come to stay.

Pen looked so much better, she had colour in her cheeks and seemed much brighter. Mark took charge of Lottie as soon as we arrived. He settled himself comfortably in the big wing-backed hospital chair, with her on a blanket in his lap. Lottie's head nestled in the crook of his elbow as a ray of evening sun shone across her. Lottie in the spotlight, Mark in the shadow. I took a photo. Despite my reservations, it was clear to see that Mark was going to love this little girl.

"Can I whizz down and grab a bath while you're here?" Pen asked. "Ellie, you can come and chat. Do you mind, Mark?"

"Mind," I laughed, "does he looks like he minds?"

As Pen lowered herself into the bubbles, she groaned, "This is bliss. Have you seen the size of my boobs? I feel like my new name should be Daisy or Ermentrude."

I grinned, "Not that I'm checking you out, I hasten to add, but they are impressive!"

She rolled her eyes. "Tell me what's happening in the outside world, where there are no netting knickers or gigantic bras with flaps and discreet embroidery. I want all the gen Ellie, seriously."

I laughed. Thank goodness she was still in there somewhere, my best friend. It gave me hope.

Chapter Six

Millie, Dom and Vale

We enjoyed the film, a slightly dark piece of escapism was just what I needed to forget my concerns. I slept the sleep of the just and woke early the next morning, looking forward to seeing one of my favourite regular patients, who I noticed, was first on my list before I left the clinic yesterday. Millie Stamford first introduced me to Gordon Setters, and she had a lot to answer for!

As I'd woken so early, I had time for a long walk before work. Grabbing a lanyard with my two dog whistles on it, I picked up the car keys from the wooden fruit bowl and an apple, which I bit into and held between my teeth. I slipped my feet into the trainers that live behind the back door. Not missing a trick, Jeeves and Bird read the signs; they were ready and waiting to follow me to the car.

"Hup! Wait!"

The dogs dropped with barely concealed impatience as I opened the back door of my battered 4x4. The back of it housed a bespoke crate, much smarter than the car itself and possibly worth more money. I finished my bite and balanced the apple in the back-door tray. My mouth watered as I enjoyed the sharp, sweet taste. I opened the inner doors of the dog crate and looked back.

"Okay!"

Bird and Jeeves surged forward, leapt up and settled in the crate, raring to go. Retrieving my apple, I took another bite, closed the dogs in and slid behind the wheel. I'd decided to head out into the country towards Maldon for a change.

I love late summer mornings, and today there was more than a hint of Autumn in the slight chill. I headed off towards one of my favourite walks, which meant climbing the only hill around. An exuberant hedge almost swallowed up the public footpath sign pointing towards the fields, but beyond the gate was our walk.

It began on the flat, following a footpath beside crop fields, then banked away steeply to the right up a hill. Halfway up the incline, a copse of blackthorn and oak trees lay to my left. The land belonged to a friend of Angus, who had permitted me to run the dogs, so they didn't have to be on leads here. They loved being somewhere different, and as I let them off their leads to enjoy a run in the trees, I could hear them foraging through the undergrowth, twigs snapping and branches rustling. Beginning to puff slightly with the exertion of the short, sharp climb, I arrived at the top of the hill. I enjoyed my reward, a stunning salmon and cream sunrise stretched for miles in front of me, presiding over the fertile fields of the flood plain, snoozing lazily under a soft duvet of morning mist.

The scene was framed to my right by the River Crouch as it snaked towards the sea, to my left, by the River Blackwater and the concrete hulk of Bradwell Power Station. Lying in the mist, at the far reach of my vision, was my clinic and the town which had become home. In bed, asleep when I left, and probably still there, was Mark.

Usually, so in sync, we weren't quite now. He didn't seem to think there was any room for doubt or need to wait before joining Pen and Angus in the family stakes. The thought sent an uncomfortable tingle of apprehension up my spine as I foresaw a tussle between his pressing desire to start a family and my reservations. We weren't even married yet, for goodness sake. Somehow, we would have to find a compromise. Suddenly, the sunrise seemed slightly less magnificent, and all my worries of the last few weeks started to invade my morning headspace.

Lost in those thoughts, with my mood in freefall, I felt a glancing blow to the side of my knee, which took me by surprise and nearly knocked me flying. It snapped me out of my funk. "Steady you," I said as I looked down at a happily panting Jeeves.

"What you doing?" He seemed to say.

I ruffled his head. "Just wool-gathering, come on, get on." I set off down the other side of the hill to finish our walk. It was time to get to work.

Millie, my first patient at the clinic this morning, was an animal fanatic and had a small army of rescues, all a little battered and missing a variety of ears, eyes, legs or tails. They were battle-scarred but beautiful and now tended with the loving care Millie and her mother bestowed upon them on their smallholding in Bradwell.

I had often walked at Bradwell, even before I had the dogs. I loved the paths on top of the flood defences, with salt marsh and the estuary on one side and the flood-plain fields on the other – miles of crops as far as the eye could see. There was always a sea breeze, and it felt wide open and spacious out there.

I met Millie walking on the sea wall one bright winter day with a small selection of her menagerie. They caught my eye as I saw them in the distance because there was one dog silhouette I couldn't quite make out. The dog in question turned out to be a miniature goat in a harness. Lily-goat was enjoying a ramble with the dogs, accompanied by three trusty hounds: Sadie, a black and white, one-eared, Jack Russell cross. Raffles, goodness knows what he was, but somehow his head was a bit small for his body, his legs were too short for the length of his back, added to which, he seemed to be mainly short-haired with a light smattering of some longer hair that gave him a moth-eaten appearance. None of which bothered him in the slightest. Last, but not least was Fergus, a rather beautiful Deerhound with one badly mangled leg. Fergus had been left to die in a bin liner. Luckily, he had been rescued, repaired and had come to Millie for convalescence after surgery, never to leave.

As our paths crossed, I made a big fuss of everyone and passed the time of day with Millie. We met by chance again several times afterwards and enjoyed a chat as we walked. The chance meetings turned into coffees at the Green Man Pub on the Quay, during which Millie mounted her campaign to get me a dog, the love of which she was certain would help me recover from losing Brett.

Before a dog could be therapy for me, I ended up treating Millie. Her mum phoned the clinic one day to announce that Millie's back had "gone", and could I help her? Working hard on the smallholding meant that Millie frequently injured something, so she became a regular customer at Touch as well as a friend.

During the first of those sessions, Millie had acupuncture, and I was engaged in placing slender needles on either side of her spine and in her feet and hands to relieve the acute pain. I also wanted to release the spasm in her back muscles and generally stimulate healing where she'd damaged the tissues. As I inserted the needles, I was feeling for Millie's body to 'grab' each one and for her to feel De Qi, a deep dull ache, signal that the acupuncture point has been stimulated.

Millie had had acupuncture before at a different clinic. She told me it gave her excellent pain relief, and she said she always had a great night's sleep after her treatment. As she relaxed, face down on the couch for half an hour while the needles worked their magic, Millie took the opportunity to relaunch the topic of finding a dog for me. She thought that as it was a while after Brett's death and I was more settled, it was time for me to take the plunge. That day she tried a new tack.

"Dogs have a lot in common with acupuncture. They are scientifically proven to relieve stress, help people recover from injury, raise mood and lower blood pressure. They encourage people to take more exercise too."

I grinned, "You're preaching to the converted, Millie; we've always had dogs in my family. They're great listeners and don't answer back the way people do. Well, sometimes they answer back, I suppose," I said, thinking about their range of expressions and variety of vocals. "I'd love one, they're good company, but they are a tie, though, puppy training takes a lot of time, and I'm so busy at the moment."

"It doesn't have to be a puppy. Plenty of rescue dogs need homes. My friend breeds Gordon Setters, like Red

Setters but black and tan coats. She trains them for working and takes them onto the moors up north, counting the different bird populations for a gamekeeper. They count Grouse in the Spring and Summer and seem to walk for miles over the moors. I think you'd love it."

"Sounds great," I said, my interest piqued, "I'd love it, but I'm not sure I could fit anything else in at the moment." I shook my head, "I'm not even sure I could afford a dog."

Ignoring my excuses, she continued, "I'm meeting her for a coffee at the weekend. Would you like to come and see the dogs working?"

I accepted enthusiastically. "I don't know much about how Setters work, so I'd love to see them."

From the moment I saw her friend's beautiful, exuberant, joyful dogs galloping effortlessly across the fields, I was a lost cause! Despite their speed and distance from her, they responded to whistle commands, always retaining their partnership with their handler.

Suddenly all my carefully constructed arguments crumbled away, and I asked about booking a puppy from her next litter. But before that litter appeared, I had another call from Millie.

"Ellie, I don't know what you think about this, but there are two rescue Gordons who have arrived at my friend's place. She's fostering them until they find a new home. They're still young, two and one, a boy and girl. They've been well trained and well-loved; their owner has been ill and is giving up her house for a flat and can't keep the dogs. I thought they'd be great for you."

"Two, Millie! I haven't decided to have one yet."

"I think having two is easier than one because they're company for each other, and you won't be worried that they're lonely when you're at work. No puppy training either. Why don't you pop up and meet them?"

"I'd love to see them, but I don't think I can take on two."

As Millie had suspected, it was love at first sight. We met, and all went for a hike across the fields. Bird seemed to take to me from the start and came back to me throughout the walk to check-in, despite the temptations of the fields. She wound herself between my legs in a figure of eight, casting her spell on me, as Millie said later. Jeeves was more playful, and I swear he was flirting with me. At the end of the walk, they looked up at me with hope in their beautiful soft eyes and a gentle dignity. Despite being refugees and away from everything they had ever known, they were gracious. Looking back, there has never been any doubt in my mind that although I technically rescued them, they, in fact, rescued me.

Despite my previous doubts, I found ample time in my busy life for the dogs and never regretted their coming. They more than re-paid my time with loyalty and affection, and they taught me to open my heart to love again.

Today, Millie was back at the clinic. This time, she was part-way through treatment for a shoulder problem caused by a fall off a ladder. I used acupuncture with her again to help with pain relief so that she could complete her exercises effectively.

"How are those rascals doing?" she said, seeing the dogs in my office on arrival at Touch for her appointment that morning. She paused to give them both a stroke over the child gate, which restrained them from bouncing all over her. Millie was a great favourite.

"Can I?" she said, showing me chunks of the dried liver she always kept in her pocket.

I nodded, "Yes, you spoil them."

"Ah well, they need a treat; they're always so good."

I raised my eyebrows. "Hmmm, I wouldn't say always!" As we walked toward the treatment room, I said, "Did you hear that Pen had her baby? A little girl called Lottie."

"Yes, one of the dog club people told me. I'll come to see her when she's home. I can't believe she's old enough to have her own baby; I remember Pen when she was a stringy teenager at the dog club, doing agility. It'll be you next, Ellie, having a family."

I groaned, "Don't you start as well, Millie!"

She pulled down the corners of her generous mouth. "Sorry, has everyone been badgering you?"

"Yes." I replied wearily. "And it's a bad idea to upset your physio before the session starts, Millie. We have ways of taking revenge."

She grinned, "My lips are sealed! The word 'baby' will never again be spoken between us. But you'd be a great mum when you're ready, of course."

I tutted despondently, "How do you know when you're ready? That's the problem."

She patted my hand. "Something will happen. I'm a great believer in fate. A baby will come along if it's meant to be. No point stressing about it."

I decided to take her advice and put babies to the back of my mind for a while.

As I got back to the barn after work, something happened that put baby thoughts out of both our minds completely. I saw Dom's car parked in front of the barn, which was odd. We weren't expecting him.

“Hi,” I called as I let myself and the dogs in.

“In here,” called Mark from his office.

I dumped my stuff on the side and went through. “I saw your car out front. Good to see you, Dom.”

He got up, smiled and kissed me on the cheek, but I could see something was wrong. “Are you alright?” I asked.

“Yes and no,” he said, “Vale’s been recalled to America by her company. She must be back there by the middle of September. We’re not sure what to do.”

“Oh Dom, no, that’s a terrible blow. I thought she was in England permanently now.”

He made a palms-up gesture of puzzlement. “So did we, but you know what these large companies are. They move people around like pawns on a chessboard.”

I nodded my understanding; hiring and firing, lives turned upside down, seemed everyday occurrences in the city. The way Mark had been treated when he initially thought Katrina was missing had pushed him to the brink of a breakdown. I’d first met him when he was recovering, and it was why he’d decided to set up his consultancy and work with smaller companies.

“I’ve come to see Mark so we can have a look at some options for my company. Vale loves her job. She said she’d resign, but I don’t want her to have to give up what she loves, and resigning wouldn’t help because her resident’s permit was linked to the job anyway.”

I nodded sympathetically, “Tell me about it, I remember how tricky permit issues can be from my time in Australia. Look, I’ll make a cup of tea and leave you two to chat. Are you staying tonight? I can make up the spare room.”

He looked uncharacteristically anxious, “Thanks, Ellie, I’d love to stay, but I want to get back to Vale, she’s really upset about all of this at the moment.”

“Shall I give her a call while you’re chatting?”

He shook his head, “You won’t get her ‘til very late; she has back-to-back conference calls about the reshuffle, so she’ll still be in the office because of the time difference with the States.”

I’d never seen Dom look so distraught. And had never seen Vale anything other than cool, calm and collected, so if she was unravelling, this had hit them hard. I was sad, Vale had been a good friend since the night of the wedding reception of Mark and Dom’s friends before Mark and I were together as a couple. Vale had only just met Dom, and as everyone else on our table knew each other from way back, we had bonded. She was warm and funny behind the sophisticated exterior and someone who understood about me loving my career, which was vital to me. I would miss having her here.

Even worse, if Dom emigrated permanently with Vale, Mark would be lost. They were closer than most brothers. Dom’s parents had worked overseas, and he had been a boarding pupil at Mark’s school since he was six. Alessandra had taken him under her wing, and he’d spent exeats and some holidays at Mark’s home. They would hate to be separated, but Dom was head over heels in love with Vale too. ‘Life’s a bitch,’ as Brett would have said.

I put mugs of tea on the desk in front of the lads and left them to their discussion. I sometimes forgot what a respected business consultant Mark is. Hearing the hum of their voices in the office as I made supper in the kitchen made me realise that Mark had been Dom's first port of call professionally as well as personally.

The dogs seemed to have caught the tension in the air and were both looking at me anxiously from their baskets.

As the men emerged about an hour later, Dom hugged me but seemed bereft of his usual charm for the first time since I'd known him. He shook Mark's hand and said, "Get those figures over to me as soon as you can, mate; I appreciate it. Ellie, sorry I'm in such a rush." Then he was gone into the night.

I looked at Mark, "Are you going to be able to help him?"

"Yes, I think so. As Dom invests in start-up tech companies, it doesn't matter where he's based. He already manages the American office from here most of the time. He'll have to change his business model slightly and appoint a right-hand man to liaise with him and take charge of the London office. He'll need some of the new technology he is so fond of investing in to allow him to attend his UK meetings by video conference. It'll mean more travel probably, but it's all doable. I'm sure it won't be long before he is taking America by storm."

I pursed my lips. "So he's going to move to America with Vale?"

"Well, it seems like the best option."

Mark spoke lightly, but he didn't fool me, his dark eyes had a clouded hue, and there was a slight droop to his shoulders. I stepped in and held him. "You'll miss each other."

Dom and Mark reminded me of Max and Brett. When Brett died, my best friend Annie told me that her partner Max had been inconsolable for months.

"It'll be alright," he lied resolutely. To me, or himself? I wasn't sure.

Mark still bore the emotional scars of the trauma with Katrina, and I'd noticed he was slow to trust new people. When Katrina had disappeared, he'd initially been frantic when he couldn't contact her until he found out why she'd disappeared. He told me he'd drunk too much for a while until Dom cared enough to pick Mark up and start him in consultancy work. Dom, for all his slick image, was a loyal friend, and they were important to one another.

Chapter Seven

Plans

Saturday dawned bright and clear. Although, the chilly start to the day and the wispy mist that clung to the fields indicated once again that Summer was gracefully changing into Autumn. I walked the dogs over dew-drenched grass, and as they ran, their feet left dark green tracks. They turned their noses into the tiny whisper of a breeze, barely discernible other than in the gentle swaying of the trees.

I ducked between the strands of barbed wire forming the fence and noticed that some of the blackberries in the hedge had started to darken to a deep purple. I decided to come back later and pick enough to make an apple and blackberry crumble for Pen and Angus. Angus had phoned to say his two girls were finally coming home, and I'd heard the beaming smile in his voice.

As I walked, I mulled over a plan in my mind but wasn't sure if it was practical. Dom had come straight to Mark for advice, and they trusted each other. Could Mark liaise with Dom and help oversee the business for now with the help of Dom's existing team? It would let Dom relocate temporarily until he and Vale decided what they would do?

They were coming down on Sunday, I'd chat to Mark today. Maybe he preferred to keep business and friendships separate, but I decided the suggestion was worth thinking about.

Jeeves had disappeared through the far hedge, and I whistled him back. He knew he should remain in sight and re-appeared with the jaunty swagger of a dog well pleased with himself. He reminded me of a swashbuckling buccaneer returned with tales of derring-do. "You!" I said as he got close, "Are pushing your luck."

He quickly assumed a guileless expression to answer me.

"Come on." I gathered the dogs in, and we walked back to the barn along the old chase from Angus' parent's house. I wondered how his father was faring up in Scotland and how his uncle was? When we popped in later to see Pen and Angus, no doubt we'd get an update.

I made my way into the big shed outside the barn and opened the outside fridge. The shed housed all my dog paraphernalia and the garden equipment. Putting two clean bowls on the counter, I measured out food plus a raw bone for each dog. Jeeves and Bird followed me into the fenced area of the garden to have their breakfast and a relaxing gnaw at the bones.

Mark, still in a bathrobe, opened the door for me and said, "Coffee?"

I couldn't resist slipping my cold hands inside the robe and around his waist. He pulled back, scowling, wrapping it around himself again. "Oi, that's mean."

"Sorry, couldn't resist."

He flicked my backside with the tea towel he had in his hand and said, "I'll get you for that."

As we sat at the breakfast bar, he thumbed through the Saturday paper idly, and I watched his face in profile, the curly hair, wild from being slept on, his tanned face and an overnight growth of stubble. I still hadn't cured him of his slight slouch, and he looked completely relaxed.

"What?" he said without looking up, taking me by surprise. "You're staring, and that usually means you're hatching some devilish plan. It's making me nervous."

I gasped at the accusation, "I'm not."

"Staring or hatching a plan?" He said suspiciously.

"Either," I said, laughing, then continued, "Well…"

"See, I knew."

"It isn't a plan exactly. I just wondered; would you be a good fit to care-take Dom's business until he gets organised? I don't know what's involved or if you have time, but I thought it could solve a few issues in the short term."

In the moment of stillness which followed as he considered my suggestion, I worried that I had said something supremely stupid.

Mark screwed up his face. "He asked me the same thing himself last night, and I said no."

I frowned, "Oh, why?"

"He's offered me jobs several times in the past, but working together isn't the same as being good friends. I worry that it could affect our friendship."

I pursued the idea. "Is that all that's stopping you? Or aren't you interested in the business per se?"

He tilted his head, considering. "I imagine it's exciting. Dom's a talented entrepreneur. He mainly invests in small tech start-ups. It's a bit different from what I'm used to because of the investment side of things, but he has a team of specialists who assess risk. My role would be more mentoring the start-up companies they invest in and overseeing the smooth running of the London side."

I dug a spoon in the sugar and watched as the grains trickled slowly back into the bowl. "If you're honest with each other and write a carefully worded contract, don't you think it could be fun to work together for a while?" I looked at Mark. "I think Dom needs the support. Did you see how distraught he looked last night?" I put the spoon down and reached for his hand. "Why don't you consider it? As long as you have time, and it won't affect your own business."

Mark shrugged, "I could make time if we're talking about a caretaker role. I would have to stop taking new consultancy clients until he appoints someone permanently." Mark ran his hands through his hair. "I don't know, Ellie. I promised myself no more corporate work, not ever."

His face darkened. "It was terrible when Katrina first left. I was away from home when she went back to Russia, and they wouldn't give me time off to go and find her. I vowed I would never relinquish control over my life like that again. When you had your accident last year, I liked that I could be there for you."

I smiled at the memory. "I know, and I was so pleased you were," I rubbed my thumb across his hand. "But would this be the same? It's only temporary, and if you helped Dom on a consultancy basis, you would still retain your flexibility, surely?"

"I'll think about it, Ellie. I'm partly hesitating because if it goes on for longer than we expect and say we did have a baby fairly soon, I'd want to be around. I wouldn't want to miss it all, being in a plane over the Atlantic or tied into some work schedule I couldn't get out of."

I withdrew my hand sharply. "Mark, we don't have to factor babies in yet. With Robin away next year, I'm going to be heavily tied into Touch for the foreseeable."

He pushed his hand through his hair. "But you don't have to be. We could manage that with recruitment, no one is indispensable, Ellie, and both our businesses are much more stable now."

I jabbed the spoon into the sugar several times. "That's easy for you to say, you don't have to cope with all the physical upheaval of being pregnant. Anyway, I'd like to relax and enjoy the business feeling stable for a while, I've had so many years where it's been hand to mouth."

He looked at me. "I can see that, but I don't want to put our personal life on hold forever because of work."

"Look, it's difficult to explain, Mark, but when I came back to England after Brett died, I felt completely disorientated and lost. Having my job, my identity as a physio and building Touch, it all gave me an anchor. "I paused, looking for the right words. "It's more a part of me than just a job."

Mark nodded, "Renovating was a lifeline for me too, but I'd hoped we were both over losing Katrina and Brett now. We've both survived, and we have each other. Don't you trust in that?"

I looked down, "Yes, I do, but I'd like to keep things as they are and relish feeling happy again. You can't say, 'Cheer up, love it may never happen,' to me because I know it can." I could feel my voice rising, and the old familiar panic that I hadn't felt for ages began to surface. "Look at what Pen went through. I couldn't treat patients if I were that sick, and it makes me feel vulnerable to imagine the prospect of not being able to work." To my horror, a fat tear welled up and rolled down my face.

"Ellie," he said, brushing the tear away, "I think you're over-thinking this."

"Don't tell me how I feel," I snapped and turned to walk away.

"Ellie, don't walk away. What is all this?"

I looked furiously at him, "It's everyone pressuring me to have a baby. I like the idea of having a family one day, but I don't know if that day is now."

He rubbed his face, looking frustrated, but crucially did not say, "It's alright, we'll sort it out, there's time," like he usually would. Instead, he said, "When Ellie? When will the time be right?"

My angry flare died away, and I pleaded, "I don't know, there's no rush, surely?"

"No, not exactly, but I would like to think about it soon. If we had a baby next year, he or she could grow up with Lottie. We're both in our thirties. I don't want to be too old with young kids."

I opened my eyes wide in shock. "Next year! Mark, Robin's due to go away next year. What would happen to Touch?"

He banged his coffee cup on the table impatiently. "There will always be something happening in the businesses, there is never a perfect time. We'd cope. Just tell me you'll think about it."

I rolled my eyes. "Fat chance of thinking about anything else, it's all anyone talks about these days."

"Come on, Ellie, that's not fair. It's not like you to be so prickly. Are you sure you're alright?"

"Prickly!" I snorted, "Well, it's not like you to be so

pushy either. We're not even married," I blurted out.

He looked me in the eyes, calling my bluff, "We can easily fix that."

I stopped and stared at him. "Mark Roxbury, if that's a proposal, it's the worst in the history of proposals."

He shrugged, "Just saying! I don't see what that has to do with how you're feeling about having children. I won't love you more because of the piece of paper."

I sighed, "Oh, let's just drop it, I don't want to argue, and anyway, we need to sort Dom and Vale out first."

He turned back to his paper, and I headed off to the shower, but with horrible, deep anxiety in the pit of my stomach and the flames of anger and resentment licking around my galloping brain. Just because everyone had decided it was time for us to have a baby, they were looking at me as if I had two heads and asking if there was something wrong because I wasn't just falling into line. Unbelievable. It was my life, after all.

I needed some time to myself to cool off, so, much to the dogs' disgust, I left them in the fenced garden and headed back to do my blackberrying alone. I've picked blackberries since I was a child on holiday, escaping my mother's clutches and pedalling on my bike to likely spots with an old ice cream tub to place my berries in. I could roam along hedgerows for hours, returning with a box full of nature's bounty, purple lips and stained fingertips.

Picking berries soothed me as a child, and the familiar routine comforted me now. I returned to the barn, feeling calmer and more relaxed. As well as purple fingers and lips, I had a few scratches on my forearms where I'd reached through the hedge for a particularly luscious berry, only to fall foul of the vicious, hooked thorns. Without calling to

Mark, I set about peeling and coring the apples, then chopped with vigour, filling two deep crumble dishes with sharp apple slices and scattering the sweet berries on top. I had just started to rub the butter into a flour and sugar mix, to make the crumble when he emerged from his office. He looked so handsome in his jeans, a grey shirt and navy cashmere sweater. His rueful expression made him look like an errant schoolboy and melted the last of my anger.

"Look at you," he said, "You look like a real wild child, with your hair tangled and your arms all scratched to pieces. What are you making?"

I grinned and shrugged, "Apple and blackberry crumble. One to take to Pen's and one for tomorrow when Dom and Vale come over."

"Will you make me a taster?" he wheedled.

I laughed. This was something Alessandra had always done, made him a miniature of whatever she was baking to taste.

"Okay."

"We'll work it out," he whispered as he bent over to kiss me.

The crumbles came out of the oven, bubbling purple underneath their rough golden crust. Mark demolished his taster with a large dollop of ice cream on top, rubbing his stomach theatrically afterwards and saying, "Delicious, you spoil me."

We wrapped one of the large crumbles in a cloth and set off across the fields to see Pen, Angus and Lottie with the pie in a basket, still hot. The farm kitchen was in its usual lived-in shambles. However, the addition of a pram in the boot room, steriliser on the table, and babygrows on the airer in front of the Aga gave the room an unfamiliar feel.

New baby cards lined the window ledges, and flowers in vases were beginning to wilt, the water showing clouded behind the glass. Both were a testament to the astonishing array of gifts that Pen had received.

Lottie herself was sleeping peacefully in her crib, one arm up and an occasional grimace flitting across her face, which brought her knees up.

"Wind," said Pen, "Thoroughly well-deserved too, she is such a piglet, every two hours last night. The other babies had the decency to lose a little weight after they were born. Lottie has already put some on."

"She needs it Pen, she's so tiny," I said, looking at this newborn soul, who seemed so fragile.

Just then, an enormous and clearly audible fart, brought Belle and Daisy off their sofa to look at the crib, with heads cocked on one side.

We all burst out laughing, and Pen said, "No company manners!"

Angus nudged Pen, "Takes after her mum then."

"Thank you, darling, love you too." She blew a kiss in his direction, then turned to look at me. "What's in the basket, Ellie? Smells heavenly. I'm as ravenous as Lottie; this feeding lark means I need regular sustenance."

I grinned, "Well, you hardly ate for nine months, so it's not surprising,"

She pulled a face, "Don't remind me. It was horrible, don't ever get pregnant, Ellie. Take my advice – adopt."

I didn't dare look at Mark. Instead, I engineered a quick change of conversation, "How's your uncle, Angus?"

Angus shook his head, "He died yesterday, during the night. My dad rang this morning. I'm glad we got to see him, even though it caused some havoc here."

I put my hand on his arm. "Oh no, I'm so sorry."

"Everyone is upset, of course, but nobody would've wanted him to suffer anymore. My cousin and his wife have moved in with Auntie Jess until the funeral, so Dad is flying home tomorrow to see the baby."

"Has your mum been alright at the farm on her own?"

Angus smiled, "Yes, she has, I'm always in and out, depending on which side of the land I'm working on, and she was here this morning doting on Lottie. She'll be glad to have Dad back again though, and then I expect they'll go up to Scotland again for the funeral in a couple of weeks."

Pen looked rueful. "Angus is so busy on the farm at the moment. When the guys from the co-operative tested the wheat, they told him it's ready to harvest now. I'm not supposed to be alone for the first few days, so, what with the harvest and Angus' uncle, this little madam arriving early has put a massive spanner in the works."

"It's certainly been an eventful time. Nice you have Angus' mum close so she can pop in if you need her. Is she thrilled?"

Pen waggled her hand in a so-so gesture. "She is, but it's all tinged with sadness because of the funeral."

"It's so difficult for all of you, it doesn't seem fair. What about your mum and dad? Are they coming to see her soon?"

A look of sadness passed across her face, "They're still away on holiday. As ever, they're always away somewhere. Mum said they went away early to be here for the baby, but clearly, that didn't work out, and now Angus is so busy too. It isn't how I imagined it would be."

I reached across and touched her arm. "Oh, Pen, what a shame."

Angus had worked in the city when he left school, but his father's early heart attack had brought him back to the farm. Pen, who had moved from pillar to post with her father in the army, had embraced farm life, relishing the permanence and being part of the rural community. Even the draughts and the dodgy heating in the old farmhouse didn't deter her.

Their house had been built in the eighteenth century of uneven kiln bricks and had a lichen-covered, shingled roof. The design made it look like 'the house that Jack built.' It had uneven gables on either side and a single-storey Victorian extension that housed the vast kitchen. Originally it had been the only farmhouse on the land. Angus' grandfather had built the more modern house that his parents lived in on the other side of the farm.

Pen was born to be a farmer's wife. She loved animals of all sorts, was more at home in dungarees and wellingtons than a dress, and, unless baking, was generally to be found outside mowing, planting or clearing something. Her curly hair wildly escaped from any restraint, cap or scrunchie, and her face was usually tanned by the sun and wind. We had met through the dogs and had been friends ever since.

I sometimes felt like the mid-point between Pen and Vale. That's always been me, neither fish nor fowl. 52/48 on psychometric tests, academically, I was neither mathematical/logical nor overtly creative/intuitive. Socially, I love the outdoor life and living in the country. Still, I also enjoy dressing up and heading into town for the theatre or an exhibition. I appreciate both sides of an argument, the disadvantage being I sometimes think I don't quite fit in anywhere either. That's probably why physio suits me well. It's an art and a science, traditional and holistic.

Today, however, Pen sounded generally tired and disillusioned, and my heart went out to her. Angus looked at her anxiously. I felt for him, too, it wasn't like Pen to sound so defeated. Unaware of the havoc she'd caused by arriving early, Lottie continued to sleep unperturbed.

As silence fell in the room, Mark reached into the basket for the crumble. "Shall we try this?"

I was glad for a break in the tension. I would catch Pen another time, when she was alone, to let her talk freely. But not today, because today, every conversation seemed fraught with emotion and unforeseen consequences.

Angus headed out onto the farm after eating his crumble.

"I'm so sorry. I'd love to stay," he said, running his hands through hair already stiff with dust from the morning's work. He was behind with the harvest, and we knew he was trying to avoid bringing in contractors to help because of the cost.

While I'd walked the dogs around the edge of the fields, I'd watched the crop grow from small grassy shoots into a sea of rippling stalks bearing knobbly seed heads. Those green stalks had gradually ripened to the rich golden sea that rippled in the breeze and was ready to harvest.

Wheat was the main cash crop of the farm, and Angus couldn't afford to lose it. He also needed to finish bailing the straw and get the bales stowed before the weather broke.

Angus looked like a man pulled in all directions, Pen looked exhausted. The timing of all this was terrible, but nature had taken no notice of that.

Chapter Eight

All Change

The next day, before Dom and Vale arrived, Mark and I both had work to do in the study. He needed to finish his preparation for the meeting with Dom and come to a final decision about what his role might be. I had research to do. I was giving a talk soon, for which my bank manager had put my name forward.

He was a big supporter of the Federation of Small Businesses, and this would be at one of their events. They wanted to hear about my experiences as a small business owner and for me to talk about the development of Touch. I was doubtful about whether I had enough business knowledge to present. I lacked any formal training where business was concerned and felt like an imposter talking to this audience.

James, the regional organiser, had encouraged and charmed me into accepting. I hadn't realised how successfully I had been reeled in until I put the phone down and the doubts came flooding back.

Chewing the end of my pen and putting off getting started, I idly wondered what age James was and how he looked. It was hard to gauge by our conversation. I was flattered he'd followed up on the recommendation. I'd have felt perfectly at ease if it had been a physiotherapy lecture. However, this was a business audience, hence, so far, procrastination had been the order of the day rather than getting down to planning.

Vale had been super-enthusiastic about the presentation when we talked. "Play to your strengths," she had advised, "If you're uncomfortable with business jargon, don't use it. Tell your story in your way, and add in your physiotherapy anecdotes. Most business talks are so dry, Ellie. Think of it as a great opportunity to network and get new referrals. People love talking about their health, and I bet this bunch are all over-stressed, with terrible posture and even worse fitness."

"Oh, just like you," I batted back, looking at her flat stomach, toned legs and long graceful neck.

She laughed, "Believe me, most of the guys I work with never get near the gym. They play an occasional round of golf and drink way too much."

I hoped she was right. I'd imagined a room full of lean, hungry, dot.com sharks who wouldn't hesitate to rip me to shreds.

In the end, I decided to centre the talk around people. How events, different personalities and skill-sets contributed to the creation of Touch. I wasn't sure I could talk about losing Brett in public without crying. The thought of standing in front of a room of business people made me feel anxious enough, so I'd cut myself some slack and glossed over the exact life-change that triggered the move and inspired me to set up my own business.

To get ideas flowing, I wrote random thoughts on a large sheet of paper, then sorted them into groups that sat well together. Finally, I took out a pile of key cards and started to jot down headings until I had a running order. Pleased with my progress, I looked at the PowerPoint logo on the computer and decided that challenge was for another day. I left Mark to his calculations and headed for the kitchen.

Outside, the Indian summer continued. Through the kitchen window, I could see golden leaves gleaming in the sun, with a backdrop of blue sky behind them. Rosehip and bramble stems, laden with fruit, nodded in the breeze. I opened the backdoor and, in the distance, heard the faint thrum of the combine, announcing Angus was at work. According to the weather forecast, rainclouds were gathering and moving in from the west, but today there was no sign. I hoped Angus got finished before they arrived.

The warm weather today posed a slight culinary problem. Yesterday, I was thinking of crisp mornings, comfort food, casseroles, and apple crumble. Today I decided light, summery food would fit the day better. I called through to Mark that I was popping to the shop and received a distracted grunt in reply.

I usually tried to avoid shopping on a Sunday, but now I fancied a different menu enough to break the rule. Slices of hand-carved ham with pickles, ears of corn on the cob and salad had tempted my imagination. The casserole could go into the freezer for another day. As I took my handbag off the dresser, the dogs eyed me mournfully from their baskets. I wasn't giving off a walking vibe, it seemed.

The local farm shop was a single-storey wooden barn painted black that contained excellent local produce displayed on islands skirted with artificial grass. Initially, they sold only fruit and vegetables but had gradually added delicatessen products, local wines, homemade cakes and bread. The largest local vineyard had produced light white wines for several years, and I'd recently noticed a new small vineyard not far from Pen and Angus. This area was turning into the Alsace of the UK.

The shelf of homemade pickles at the farm shop had my full attention when a familiar voice said, "Go with the gooseberry chutney, it comes highly recommended." I spun around, "Pen, what are you doing here?"

She grinned, "Angus' mum and dad are with Lottie, and I have cabin fever, so I've come to buy veggies and to get some fresh air."

I told her Dom and Vale were coming to lunch and filled her in on their situation. "Do you fancy a coffee?"

She looked longingly at the small coffee shop in the corner. Usually, we'd have sat down for a good chinwag. Instead, she said, "Would love to, but I'd better not push it. This is my first time out. Lottie may need a feed, and she'll be vociferously indignant if I'm not there. Next week, I can start to take her out, let's do it then."

I pulled a face, "That sounds very scary, and you're right, they'll worry if you're longer than they expected.

She nodded, "Plus, Angus' parents may never offer to babysit again if Lottie shows her true 'hangry' colours."

I swallowed my disappointment behind laughter at her joke. For a minute there, I'd forgotten about Lottie, and I would love to have had a chat with Pen.

Taking the gooseberry chutney and all I needed for a large mixed salad, I watched as slices of ham fell onto the paper under the butcher's sharp knife; then made my way to the till.

"See you're eating healthy."

One of my ex-patients was peering into my basket from their place behind me in the queue. Why are my patients fascinated by my shopping? Unfortunately, I usually bump into someone when my basket is full of Jammie Dodgers and chocolate, but today I could escape with a polite smile and a jokey, “Practice what you preach.”

When I arrived home, I saw Dom and Vale’s car parked, and there was an inviting smell of fresh coffee wafting toward me. Vale called out to me from the seat in the garden, “I’ve helped myself to your coffee. I hope you don’t mind. There’s a cup in the cafetière for you, the boys have had theirs.”

I dumped the bags on the kitchen counter and said hello to the dogs before filling a mug for myself. As I stepped into the garden, Vale had her face turned to the sun and, at a glance, looked perfectly relaxed, but as she looked towards me, I could see her eyes were puffy with dark smudges underneath.

I walked over and hugged her. “Aww, you’ve been having a nightmare, you poor thing.”

She rubbed under her eyes. “Don’t set me off again. I only came to England for six months and expected to be more than ready to head back to the States. But it’s been nearly two years now, and I’ve settled here. I’m a Brit now, dammit. I can’t believe they’re uprooting me like this.”

Her strong southern drawl tended to suggest otherwise, but I knew what she meant. I hugged her again. “What a nightmare. Are Mark and Dom in the office?”

She nodded, “Dom is desperate for Mark to caretake for him, and he has been thinking up all manner of persuasive arguments.”

I smiled, "There's a good chance he will if he can get over his allergy to corporate life. We were talking about it yesterday. He had such awful problems when Katrina left, and his company gave him a hard time. He's worried about messing up his friendship with Dom too."

Her eyes opened wide with surprise. "I can't see that ever happening."

I shrugged, "Me neither, but you do hear stories of close friends becoming sworn enemies after working together."

She began to look alarmed. "I don't want that on my conscience,"

"I'm sure everything will be fine, but they'll have to work it out between them. Where will you be based when you go back?"

"New York," she said without enthusiasm.

It sounded exciting to me. "Oh wow, I know it isn't very close to your family, but New York will be brilliant, won't it? Think of the fab shopping and the shows. Have you had a chance to think about where you'll live?"

She looked miserable. "No, not yet the company will house us until we find somewhere, a hotel suite to begin with, I expect."

I had never experienced corporate life, so it all sounded pretty glossy to me. But I suppose glossy can be lonely if you haven't got the people you love around you.

Vale sighed, "Dom's determined to come with me. I wanted to resign and stay here, but he said no. It's a mess, Ellie. My job is challenging, I love it, and it's what I've worked towards for years, but I feel selfish taking him away from everyone he loves."

"Come on," I sat next to her and squeezed her shoulder, "Dom's a grown-up guy, he wouldn't do it if he didn't want to, and anyway, it's quite clear that the person he can't bear to be away from is you."

She took a tissue out that was tucked into her sleeve and dabbed her eyes.

I continued, "Who would have thought Dom could be such an old softie? I think it's brilliant that he's putting your career first, and it looks like he can adapt his company structure to support you, so why not?"

She sniffed, "It won't be forever, I promise. I'd much prefer to settle in England. It's so much more liberal than the States. In the meantime, you will visit us, won't you? I'll miss you so much, and Dom is going to miss Mark terribly."

I grinned, "Of course we'll visit, try to keep us away. I've never been to New York."

Noise from inside made us both look up, and Dom came out half-running clutching some papers. "He's agreed," he said gleefully and pulled Vale to her feet to swing her around.

Mark followed more quietly and looked at the joy on both their faces, then looked at me, shrugged and smiled. "Mad," he said.

I smiled, "Madly in love." I was glad he'd taken the plunge to help Dom and squeezed his hand, "Well done you."

He grimaced, "I don't know what I've let myself in for, but when he asked me how I would feel if it was you going away, he knew he had me." Mark bent to kiss me. "I couldn't bear it. I know what being left behind feels like, and I wouldn't wish it on anyone."

Mark's reference to his pain when Katrina left, made me worried, I hoped Dom going wouldn't open the old wound.

But then a guilty thought crossed my mind, perhaps while Mark settled in at Dom's, it might buy me some time on the baby issue. I chased the ignoble thought away. I was not going to be a coward about this, we would have to work it out together.

"This calls for celebration," said Dom. He ran outside and produced champagne in a cold bag from the boot of his car, like a rabbit out of a hat.

I couldn't help laughing at the bare-faced cheek of him, he had assumed all along he'd be able to talk Mark round.

We moved inside and drank champagne round the breakfast bar while I assembled the salad. The effect of the bubbles, with Dom and Vale's elation, made us all giggly, and the talk was light-hearted. We toasted to love, and travels, then inevitably Lottie. I waited for the 'you next' baby remarks, which could spark off the tension again, but thank goodness they didn't come, so the day passed without further incident. As we waved Dom and Vale off, I felt more relaxed than I had for the last few weeks.

As we turned towards the barn, I said, "That was lovely. What a shame they'll be away for a while. We must go out to see them. I've never been to New York."

Mark rested his arm across my shoulder. "Well, it will be my pleasure to show you the sights, Miss Rose."

"Breakfast at Tiffany's?"

He shook his head, "They still don't have a café, but we could window gaze with a bagel, I'm sure there are plenty of items that may interest you."

I laughed and nodded, "I'm sure there are."

He wagged a cautionary finger. "Beware, if you have to ask the price, you can't afford it!"

“How disappointing that there’s no café, someone should do something about that!”

He squeezed me close to his side. “I will personally e-mail them in the morning.”

I laughed at his nonsense, and he caught me around the waist, pulling me into him. “I love you, Ellie.” He bent forward to kiss me, and I thought, *this is perfect, why would we change anything*?

“There is just one small favour that would make the day better…”. I looked at him thoughtfully for a moment to keep him guessing, and watched the fleeting expressions of concern, then curiosity flick across his face. Slowly reaching forward, I undid the top button of his shirt, tracing my finger in the ‘v’ of skin now exposed.

Chapter Nine

Home and Away

Every time I thought about my presentation to the business association, I felt butterflies and the need to eat chocolate to calm myself. Used to a dedicated audience of physios who chose to attend courses based on my expertise, I found my reincarnation as a business speaker to be out of my comfort zone. I simultaneously felt irritated by my lack of confidence and cross because Mark refused to acknowledge a problem existed. He seemed unshakably confident that all would go well despite my misgivings.

I was looking forward to my coffee with Pen to have a proper chat about how I felt. I knew she'd get it. Unfortunately, it became apparent when we met that taking Lottie out for the first time was Pen's main preoccupation. My worries about business talks were quite rightly the last thing on her mind.

I'd offered to pick them up, but of course, my car was no use because we needed a baby seat, so in the end, it was Pen who drove. We decided not to be too ambitious initially, so we headed for the local garden centre. It was more of an expedition than we had bargained for even so, and I had not realised how much paraphernalia one small infant required. When we finally managed to extract the travel seat from the back of the car and fix it onto its base, which was a PhD thesis all by itself, Lottie was awake and had begun to cry fretfully.

"Probably needs a change," said Pen, as she looked at me for confirmation.

I shrugged, "No good asking me. You know I'm clueless."

Pen tried to reassure us both by saying, "Alessandra said change, wind, hungry or thirsty are the go-to things. Then if those are all sorted and providing there is no temperature or rash, apply love, and that's all baby's need at this age."

I was impressed. "Sounds very sensible."

Pen looked worried, nonetheless. "It's terrifying sometimes, Ellie, not knowing what the problem is and being completely responsible for her life."

"I'm convinced," I said, looking at Lottie, whose face was bright red and dominated by the most indignant set of gums ever to be bared in frustration. "Would you prefer to go home? Would that be easier?"

She shook her head, "No, we're here now, and I have to start getting out and about with her, or I'll go crazy. Can you find a table? While I go and check her, she smells ominous. I won't be a tick, sorry."

"Don't worry, take your time." I looked around the café for a suitable table with room for the buggy and plumped for one in the corner. I manoeuvred the buggy alongside it then went to the counter and bought two coffees and a Belgian bun each. Pen's appetite had returned, but she still needed to regain some weight, and as she was feeding Lottie, I knew she was enjoying illicit snacks.

The coffee was cold before Pen reappeared, looking

very flustered. "I'm sorry, she had poo everywhere, I got the worst off with a wipe and ended up dunking her in the sink."

I pulled a sympathetic face. "Nice! No wonder she was crying, poor little thing. I'll get you a fresh coffee, that one's gone cold."

Pen sighed, "I never seem to get a hot coffee these days."

Pen settled Lottie, and peace reigned again. She started to explain about the funeral up in Scotland. "We're not going, it's too much. I don't feel up to the journey, and Angus is still so busy on the farm. At least his Auntie Jessie understands, she's been a farmer's wife all her life."

"Are Angus's parents flying up for it?"

Pen rattled the row of brightly coloured ducks on the buggy and smiled at her daughter. "Yes, we'll drop them at the airport, and one of his cousins can pick them up."

I looked across the table at my friend's tired face. "If it's a problem, tell us, one of us may be able to drop them off. It would save you the trip."

Pen gave me a brief smile. "Okay, thanks, Ellie, hopefully, I'll feel more like driving again by then. I feel a bit shaky, driving with Lottie in the car at the moment."

I wasn't sure what to say, Pen not confident in the car? This was the girl who would drive anywhere and anything, from a battered Landrover to a combine harvester.

I tried to comfort her. "You're probably still beaten up from the delivery and sleep-deprived. You can't expect to be fully recovered, give yourself time. You don't have to be superwoman."

"I certainly don't feel like superwoman, that's for sure." Pen stirred her coffee and spooned the froth off the top into her mouth. A silence fell, so I tried a different tack

"I heard Angus out on the fields in the tractor until late on Sunday; how is the harvest coming?"

Pen nodded, "He's been putting in the hours, but we got the wheat and straw in in time. He's ploughing in and drilling seeds now. Angus prefers not to burn because our fields are so close to houses – if a fire got out of control, there could be a disaster."

I hated seeing clouds of smoke drifting from the fields and across roads. "I bet it avoids complaints from the neighbours too."

She laughed, "Well, that's you guys, so think yourself lucky. You could have been smoked out. Who knows, once Angus has finished the harvesting work, he might have time to get to know his daughter." She tried to laugh again, but it sounded a bit hollow, and she didn't meet my eye.

I reached across the table and rubbed her arm. "Is everything alright Pen?"

She shrugged, "I suppose so. We're both shattered, which doesn't help. Angus is besotted by Lottie when he sees her, but his life just carries on. Yesterday, he ate his meal and went out to Young Farmers, didn't even think I might need some adult company."

I felt indignant on her behalf. "Oh Pen, why didn't you say something to him? Or you could have given me a call."

"I couldn't say anything, he'd asked did I mind if he went, and I said no, but I never dreamed he'd actually go. You know?"

I shook my head, "You'll have to have a word, he hasn't realised how you feel."

There was a definite tremor in her voice as she said, "I know, but I don't want to seem like a boring nag-bag."

I started to reply, but she changed the subject. "Anyway, enough about my life, how are you? How is life in the outside world?"

We chatted about Dom and Vale, and then I tried to tell her how nervous I felt about the talk coming up, but she looked at me as if I was crazy and said, "I'm sure you'll be amazing. You do presentations all the time, what are you panicking for?"

Before I had a chance to explain, Lottie started to stir, which galvanised us both. Pen wanted to get home before Lottie kicked off, and I thought that was a good plan.

I put Lottie's seat in the car while Pen wrestled the frame into the back. Lottie smelt of baby lotion, and as I brushed a kiss on her cheek, her skin felt delicate and smooth. She was quite appealing when she wasn't crying.

As Pen dropped me off and I waved goodbye, I felt concerned. I would pop down and see Pen again soon. She didn't seem in great spirits, and with the harvest, the funeral and a new baby to cope with, she'd been thrown in at the deep end.

I was glad she and Alessandra were chatting, hopefully, that made up a little for her mum being away. Angus' mum was preoccupied with the family in Scotland as well, which left Pen a bit stranded. Having the support of someone like Alessandra, who'd done it all before, must have been reassuring.

Of course, my issues weren't on the same scale as Pen's, but I still wished I had someone to talk to. I suppose we all need a listening ear occasionally, and all mine seemed to be either firmly in the baby camp or preoccupied with other things.

On the day of my talk, I arrived at the Federation of Small Businesses meeting, having emailed my new PowerPoint presentation to the business centre earlier that day. I hoped I looked business-like in a smart suit, carrying my notes in a briefcase.

As I left the barn, Mark said from his recumbent position on the couch. "That's a sexy look, I love the power dressing. You'll knock'em dead." I rolled my eyes, feeling anything but sexy or powerful. I wanted the audience to engage with my talk, not how I looked.

With Vale's advice in mind, I spoke simply about why I had gone into business and what I had done. I did not try to emulate the usual business talks, which were driven by statistics and protocols.

The presentation went surprisingly well, and as the talk progressed, I warmed to my theme of a business built around key personnel, providing the best services for the people who used it. No one in the audience seemed to find the idea stupid, or if they did, they were polite enough not to give me a hard time in the question-and-answer session afterwards.

I left the room feeling elated. James, who turned out to be in his mid-forties, was indeed a confident, charming man. He ran a wine importing business, and it was easy to see that he regularly hosted events.

James worked the room efficiently, deftly fielding anyone on their own and introducing them to others. He also managed to bring together people whose businesses could be complementary to facilitate successful networking.

Despite all that, James still found time to make me feel at ease. Well, more than that, he made me feel special and interesting. He managed to spin my business so that virtually everyone asked for a card. I had the feeling I was watching a Jedi Master at work. On the way home, I realised with some surprise that what I saw as relying on my instincts had given me a valid business model after all. Lucky for me, because I knew that I would struggle to manage my business any other way.

An unexpected spin-off from the talk happened when James phoned the next day to thank me. "Ellie, I wondered, as your talk was such a hit if you'd be prepared to go to other regional meetings to give the same presentation? We would pay your expenses, of course, as well as the speaker's fee. I know it's short notice, and please don't feel pressured, but there has been a cancellation on Thursday of next week in Surrey."

I explained that I wasn't sure how Thursday would pan out because I knew I had patients booked in already but that I'd ring him back.

I chatted it over with Mark. He would be in London next week with Dom, and it would save a lot of travelling if he stayed over. As he wasn't going to be around, the idea of a trip away sounded appealing.

I rang Sarah, who was obviously surprised – it was rare that I cancelled a list. She did a bit of juggling with my patients and said that if I worked extra hours earlier in the week, I could free up Thursday afternoon and Friday without letting anyone down.

"You're turning into a bit of a star then," Sarah said, looking impressed, "You wouldn't catch me standing up in front of all those strangers."

I laughed, "Ah yes, but then I'm rubbish at admin and can only type with two fingers. Making these presentations scares the living daylights out of me too. I'm confident with physio talks but trying to speak to a business audience frightens me more. I have full-on imposter syndrome!"

Sarah shook her head. "They don't see that, or they wouldn't have invited you back. Shall I phone this chap for you and let him know you can free up the time?"

"Don't worry, I'll phone him." I wasn't averse to another chat with the charming James.

As the meeting was in Guildford, it was nearly halfway to Portsmouth, where Mum and Dad lived. I decided to drive on down to see my parents. A visit was overdue, as Mum reminded me every time she rang. I could kill two birds with one stone.

I certainly didn't want to ask Pen for help, as she had enough to cope with, so with Mark away in London, I decided I would take the dogs with me. They would enjoy the beach walks, and it would be a nice change for them and me.

Mark left for London on Monday. We'd had a lovely lunch together on Sunday and spent the afternoon walking it off along the seawall from Burnham to Fambridge. I waved him off, knowing he had a hectic few days ahead of him, but I'd seen the sparkle in his eye – I thought Mark probably thrived on a challenge more than he realised.

As I had a few days to myself before the talk, I wanted to spend some of it with Pen and rang to say I'd bring dinner with me and visit after work tonight if she was home.

When I arrived, Lottie was awake and enjoying a little freedom, stretched on a playmat. My dogs sniffed curiously at this small addition to the household, then succumbed to the temptation of the dog sofa and piled happily in a heap with their Pointer friends. Pen and I chatted over a bowl of chicken casserole with rice. As Lottie was still awake, I picked her up. I wasn't sure if she'd remember me, but she came to me quite happily. I stood rocking gently from foot to foot as we had a cuddle. She still seemed frighteningly tiny, with such delicate limbs, even though she had been steadily gaining weight.

"Lottie's two weeks old already," said Pen, as she stretched out on the sofa with a contented groan. "I have to pinch myself sometimes to remember what my life was like before she was born. At least she seems happier, and more settled the last couple of days."

"I suppose as she came early, this is getting closer to when she would have been full term. Perhaps she didn't feel great initially either."

Pen grimaced, "That makes two of us."

"Pen," I took my fence at a rush, "You would tell me if you felt depressed, rather than just dog tired, wouldn't you? You can say anything to me, and you don't have to pretend. You've had so much to cope with, the awful sickness, the birth, and everything that's happened since. Lottie being your first baby was going to be a big adjustment anyway without everything else."

Pen looked at me seriously, seeming to consider what I'd said. "I'm a bit up and down. Some days I'm fine, then others, I can burst into tears just because I've knocked the milk over or something. I thought being a mum would be easier. It's taking me time to bounce back and get to grips with everything."

I nodded, "Your hormones are all over the place as well, which doesn't help." I took both her hands. "If you get stuck on a downer for more than a few days, you must say."

She blushed, "Thanks, Ellie. Alessandra mentioned that

today too. She said, as long as the baby is clean and fed, forget about everything else."

I grinned, "She's right, blow the housework, sleep when Lottie sleeps. If it's getting too much, let me help with the stuff I can do. I can walk the hounds or do housework, ironing, and food. Would it help if I bring stuff for the freezer?"

Pen laughed, "Blimey Ellie, the ironing? Are you sure? You hate ironing."

I rolled my eyes. "I do! Maybe that was a step too far. Seriously though…"

"Don't worry about food, everyone is determined to feed me up. Alessandra has already brought food for the freezer, and when Sarah popped in to see Lottie, she brought some too, so I'm doing well."

"Good, people want to help, so let them."

Pen looked at me seriously, and I saw tears well up in her eyes. "I tell you something, Ells, being a mum is the most ferocious, passionate feeling. I love Lottie so much, I can't explain, but it's a bit overwhelming too."

I kissed her on the cheek. "I think you're doing great, and she's a lucky baby."

The idea of loving another being with that passion wasn't new to me. It was how I'd felt about Brett. Only now, hearing her say it about Lottie, it filled me with dread. Losing him had nearly torn me apart. I looked at Pen, and all I could think of was the awful grief I'd felt at the time of losing him and how it still caught me unawares sometimes.

Over the next two days, Pen and I ventured out over the fields to walk the dogs together, with Lottie in a papoose. Pen had more colour in her cheeks and seemed relaxed.

Perhaps there was no post-natal depression after all.

I was much happier when I left for my talk in Guildford. Sarah had promised to pop in to see Pen, and I knew Alessandra was helping her too. Angus' workload on the farm was finally slowing down, so I hoped he would be able to spend more time with Pen from now on.

Mark rang every night from London; he was working long days getting to know Dom's team and bemoaned the fact that he was all alone in a palatial room, with an empty king-sized bed and only a computer to keep him company.

"You make sure it stays empty." I said, "no cavorting with eagle-eyed, sharp-suited, young businesswomen."

"Ellie!"

"Just saying."

On Thursday, I loaded the car before going to work and managed to finish my patient list in good time to get to Guildford and settle into my accommodation before the talk. I think James' secretary had been taken aback by my need for a dog-friendly room but had nonetheless found me a neat little holiday apartment on a farm, which suited me perfectly.

"Here I go again," I said to the dogs as I changed my jeans and sweatshirt for a business suit and picked up my briefcase, ready to head off. They were not impressed by my transformation. Business clothes did not signify a walk for them, so they weren't interested. They had eaten and had a good run, and a long snooze was their order of the day, whatever I was off to do.

I was astonished to see James when I arrived.

"Ellie!" He came over and kissed me on both cheeks, "Good to see you."

I smiled, "Hi James, I wasn't expecting you to be here."

He made an 'it's nothing' gesture with his hands. "We try to get to one another's meetings from time to time, so I thought I'd come today to introduce you. Dave, who organises this region, is a good friend."

"Well, thank you, that's very thoughtful."

"No, no, my pleasure, you've got us out of a hole today. It's the least I could do. Perhaps we could grab a bite to eat afterwards?"

I blushed at his unexpected invitation, "Um, well…"

"Good, that's settled, look forward to it."

I didn't have time to think any more about it as Dave called the meeting to order, and I joined him on the rostrum.

If I felt a little awkward about being swept off to dinner by James, I needn't have done. We ate in a very good pub-restaurant, not far from the farm. James was easy company, funny and spent some time explaining how to taste the wines he chose. We gently rocked the wine first, blew in the glass to clear the evaporated alcohol and then breathed in the rising aromas. I could smell cherries and plums with something mineral behind them.

He clapped his hands. "Ellie, you have a natural nose. That's gunpowder you can smell, classic in these wines."

I flushed with pleasure. Next, we rolled the wine around our mouths, me trying not to laugh and spit it out, James with a look of concentration.

"I'm getting fruits and honey, then right at the back end of the mouthful, something earthy. What about you, Ellie?"

I took another mouthful. "Fruits and then something different, but I'm not sure what."

"It takes regular practice," he said mock-seriously, "but it's fascinating to develop your senses."

He looked at me over the rim of his glass, his blue eyes

and neatly cut hair so different to Mark's curls and dark eyes. Poised and confident, I decided he was a very attractive man.

Changing the subject from wines, he asked, "So I know all about how you started your business from your talks. What's next for you?"

I looked up, surprised, "Next?"

He nodded, "Yes, where are you hoping to go with your business?"

I paused before answering and bit my lip, unsure of how much he really wanted to hear. "I'm at a bit of a crossroads. I'm interested in holistic therapies and wouldn't mind looking at developing that aspect. They blend ideally with the well-being side of physio. When I did my masters, I took an elective module in psychology, listening skills and basic counselling, that interests me too. And then my boyfriend would like a family."

He cocked his head to one side. "And you? Would you like a family?"

I sipped my wine again, then swirled it around the glass, looking at the legs form as it ran back down the glass. "I don't know, I love my work, and I feel like I could end up doing everything badly if I'm juggling both things."

He made an open gesture with his hands. "Ellie there's nothing wrong with not wanting kids. You don't have to, you know."

I grimaced, "I know that. Perhaps you'd like to tell everyone that's nagging me, though. I'm not normally indecisive, I don't know what's the matter with me."

He grinned, "Sounds like you need a holiday."

I could grow to like this man, I thought, as we both laughed.

Chapter Ten

I need a break!

As I closed the door to my cottage, I fanned my face and said, “Phew,” to the dogs, “think that wine has gone to my head.”

The image of James’ intriguing eyes teasing me over the glass stayed with me as I looked at myself in the mirror and removed all traces of my make-up mask, and cleaned my teeth. I looked at the pale and freckled face before me from all angles. This was the face Pen, and Mark saw, but it had been fun to be more sophisticated tonight. Maybe Vale always felt like this with her immaculate make-up and clothes? Empowering and sexy, it felt intoxicating.

More like intoxicated, I thought. I was aware that James could become a serious distraction for me in a cleverly understated way. Although he was older, he reminded me of Brett with his teasing and sense of fun. I suppose his challenging me to do new things had also made me feel adventurous again and compounded my restlessness.

I had certainly felt a tantalising tingle as we rolled rich red wine around our mouths, and he watched me taste for its layered flavours.

I wandered away from the mirror and into the bedroom, pacing around the room, feeling unable to settle. I thought, *Luckily, you won't be seeing James very often if he bothers you this much.* Did I mean that? I wasn't entirely sure. It was glamorous and fun to be flirting over a glass of wine without a care in the world and no talk of babies.

The phone rang and made me jump. I grabbed the receiver, my heart pounding,

"Hi, Babe." Not James! Mark's voice sounded bone-tired and nudged me out of my imaginings.

I sat on the bed and arranged the pillows behind me. "Hi you, how did today go?"

"I'm shattered. It's been back-to-back meetings. Everyone is sizing me up and trying to second guess what I'm going to be like."

I frowned, "Oh no, being the new kid on the block sounds daunting. I suppose Dom's team is feeling a bit insecure with him moving away."

"Yes, it will all settle down, but I need to learn the ropes fast, or they'll lose confidence. Dom's a hard act to follow." He sounded weary and a bit vulnerable.

"Come on. You'll be fine, look at how much people love Robin at Touch, yet he's so different to me. You've got other qualities, they will see that." James' face slipped out of my mind as I applied myself to comforting Mark. I pictured him lying across his hotel bed. He'd be lying propped up on one elbow, phone to his ear, tie hanging loose around an open collar, eyes hooded with fatigue. *Mark, your boyfriend!* I reminded myself sternly, *Don't you forget it!* Right now, he sounded like he needed a hug.

He sighed, "I know, I'm just tired. It's been a long day. How did your talk go?"

Eager to sound upbeat, I said, "It was great, and the talk went down well again."

"Did you find it alright and meet the chap who runs it?"

"Yes, I did. James came down to introduce me, and we had a pub meal afterwards. He comes to different meetings sometimes."

His voice sounded guarded. "I bet he does. So would I if you were there."

I blushed and was grateful Mark couldn't see. "Don't be like that; he was only being thoughtful because I helped them out at short notice."

Mark didn't sound convinced. "Hmm, he'd better not be trying to steal you."

I clicked my tongue impatiently. "He isn't!" And changed the subject hastily. "Have you managed to eat something? You're always crabby when you're hungry."

"After a fashion, Dom had a takeaway delivered, and we ate it going over some papers."

Thinking of my lovely dinner and wine, I felt guilty. "Oh, poor you. Is this project more than you bargained for?"

"No. Well, perhaps. I knew it would be difficult to start with. Dom's got a good team. I've just got to get through this first bit. There's one good thing. We'll have a nice injection of funds while I'm here, Dom is paying me well. I'll whisk you away for a romantic holiday."

"That sounds good," I said, thinking, *don't mention babies now and spoil it.* I mentally crossed my fingers.

"I miss you, Ellie."

I smiled into the phone, "I miss you too."

He yawned, "I'm going to sign off and grab some sleep. Hope you have a good couple of days with your parents."

"Okay, I'll ring you tomorrow."

As I hung up the phone, I realised I felt calmer again and sleepy now. It had done me good to chat with Mark. I needed to be careful with dangerous imaginings.

Mark was especially sensitive about honesty after Katrina, he didn't deserve to be hurt, and we didn't need any more complications than we already had. I disturbed the snoozing hounds and took them out for a last walk, then settled into the comfy bed and clicked off the light.

The next morning, a buttery light filtered through the gold curtains onto my face and woke me gently. The dogs had slept in with me and now watched as I pulled on my jeans and a jumper. Their hopeful eyes brightened further when I pushed my feet into wellies, they circled excitedly, more than ready for a walk around this new place with all its enticing smells.

Wet from the dew on our return, I towelled them briskly and loaded them into the car to dry off. I made my way through the walled garden of the main farmhouse to the dining room and took my place at the table laid for one.

One other man was finishing his breakfast; he had pushed aside his plate with smears of egg yolk, brown sauce and a curly bacon rind, suggestive of a full English breakfast. As I looked at the menu, he sank uneven, nicotine-stained teeth into a slice of toast and disappeared behind his newspaper with not so much as a 'good morning' to me. At first glance, I put him down as middle-aged but realised with a shock, as I observed him more closely, that he was probably about the same age as James.

Unusually, I was ravenous. Even Nylon-shirt man couldn't put me off my breakfast. I ordered scrambled egg on toast, which arrived plentiful on the plate. I eyed the rich, creamy yellow mound with enthusiasm, made with fresh eggs from the farm. I dispatched the lot, along with strong tea, two rounds of toast and homemade marmalade. I felt like a new woman and was fortified to cope with the impending visit to my mother.

I negotiated the country lanes back to the A3 and took the southbound carriageway. As I drove, I sang along happily to the Eurythmic's Greatest Hits.

Jeeves took up the refrain, howling hopelessly out of tune but with great enthusiasm. The miles of familiar road slipped away until I paused after the majestic sweep around the Devil's Punchbowl, stopped by traffic lights at the narrow crossroads in Hindhead. There outside the antique shop were my favourite statues, two Great Danes, a dog and a bitch. I hoped no one ever bought them unless it was me. They had marked the last leg of so many journeys home since I was a little girl. As the lights turned green, I pressed on, past the empty and forlorn-looking army base, over Butser Hill, past Langston Harbour and through the familiar streets of Portsmouth, to my parents' house. Mum was twitching the curtains on the lookout for me. She opened the front door before I had unloaded the dogs.

"Graham, she's here. Hello darling, come on in." she turned impatiently towards the house. "Graham, come and get Ellie's bags."

Dad emerged from the study, slightly stooped, I noticed, and bent to kiss my cheek. "Good to see you, Ellie, I'd better go and get your things, or I'll be in trouble."

They were both delighted to see me. Mum had made shortbread to go with coffee and had a million questions tripping off her tongue as always. Poor old Dad couldn't get a word in edgeways, but he sat back and listened. He and I would get our chat later when we went for a walk along the beach.

The beach has never quite felt the same for me since the day I walked it endlessly when the news of Brett's death came. But at least I could go there and appreciate its beauty again now. Dad accompanied me then, a steadying presence at my side; since I was a little girl, it had been our special place.

Unfortunately, despite the happy start to my visit, lunch became a little tense. We were chatting about my friends that Mum and Dad had met in Essex, and Mum naturally asked about Lottie. I showed them both the photos I had taken.

"Mark and I are going to be Lottie's Godparents."

Echoing the same sentiment that half the world seemed to have, she said, "Oh, how lovely, that will be nice. You live so close to each other; when you and Mark have kids, they'll all be able to play together."

I froze, and out of the corner of my eye, I saw Dad flick a quick frown in Mum's direction.

Mum stared at him, "Why are you frowning me down, Graham? I'm sure Ellie has thought about it. After all, they've been together a long time now, and it doesn't do to leave these things too late."

Tired of everyone assuming that children were the next step for me, I added, "Well, we may decide not to have children at all."

Mum laughed incredulously, "Oh, what nonsense. Of course, you will. Mark will come around to the idea. We'd love to have grandchildren; nearly all the girls in your old class already have children." She nodded enthusiastically, "I see some of the mums at W.I. You're our only hope, remember. I expect Alessandra feels the same as Mark's an only child too."

"Susan, really!" Dad sounded exasperated. He could see I was retreating behind my defences, so often the case when my mum blunders in.

"Actually, Mum, it isn't Mark. He'd love to have kids; it's me. I don't feel ready yet."

She stared at me in shock, "Well, you be careful. You aren't as young as you were. He's a lovely man, and if he wants children, you could lose him to another girl who's less career-minded."

"Susan!" Dad looked mortified.

"I'm just saying…"

I listened with mounting anger; my appetite killed stone-dead. I stood abruptly. "I think I'll take the dogs down to the beach."

Trying to bridge the yawning gap which had opened up, Dad said, "I'll help your mother clear, then come and join you."

"Fine," I said and headed for the door. "Leave the washing up; I'll do it when I get back."

I knew she wouldn't, but I couldn't bear the thought of her pursuing the grandchildren agenda in the kitchen if I went in to help her now. The walls of my old home felt like they were closing in. The thought of Pen looking at Lottie with so much love and the memory of the pain I felt when I lost Brett were jostling in my head. Suddenly images of me juggling a crying baby in one arm and an ultrasound in the other flashed in my mind. My thoughts seemed to have accelerated and were making me feel panicky. I needed to get out of the house.

I took in deep breaths and let the onshore breeze blow away my frustration and panic as I wandered to the water's edge and watched the dogs pouncing on seaweed as it was pushed up and down by the waves rolling in.

Never famed for her tact, Mum had just applied one more turn of the baby screw. Was there nowhere I could go where people weren't pressuring me to have a baby? No wonder James had felt so attractive last night. Gulls screeched overhead, mocking me.

"Ellie, there you are." I heard Dad's feet crunching over the pebbles. "Don't worry about what your mother said, no one is pressuring you. It's up to you and Mark to decide. Nothing to do with us or what we'd like."

"Yes, well, that's the point Dad; everyone *is* pushing. I feel like they all think they have a right to my life. But it'll be me who has to change my life completely if I have a baby. They will buy cute clothes and have cuddles, then go home. You haven't seen Pen yet. She looks like a shell, and anyway, I like my life, how it is."

"Gosh," he said, smothering a smile, "Is that all that's bothering you, and I thought it was something serious!"

I looked at him, my forehead pleated in a scowl, then saw his soft smiling eyes, full of concern but gently coaxing too. I relented; Dad could always make me smile.

"Why do things have to change, Dad?"

He shrugged, "That's life, Ellie. There's no way out of that, you must keep finding a way forward."

I looked away into the distance, then glanced back at his familiar face. "Very philosophical, I'm quite happy moored up in my little creek, thank you."

He shook his head, "Sadly, you aren't the only force at work here, my darling. It sounds like your boat is on the move, like it or not. No point resisting, decide where you're heading next."

I snorted, "If everyone doesn't get off my back about babies, I may bail out and head for Australia again." I was only half-joking. I had returned to England after Brett's funeral, and memories of mine and Brett's idyllic life there seemed very appealing.

"Well, you can run, but problems have a habit of catching up with you." He patted my arm awkwardly. "You'll work it out, Ellie, but I would say you're only looking at the downside of having a family and forgetting all the joy. I can't explain how much we loved you when you were born. Still love you. No sleepless nights or inconvenience could ever make us regret that."

He put an arm around my shoulder and gave me a squeeze. "Take your time. You and Mark are the only ones who can decide."

We walked on, chatting about this and that until he said, "Better head for home. Susan will be fretting. I know she says the wrong thing sometimes, but she means well."

I looked at him sceptically. It seemed to me that Mum cared too much about presenting the right appearance to other people, and it was clear that right now, she was ready to boast to the W.I. about her grandchildren.

As we walked back to the house, my words, spoken in jest, turned around in my head. A trip to Australia would be fantastic. Whatever Dad felt about me running away, I felt like I needed a break.

Chapter Eleven

Max and Annie

As I said goodbye to Mum and Dad and drove around the long sweep of Langston Harbour to leave Portsmouth, I looked at the calm waters reflecting the blue sky. As I joined the A3 North, the curve in the road meant that I turned my back to the sea quite abruptly, began to climb over the South Downs and headed north towards home.

My thoughts were anything but tranquil. I couldn't find the right soundtrack for my mood either. Annie Lennox began singing *'Sister's are doin' it for themselves'*, which felt exactly right for Ellie; public speaker and flirt of a sophisticated older man (whose lifestyle seemed very appealing just now). However, *'The Miracle of Love'* had me almost in tears. I thought of Mark and how he had tenderly helped me piece my crumbling world back together after Brett died, and I felt like a complete traitor for enjoying my meal with James yesterday and feeling a twinge of attraction.

I stopped the music. I preferred to listen to my thoughts rather than hear Annie Lennox's musical reproaches as the trees and fields sped by. Scenes from the last few weeks were jumbled in my head. I imagined Pen's pale, tired face and Lottie's angry one and my instinctive recoil from how dramatic and demanding it all seemed. I was shocked at how vulnerable I felt when I saw that love. I knew what pain that kind of love could bring.

Dad's comforting hug and his assurance that everything they had gone through, every worry and inconvenience, had been worth it because they loved me, were supposed to be a comfort, but they weren't. I thought of the horror of losing Brett. Had that been worth it because I'd loved him so much? Would it have been better never to have met him?

Never knowing Brett seemed unthinkable, but could I put myself through it again? What if I lost a baby that I loved like that? I wasn't sure I could cope. Losing Brett had nearly broken me. I remembered Mark's quiet confidence that we could surmount any obstacles a baby might bring and my angry reaction that it was alright for him, his life wouldn't change. Why, when he had lost Katrina and nearly lost everything, wasn't he as afraid as I was of committing himself again?

Over and over, the thoughts tumbled in my head like waves on the shore I had just left. I felt bewildered and didn't know what to think anymore. More conservative than Brett but sensitive and caring, did I love Mark enough to settle and have a family? He had made me feel safe until now, but he wanted more. My eyes glazed over with tears. I pulled into the services near Guildford and let them fall unchecked into the plastic-tasting coffee from my mother's flask. The dogs, always sensitive to my mood, whined softly in the back of the car. I was upsetting them, and after several minutes I thought angrily, "*Enough self-pity. For goodness sake, shape-up woman! If your patients could see you now, they wouldn't recognise their calm, confident therapist – she of the wise words…"*

I used my fail-safe distraction to relax, closed my eyes and, in my mind, walked along the cliff path from Bondi to Bronte. The dramatic scenery had made this our favourite Sunday morning walk when I lived in Sydney with Brett. I imagined the sun on my face, a warm breeze and the sound of crashing waves. I wished I was back there right now and not in motorway services near Guildford, crying.

The last time I'd been at Bronte was a stolen afternoon just before my exams. It was a beautiful, sheltered bay, much less frequented than Bondi next door and with lower surf. I'd sighed contentedly as I stretched out on my towel and let the sun play over my skin. Pale at best, it seemed almost translucent after too many hours of revising at the library under artificial light.

I remembered feeling guilty about being at the beach, not in my room preparing for the looming final exams. I had spent far too much time the previous week staring absently into space and daydreaming about Brett.

Brett's torso had cast a shadow on my face, and I'd opened my eyes to see him smiling at me. "Swim?" he'd said, holding out his hand.

I'd nodded, and he'd pulled me to my feet. "I'll give you a head start; count of ten, last one to the sea buys the gelato!"

What a mistake; he'd never seen me run. I had been county champion over two hundred metres, admittedly ten years before, but still, I'd taken off over the sand in earnest and reached the water before he caught me. I could still remember the pull of the sand on my feet and that first cold spritz as the water splashed my legs.

"Not bad for a Pom," he'd said when he caught me splashing through my first wave. "We'll make a lifeguard of you yet. You win. I'll buy the gelato."

The Baywatch fantasy had died abruptly when we started swimming. Seeing Brett in the water came back to me as if it were yesterday. He'd taken off, cutting through the surf with clean, powerful freestyle strokes, leaving me for dead. I'd set off after him in a less athletic style, with my corkscrew-kick breaststroke, spitting out the occasional mouthful of saltwater as I mistimed a wave. The sea had been glorious, as crisp and refreshing as the day was hot and dusty. I'd paused for breath and trodden water looking around for Brett. The sun-spangled waves bordered by the rugged, red-clay cliffs of the bay made a perfect picture. Hard to believe that in those idyllic waters, serious predators roamed, although not at Bronte, because of the shark nets. The unfortunate idea of sharks had only just crossed my mind, accompanied inevitably by a riff of the pulsing theme from Jaws when I'd felt a sharp tug on my leg, which surprised a startled shriek from me. The surface of the water broke, and the wide, grinning smile, not of a Great White, but Brett, appeared.

"Gotcha!" he'd laughed, and his eyes teased me as he enjoyed the joke, humming the same theme that had just been playing in my head.

I'd chopped my hand across the surface of the water, sending a massive spray over him, and tried to look cross but failed dismally under the combined effect of his laughter and the sight of his tanned shoulders. Lean, muscular and dotted with droplets of seawater, they reflected the light like miniature prisms.

"Don't be cross, Ells; I'll make amends. Let me float you so that you can relax."

"Oh, sure! Then you can duck me. I'm not getting caught out twice."

"I won't, Scout's honour." He'd made a salute and then held out his hand. As he placed it behind my head, I'd let myself sink back into the water until I was supine, and my legs floated to the surface. As I stabilised, Brett slid his other hand along my back until he found my balance point, and I could relax completely.

Floating had been delicious. The slide of cool water lapping against my body, combined with the sun on my face and Brett's steady hand under my spine, was too good a feeling to waste on a busy mind. Then as now, I took a deep breath, allowed my thoughts to clear and my body to simply be.

"Hey, pretty girl, ready to come back into the moment? You looked like Ophelia there, all pale skin and red hair flowing on the water."

I dragged myself reluctantly from my daydream. When I opened my eyes, I could almost believe Brett would be next to me. Yearning for the past was not going to help solve my current problems, but the memory of how I'd felt that afternoon had enabled me to relax. For now, I decided to stop fretting and see how things panned out. For all I knew, Mark would back off the baby thing. He was fun and loving as well as conservative. I'd probably imagined the chemistry with James. The charm that had made him so alluring yesterday was just how he treated everyone. And Mum was just Mum; I don't know why I had let her irritate me so much. Time to hit the road.

As I let the dogs out of the car, the barn lay still, and I was disappointed not to see Mark's car. I let myself in by the kitchen door, dumped my bag on the work surface and walked through to the office. Sure enough, the answerphone was winking. I pressed the 'play messages' button and jotted a name and phone number from one of Mark's clients down on the pad. Then after a second beep, I heard Mark's voice,

"I'm on my way home, can't wait to see you, will pick up a takeaway, should be there around eight."

I glanced at the clock, seven-thirty, just time to feed the hounds and grab a quick shower. My heart beat a little faster as I thought about seeing Mark again; he had only been away for a week. It felt like years. As I headed out of the office, the phone rang shrilly in the silence of the barn and made me jump. Expecting Pen or maybe Mum telling me I'd forgotten something, I was surprised and delighted to hear Annie, my old flatmate from Sydney. It was as if my earlier reminiscing had conjured her up.

Diminutive in stature, Annie more than made up for it in heart. She was a dedicated distance runner covering mile after mile with an efficient stride, blonde ponytail threaded through a peaked sunhat, swinging in an easy rhythm to the beat of her feet. Annie worked as the PA to a top lawyer in Sydney and seemed to deal with demanding clients and a highly pressured boss with one hand tied behind her back.

What I loved most about her was the openness she had in all her dealings; coming from a home where my mother communicated in hints, sighs and implied disappointments, I felt so comfortable with my forthright friend.

"Ellie," her voice was squeaky with excitement. "Ellie, you've got to come."

"Slow down," I laughed, "Come where?"

"To our wedding, you're going to be my bridesmaid. Mark must come too."

"Annie, wedding? Really? That's amazing news. Congratulations. Of course, I'm coming. When is it?"

If I expected reasonable notice, I wasn't going to get it. "December 11th."

"What, this year? That's only three months away. When did you decide?"

"Overnight. Max and I have been up all night talking. I wanted you to be the first to know."

I made a quick calculation. It was only five-thirty in the morning in Sydney.

"You crazy, romantic fools." I could imagine them, Max slouched on a bean bag, Annie in the hanging chair on the balcony, both watching the city lights on the water and talking as she rocked to and fro. Brett and I had done the same several times in the cool of the night. The sounds of the garden at night and the lap of water against the harbour wall were hypnotic.

"So, you will come?"

"Yes, yes, I will. Robin is heading off for a long holiday next year, so I think I deserve to grab some time before he goes. Mark'll be back soon. I'll ask him. You know he's covering for Dom when he goes to America? So, it's all a bit manic, but by December, hopefully, he'll be fine to come." Suddenly a pin of fear pricked the balloon of my elation. "You are both alright, aren't you?"

Her infectious giggle sounded after the slight delay, "Yes, silly, of course, we are."

"Only I thought, with the sudden date…"

She giggled again, "We're both fine."

As I placed the phone on the kitchen counter and turned towards the shower for the second time, I did a delighted little skip and said, "Yeees!" to the dogs. As long as they got their supper without delay, they were more than happy to celebrate with me.

I placed assorted entrails and veggies into bowls for them and mentally thanked the universe. I had thought I needed to get away, and here was the perfect reason to plan a trip.

Before I made it to the shower, the headlights of Mark's car fanned across the kitchen and having wolfed back their food at lightning speed; the dogs headed towards the kitchen door, tails pluming. No time to get glammed up, I thought ruefully.

I opened the door, and we went out to greet him, the dogs with their customary enthusiasm swarming around the car as the driver's door opened and Mark got out.

"Need a hand with anything?" I said, wading through the dogs to the car and feeling slightly awkward, the memory of my meal with James still in my mind.

He straightened up and smiled, holding his arms out. "Hello, you," he said, hugging me to him and ruffling his fingers through my hair.

I sighed as I settled into the hug and the familiar warmth of Mark's body. My tears and confusion in the services at Guildford seemed a bit stupid now he was real and here.

A rustling sound disturbed us, and I saw Birdie with her nose in the car. "Hey!" said Mark, "That's our dinner, get off."

He grabbed a brown paper carrier and handed it to me, "Fish and chips, hope that's okay?"

"Fab, I'm hungry now."

He grabbed his suit carrier and bag and followed me into the kitchen. Both dogs were with me, noses following the scent trail from the carrier bag like the Bisto kids.

As the kitchen lights caught his face, the lines on either side of his nose seemed deeply etched, and his skin looked a pale parchment colour rather than its usual olive tan.

"Oh, wow! Dom's been working you to the bone. You look shattered." I traced my fingers over the weary lines, soothing them gently. "Just dump your stuff and sit down. I'll get you a beer."

He settled on one of the stools by the breakfast bar, and I grabbed a beer from the utility room and poured it, tilting the glass gently to get just a small head.

"Perfect," he said as I handed it to him, and he swallowed a deep draught, leaving a white moustache on his top lip. I brushed it away, laughing, and fed it into his mouth with the tip of my index finger.

"Out of the paper?" I gestured to the waiting fish and chips.

He nodded, "Fine."

I busied myself around the kitchen, putting salt and vinegar on the breakfast bar and sitting the crispy golden fish and chips in their wrappers in two baskets. The papers open like huge white lotus flowers. Mark's eyes followed me as I moved from cupboard to cupboard, and I became more and more aware of every movement as if I were a performer on stage. I hoped none of my thoughts of the previous few days was visible on my skin, like cloud shadows tainting clear water.

In the end, I turned to face him. "You're staring."

He grinned, "Too right, I am."

I sat opposite him, took a chip, and placed it in my mouth slowly, burning the intensity of my full attention into his tired eyes. "Eat," I said.

We chatted about the small stuff as we ate. How was Lottie? Was Dom's office very sophisticated? We were settling back into each other's company gently. Vale was leaving in a week, so she and Dom wanted to come down to see us this weekend, he told me.

"Do you mind if we invite Mum and Peter as well? Mum will want to see Dom before he goes."

I smiled, "Course not, are they coming Saturday or Sunday? Pen and Angus will want to see them too, I expect. It seems funny that Dom and Vale won't be here to pop in soon." I looked at Mark; his face dropped momentarily, then he shrugged and said,

"It won't be forever."

I knew he was dreading it, maybe more than I was, but I didn't press him to voice it.

After dinner, we went through to the sitting room and settled in front of the fire. Mark said, "I forgot, I have a present for you from Dom."

I looked at him, intrigued, "Oh?"

Mark laughed, "Peace offering for having hi-jacked me."

He went to his bag in the kitchen, and then handed me a small box in a gift bag with the tag inscribed. "It's only miles… Stay in touch and stay safe!" in Dom's hasty handwriting.

I unwrapped the bottle of expensive perfume and sprayed some on my wrists; green and citrus notes, clever old Dom – not dissimilar to my usual fragrance.

I left Mark in the sitting room and went out to clear the kitchen and settle the dogs for the night. It was good to have Mark home, and now he was with me, I laughed at myself for my doubts last week. He looked good enough to eat with his weary 'back from the coal-face' look, and I fully intended to chase all remaining thoughts of James out of my head tonight.

I called to see if Mark wanted a drink, but no answer was forthcoming. I walked back through, wondering which piece of his clothing I might remove first, only to find him sound asleep on the sofa. All attempts to rouse him and send him up to bed were met with unintelligible mumbles and finally a firm roll away from me, so I took the duvet from the spare room, covered him, and left him to sleep.

The next morning, I crept downstairs in stockinged feet, and looked at Mark's sleeping form, he hadn't moved from the night before. His long dark lashes lay in contrast to the skin of his cheekbones, and I could see a dark shadow of stubble across his jawline. His curly hair looked unruly against the cushion, and I guessed he would wake with the imprint of its pattern on his cheek. He looked incredibly peaceful, and my heart went out to him. He was exhausted.

I grabbed my tweed coat and wellies and shooed the dogs through the door with as little noise as possible. Eager to be off, they began to explore as I paused on the doorstep to slide arms into my coat and push feet into boots.

The morning mist still hung low across the fields, with the autumn sun just breaking through. Spiders' webs glittered diamond-bright with droplets of water as they spanned the blades of grass, and crane flies lifted lazily as I strode across the field.

I was ducking to get under a barbed wire fence when I heard my name. I straightened up to see Pen waving madly and her Pointers galloping towards us. The dogs reached me first, fawning and rubbing themselves around my legs, leaving brush strokes of tiny white hairs on my trousers. Pen arrived, panting, with Lottie strapped in a papoose across her chest.

"Hiya," she managed between gasps, "I'm so unfit."

"Hello, and hello you," I said, giving Lottie's cheek a little rub with my finger. "I was going to ring you later. Dom and Vale are coming to say goodbye on Sunday. Would you like to come to lunch?"

Her face fell, "Oh no, what a shame, we can't. We've already accepted an invitation to one of Angus' Young Farmer mates. Perhaps we could pop in before we go?"

"Yes, of course, whatever suits, that sounds good." I smiled and played with Lottie's fingers. "How's this little monster?"

"Aww, she's amazing. We had a full night's sleep two days ago. I shot out of bed when I realised it was morning; I thought something awful had happened in the night. My heart was properly in my throat, and I had to get Angus to wake her."

My heart lurched. I could feel the panic she must have felt but decided not to let her see my morbid fear.

"Pen, you've been praying for an unbroken night."

She raised her eyebrows, mocking herself. "I know, be careful what you wish for!"

I had to laugh, "You're mad."

Pen wagged a finger at me. "It goes with the territory, you wait. When babies are awake, you're trying to get them to sleep, and when they're asleep, you feel obliged to prod them to see they're still breathing. It's insane, but I still wouldn't change her for the world.

Lottie smiled at me yesterday, a proper beam when she woke up. I thought my heart would burst."

"Great softie," I replied, looking fondly at my friend. Could I ever join Pen in the place she now inhabited? I was afraid that I wasn't brave enough even to try, and I shivered.

"Someone walked over your grave," she quipped.

"Something like that."

We fell in step together. "How were your talk and the trip to Portsmouth?"

I gave a tight smile. "Portsmouth was good, Dad was fine, Mum and I nearly fell out. What's new?" I gave her a despairing glance, then continued with casual enthusiasm, "The talk was great. I'm beginning to like the new Ellie, businesswoman extraordinaire. James dropped in to see everything was all right, as he'd asked me at short notice. He took me out to dinner, which was thoughtful."

Pen stopped in her tracks. "Crikey, bit more than thoughtful, all the way to Surrey! He's got the hots for you, Ellie Rose."

A tell-tale blush crept up my face. "He has not!"

"Ha! You're blushing. Oh, my goodness, Ellie, did he make a pass at you?"

"No, he did not. Pen, he's far too sophisticated to be interested in me."

Pen looked incredulous. "Rubbish, you're beautiful, and I don't trust him one bit. You watch out; he's playing the long game, and I'm going to tell Mark."

"No, don't do that," the words came rushing out, and I spun to look at her. "Mark can be a bit sensitive about James."

She turned to look at me with a frown. "Ellie, you don't fancy James, do you?"

I tried to assume an outraged look. "No, I don't. No, of course not! It's just that Mark was a bit off when he knew James had taken me out. He's shattered and upset about Dom leaving, so I want us both to relax and the weekend to be special. Don't say anything, please don't."

"Hmmm," she narrowed her eyes. "How handsome and wealthy is this, James?"

I gave her a gentle push. "Pen! Stop, will you? I don't fancy him."

"Alright, alright, I believe you, thousands wouldn't. I'm not surprised Mark feels a bit insecure, Ells, he had an ordeal with Katrina which took some getting over."

She left it at that, and we turned back towards the farm, whistling up the dogs. As we parted with a kiss for both her and Lottie, she said, "Mark's one of the good guys, you know."

Chapter Twelve

Sleepless

I felt full of righteous indignation as I walked back toward the barn. I know Mark is one of the good guys! I only had dinner with James, for goodness sake. Nothing happened. What was the matter with Pen? I'd conveniently forgotten my confusion of the days before.

Mark was no longer on the sofa when I got in and didn't answer my call. The barn had that empty feeling when you know you're alone. Odd.

I stripped off my walking clothes and stepped into the shower. I emerged a few minutes later swathed in towels, one huge fluffy one as a sarong and another in a turban around my hair. A steaming mug of coffee sat on the dresser with a note propped against it which read 'Fresh croissants downstairs. Better be quick.'

Mystery solved; the excellent new delicatessen in town sold the lightest, most buttery, flakey croissants outside a Paris bistro I have ever found. Mark had had the excellent good taste to go and fetch some. Making haste to get dry and dressed, I headed for the kitchen.

Mark looked better this morning, less tired. He looked up and smiled.

"You should have woken me."

"Oh? How?" I laughed, "You were out cold, and I had all sorts of wicked things planned for your homecoming too."

"Mmm, well, I'm awake now," he grinned.

"Good thought, but unless I'm very much mistaken, that's your mother's car pulling up outside." I leant over to plant a kiss on his cheek, then wiped the trail of croissant crumbs I'd left behind.

He looked ludicrously disappointed. "I'm holding you to that promise."

"Morning, Alessandra," I said as she tapped the door and came in.

"Am I interrupting something?" she said, her head on one side, "You two look slightly guilty."

I laughed it off, "No, come in, there's fresh coffee, but we've eaten all the croissants."

We settled around the breakfast bar, and Alessandra said, "I popped in early to check on arrangements for tomorrow. Peter said we'd bring the wine, and I'll make a pudding, how many of us are there?"

"Pen and Angus can't make it, so just the six of us."

She looked disappointed. "Oh, that's a shame. I was looking forward to seeing Lottie, such a little poppet."

I muttered, "She is when she's asleep," and two sets of eyes swivelled towards me like the guns on a warship.

"Well, she gets pretty angry when she's hungry," I tried to defend myself. *Sheesh, the wrong remark to make to baby worshippers*, I thought.

Ignoring my inappropriate remarks, Alessandra said, "You should have seen her this week, Mark, she has a big beaming smile now."

His face went all soppy. "I expect we'll pop in to see her today sometime, bless her."

Changing the subject, I said, "Oh Mark, I forgot to say last night! Annie rang from Australia. She and Max are getting married in December, they want us both to be there."

He frowned slightly, "What date exactly? Last week, Dom and I scheduled a big conference meeting in America for December. I hope they don't clash."

I couldn't believe it. "Oh no, surely not. Their wedding is on the eleventh. I'm speaking to Robin on Monday because I'd like to take at least three weeks off. I'm going to be a bridesmaid, so I thought about going from the first to the twenty-first. I'm hoping Robin will cover me before he and Louise go away."

Mark got his diary out of his briefcase. "No can-do, Ellie; I'm in America from the second to the eighth."

I must have looked aghast because Alessandra chipped in, "Well, why don't you go out first, Ellie, see your friends and do bridesmaid fittings? Then Mark could fly into Sydney from America rather than London. You could have a short holiday after the wedding and come back together for Christmas. It would do you both good to get away."

I was disappointed. I so wanted to show Mark all the places I loved, and for him to meet Max and Annie, but his Mum was right. There would be nothing to stop me from going alone, and at least he'd be there for the wedding.

Maybe this way was best, it would be my first time back in Sydney since Brett's funeral and underlying the initial excitement to go back, I wasn't quite sure how I would feel.

"We'll sort it out," Mark said, then stood up reluctantly. "I'm sorry, but I've got a couple of calls to make before the weekend begins, can I leave you, ladies, for a while?"

I looked at his rear view as he disappeared into the office and turned back to his mother. "I thought he'd be more excited about the wedding.".

Alessandra said, "Go and enjoy yourself, Ellie. It won't hurt to go back on your own and lay some ghosts to rest for good." She straightened the rings on her finger, then looked up at me. "Tread gently, maybe it's hard for him to see you go back, knowing it's where you lived with Brett. Don't forget, Brett's been a hard act to follow, Ellie, trying to live up to his memory. Mark's busy and preoccupied at the moment."

I was about to hotly refute the idea that I still needed to lay ghosts to rest or that Mark may find my going back difficult but I chose to say nothing. I suddenly remembered that I had felt very awkward when I'd met Mark's friends for the first time, those who'd known him with Katrina. I'd wondered if they were comparing me to her. Alessandra may have a point; I'd have to talk to Mark.

Alessandra left soon after to pop in on Pen and Lottie. The office door remained closed, and I could hear Marks voice as a low murmur. I decided to busy myself.

I thought about James and felt slightly put out that I'd heard no more from him. Not that I wanted to, or that there was any reason for a call, but still. Served me right for being conceited.

Mark still had not emerged from the office when I'd completed all I had to do, so I decided to go shopping for tomorrow's food and get a paper to see what was on at the pictures. The day had clouded over, and a steady drizzle looked set in for the day. I opened the office door a crack and mouthed, "Going shopping."

Mark looked around, made a thumbs-up sign, and then returned to his conversation. I was beginning to wonder if I'd done the right thing encouraging him to help Dom, he looked weary again.

This job was more intense than I'd imagined. I'd never known Mark to be chained to his desk like this at the weekend. Still, early days, once he had his feet under the table, perhaps things would calm down a bit.

The shops were quiet, and I didn't meet anyone to chat to, so I arrived back at the barn in record time. I packed the shopping away, mentally ticking off my ingredients for the meal tomorrow. I was trying a chicken, lemon and dill pie to make a change from the inevitable Sunday roast.

That done, I settled in front of the fire with the paper. There was an old romcom on at the cinema in Chelmsford, with a showing at four o'clock. Great cast, I loved Meg Ryan and had seen this film so many times over the years. I called Mark out of his office for sandwiches and tea, then said, "Pictures at four, leaving at three-thirty, you have to be finished by three."

He looked rueful, "Finished, I won't be, but you're right. I need to stop, or I'll be working all weekend. Sorry, Ellie, I'm not very good company, but I'm trying to take so much on board, I don't know which way is up."

"It's not your fault. I'm going to have a word with that Dom when he gets here tomorrow."

He shrugged, "I suspected what it would be like. Dom is inexhaustible, and he forgets we mere mortals need sleep."

I tutted, and he continued, "He's close to being organised in the States already. The American office won't know what's hit them when Dom's there all the time. I won't be surprised if he leaves with Vale next week. I'm sure that's what he's working towards. I tell you what, he's got it bad, he can't bear the thought of her going without him."

I smiled, "He'll be proposing to her next."

Mark glanced at me quickly. "Maybe," he said.

Something in his studied, noncommittal voice made me leap on him, the element of surprise pushing him back against the sofa cushions. "What? What do you know?"

"Nothing!"

"I'm going to tickle it out of you."

From my commanding position sitting on his chest, I started to tickle, but after an unseemly struggle, he deposited me on the floor. Both out of breath and Mark's eyes alight with laughter, he said, "I don't know anything." He was a terrible liar.

The film we saw was poignant for us. In parts, I felt like the actors were playing out scenes from both our lives. I ached as they plodded miserably through days at work, smiling, laughing, pretending, all the while feeling like robots going through the motions. Mark squeezed my hand as we watched the desperate efforts of others to comfort, all well-meant but no balm for their pain. Both of us knew what that felt like, and as we left the cinema, we had an unspoken sense of connection.

As I held Mark's hand, I felt safe and comfortable. It was getting dark, and we decided to head home in favour of a meal out. With the drama of the last few weeks, we needed some time to reconnect, and the tenderness of the film had drawn us together. Unfortunately, before we got back to the car, my mobile rang.

I searched for the phone in my handbag and answered, to hear Pen's voice, strangely high pitched.

"Hi Pen, wait, say that again. Oh no! You're doing the right thing, keep putting on pressure and more clean padding on top of the old. Lift his arm in the air too. Of course! We're on our way from Chelmsford now."

Mark had been following my side of the conversation and now looked alarmed. "What on earth's happened?"

"It's Angus, he slipped on the wet grass and put his hand through the vegetable cloches as he fell. He's sliced his wrist on the glass, it's deep, and she's struggling to stop the bleeding. An ambulance is coming; Pen wants us to take Lottie."

We ran to the car, and I swore as I fumbled the coins for the payment machine in my haste, and they dropped onto the floor.

"I'll drive," Mark said firmly, taking the keys out of my hand as we reached the car. "Get in."

As he drove, I fretted aloud, "I hope he hasn't damaged his tendons, he needs both hands on the farm."

Mark refused to speculate. "Let's see when we get there. No point worrying until we know."

I shook my head and shot him a slightly irritated glance. Mark's calm in a crisis was usually comforting. On this occasion, with nightmare scenarios of severed tendons, infection and damaged nerves flashing through my brain, I felt it was easier for him to be calm. He didn't know about the risks.

As we pulled into the farm, the ambulance was outside, its back doors open, and we were just in time to see Angus in a chair wheeled out of the house by two ambulance men. He looked suspiciously pale as they loaded him into the vehicle and had a considerable compression bandage on his right arm.

"Thank you for coming," said Pen breathlessly. "Lottie's asleep upstairs, but she'll need a feed soon. There's expressed milk in the freezer, and she sometimes has a formula top-up. You know where everything is, help yourselves to whatever you want. I'm going to follow the ambulance in."

"Shall I drive you?" Mark offered.

Pen shook her head, "No, I'll be fine, stay with Ellie. I'm so sorry, guys."

I hugged her, "No problem, Pen, don't worry about us. Go and sort Angus out."

She looked at me with shocked eyes. "Ellie, it was horrible. I could see the bones through the cut."

Swallowing my concerns, I assumed my reassuring, calm, professional mantle. "It often looks worse than it is. They have a great hand surgery team at the hospital. You drive safely; we'll be fine here. Keep us informed."

We saw Pen off and entered the kitchen, which looked like a scene from The Texas Chain-Saw Massacre. There was a trail of blood from the back door, bloody swabs everywhere, bloody nappies that Pen had grabbed to stem the flow and smears all over the table and one chair.

"Dear me!" Mark surveyed the carnage. "Let's get this cleared up before Lottie wakes up."

It took us twenty minutes to get clear, and as I poured away the last bucket of red-tinged water and Mark closed the bag with all the bloody swabs, he said, "Some cut!"

I breathed out slowly. "I hope he hasn't damaged anything major. I wonder when Pen will call?"

We didn't have long to dwell on Angus' misfortunes because the sound of stirrings from the nursery, amplified through the baby monitor, stimulated us into action once more. I rummaged in the freezer and found a tub with the packets of frozen breast milk. I'd seen Pen use these pouches, they were like liners and fitted over the rim of some special bottles she had. I put two in the microwave on defrost, listening to Mark's gentle chatting through the speaker as he undressed the sleepy baby and changed her.

Mark appeared downstairs holding Lottie, who blinked like a mole at the bright light in the kitchen and sported one red cheek that she'd lain on. She waved a small fist outside the blanket Mark had wrapped her in.

"Here she is," said Mark, "Your Auntie Ellie is getting your dinner ready." He continued with a long string of placatory nonsense that seemed to have Lottie fooled. I'd seen Pen use these packets of expressed milk once, and it had all seemed straightforward until now, as I wrestled with the fiddly liner, trying not to spill the milk inside. Bottle finally assembled, I checked the temperature, then made Mark check it too and settled myself into a chair.

"Go!" I said to Mark, who handed me the little bundle. She didn't feel quite right in my lap, and to feed her, I had to hunch at a funny angle. I sent Mark in search of a cushion to prop Lottie up, so we could both relax. Fortunately, Lottie was a pro where eating was concerned; I couldn't believe how quickly she'd drained the bottle. She finished with a loud and satisfying burp as I put her up on my shoulder.

"Oops!" said Mark, dabbing at the back of my shoulder with a muslin. "Bit came back the wrong way."

"Lovely," I said. "Thanks, Lottie," as I felt the small damp patch on my back.

It seemed Lottie was ready for some play now. She pandered outrageously to Mark's ego as she gurgled in delight and broadly smiled as he played peek-a-boo and tickling games with various scrunchy, rattly toys. She was adorable and smiley but gradually started to intersperse smiles with yawns, and he took her upstairs.

I heard the nursery scene play out through the monitor as I tidied up the kitchen. Mark still softly chatting as Lottie settled with the tinkle of a musical mobile, which I knew projected moving lights on the ceiling as it turned. I glanced at the clock, at least we might get a little time to ourselves while she slept.

"Phew!" he said as he crept downstairs. "Round One over. Seconds out, Round Two."

"Oh, get on with you, you've loved every minute." I felt envious of how natural he seemed. The generosity of his gentle care for her was touching. I still felt terrified around her and awkward in a way that I never did with the adults I worked with. I wondered if I could ever feel like Mark did around babies.

I could see Mark the father as he interacted with Lottie, a smile here and a brushed kiss there. I wasn't feeling any maternal tug. What was the matter with me? There was a core of fear inside me, like a fist around my heart. I couldn't cope with the pain if I loved someone else that intensely, only to lose them. I shivered, I was resisting the urge to succumb to loving Lottie, and I felt slightly ashamed. Mark seemed willing to put his heart out there again with no reservations.

"She is gorgeous," he said, blithely unaware of my inner demons raging.

We decided that Mark should go back and feed our dogs and bring them back with him. I let Daisy and Belle out of the kennel and gave them a run in the garden before settling them on the dog sofa. Apart from the odd snuffing noise and a couple of single cries, Lottie seemed settled, so I rooted about in the freezer for something for our supper.

Pen had clearly had little inclination for her usual batch cooking and had been working her way through her stores and the gifts of food. The normally bulging freezer was thin of produce, and I was reluctant to use up anything she had left.

I phoned Mark, asked him to bring provisions from home, and pondered the unusual emptiness of the freezer. So unlike Pen, she was always cooking and baking. I resolved to get some batch cooking done for her myself. Perhaps people's initial thoughtfulness and their food gifts had dwindled now Lottie was coming up to ten weeks. Unless you tell them any different, people assume you're coping and get on with their lives.

I was just about to learn how easily cooking or indeed anything constructive might go by the board with a new baby in the house. I sat in the chair with a cup of coffee and reached for a magazine lying on the table, but no sooner had I done so than I shot straight back up. An ominous grizzling began to play through the baby sound system.

By the time I got to her, Lottie was in full voice, hot and sweaty, with her little face twisted. I picked her up and rubbed and patted her back, all to no avail, then laid her on the changing table and checked – no obvious problems at that end. Her dark lashes were jewelled by tiny tears, which glistened in the turning light show from the music mobile. I rubbed her tummy gently, and it felt tight as a drum.

OK, Ellie, what have you seen Pen do? Nappy bag, nappy bag, Pen keeps a bottle of colic stuff in there. Picking Lottie up again, I rifled clumsily through the bag beside the changing table one-handed and found the tiny bottle. Lottie's very loud protests continued all the while in my left ear, adding a sense of increasing urgency to my efforts. I squinted at the tiny writing: two pipettes. *Come on, Ellie, come on!*

"Here we go, Sweetie, this is gonna' help." I squirted the cloudy gloop into her open mouth. She looked at me as she swallowed and continued to cry. I rocked her gently, rubbing her back and hoping Mark was on his way back when suddenly a rip-roaring fart erupted under my hand, which supported her bottom. Magic! After a few grumpy mumbles, she went back to sleep on my shoulder like someone had flicked a switch. Hardly daring to breathe, I laid her down in the cot again and tottered out of the room to the sanctuary of the kitchen, where I found my stone-cold coffee and unopened magazine.

Mark arrived with the dogs and a frozen shepherd's pie. "Everything alright?"

"Colic incident averted." I grinned slightly hysterically, "Get that pie in the oven quick before the next feed is due. How scary is this?"

He opened his eyes wide. "Um, on a scale of nought to ten, seven maybe. I'm glad it was you with the colic, that's outside my comfort zone."

I shook my head, "At least you have some experience from helping Katrina in the nursery and a bit of a natural knack." I turned to look at the dogs who had started to play fight in the corner. "Dogs! Settle down. I can't be doing with you lot messing about."

They piled onto the dog sofa, Daisy and Belle with looks of resignation, my two looking slightly affronted at their summary dismissal.

It was gone ten before we had any news from Pen, and it wasn't all good.

Bad signal inside the hospital made her voice distant. "Angus has seen the A&E people and had a scan, and we're waiting for the hand surgeon. He needs emergency surgery. Luckily, the cut missed the main nerves and blood vessels, but he needs a tendon repair. It could have been a lot worse."

"Oh, Pen, I'm so sorry, what a worry. That's going to need some rest and physiotherapy."

Her voice sounded pinched with anxiety. "He's already fretting about the farm, but we'll manage somehow, at least it's a fairly quiet time. Is Lottie alright? I hope she's behaving herself."

"Yes, we're all fine here, good as gold, she's asleep at the moment."

"Did you find enough to eat? The freezer is getting a bit low, and I keep intending to cook, then don't get around to it."

I laughed, "I'm surprised you manage to get dressed, never mind cook. Don't worry about it, we had a ready-made dinner in the freezer at home, we've just finished eating."

She sighed, "I've eaten most of the Kit-Kats in the vending machine. Would you mind if I stay, at least until Angus goes down for surgery?"

"No, of course not, that's fine. Stay as long as you need to. Mark and I can hold the fort here."

Pen continued, "I always keep the bed in the spare room made up, why don't you sleep in there if you get tired?"

"Thanks, Pen, we'll see how it goes."

Mark's eyes started to droop as soon as he sat on the sofa after dinner. I suggested he take up Pen's offer and go to bed, especially as he'd slept on the couch in the barn the night before.

After a token protest, he admitted defeat and headed up to bed. I gave the last feed near midnight. The whole thing went better this time, as I was ready with the colic mixture and had the bottles prepped in advance. I settled Lottie again, then crept in beside Mark. I spooned myself around him as he slept.

Seemingly minutes later, I woke and realised he'd gone. The clock said four-thirty, and as I walked sleepily into the nursery, Mark said, "Go back to bed, we're nearly done here." All bets off for our romantic night reconnecting.

We both woke around seven, and I could hear Pen's voice downstairs, talking to the dogs. I pulled on yesterday's clothes and joined her, hair all askew and smudged make-up under my eyes.

"How's Angus?"

She smiled wearily, "Surgery was successful, he has to stay in for a couple of days, then he'll be home."

"Pen, you look ragged. Did you get any sleep?"

She laughed, "Back at you, girl! I dozed in a very uncomfortable plastic chair. What about you?"

"We're alright; I did the late feed, then Mark heard her in the night, so we shared it."

Pen laughed, "Welcome to the sleep deprivation society."

I had to chuckle, too, "Something like that. Look, why don't you come to lunch before you go back to the hospital today, save you cooking, and the others would love to see Princess Lottie."

She looked a little brighter at the prospect of some company. "That's kind, we might just do that."

Mark appeared, also looking a little tousled and bleary. Yesterday's shirt was crumpled and adorned with dog hair and evidence of baby milk. We laughed as Pen pushed cups of coffee towards us, saying only, "It helps."

Mark and I walked all the dogs, and then took our two home. I abandoned all ideas of trying a new recipe and threw the chicken into the oven. Sunday roast it would have to be.

Chapter Thirteen

Goodbyes

As the hot water curled around my shoulders and cascaded down my body, a sense of guilty well-being came over me. I doubted Pen had time for a leisurely shower. I resolved to never take time to myself for granted ever again.

Mark had disappeared back into the office to finish off some paperwork before Dom arrived, so I had the luxury of an hour to myself to get ready before everyone came.

The long mirror reflected a pale-faced girl with a smattering of freckles on her nose and long red hair, currently wet and slicked back with comb marks like tram lines running through it. Hazel eyes flecked with green and gold looked back at me, slightly red-rimmed from the sleepless night and worry of the day before, and something else, a slight reproach.

"What?" I said to my reflection.

You know what, Ellie Rose! You need to get a grip. Everything is good, and you should be grateful, don't mess it up by pressing the self-destruct button.

"Oh, no shit Sherlock!"

You're scared. You give out all this great advice about acknowledging fears and not letting them stop you, but you're afraid to take the next step.

"Yes, I'm scared. If I don't want a baby, I could lose Mark. If I have one, I might lose it. I couldn't bear that grief again." Tears started to run down my face as I battled with myself. "I want things to be easy for a while, I like feeling safe. Is that too much to ask?"

Oh, stop whinging! Life's hard, get used to it.

"Yes, thanks, I know."

Vale's voice calling up the stairs rocked me out of my internal argument. "Can I come up?"

Damn! Why did I always look such a mess whenever I saw Vale?

"Yes, if you like, I'm just going to dry my hair." I pretended to be wiping some cleanser off my eyes to disguise the crying.

"Sorry we're early," she said as she poked her head around the door. "Traffic was light."

"Don't worry, nice to see you. I suppose Dom has disappeared into the office with Mark?"

She nodded, then took the hairdryer out of my hands. "Sit, I'll do it for you."

I could feel tears welling up again at this unexpected kindness, but I bit the inside of my cheek to stop them as I shrugged and handed her the dryer and brush.

"You have such beautiful hair, Ellie." I glanced at her immaculate ash-blonde tresses, looking for a trace of irony in her face, but there was none. "Mine is so straight and heavy, your curls are soft and pretty."

I laughed, "The grass is always greener. I'm always envious because you look so sophisticated, never a hair out of place, while my hair goes into a riot the minute it gets damp."

Her long strokes were soothing as she pulled gently, curling my hair around the brush and directing the warm air onto it. Standing behind me and to the side so that I couldn't see her expression, she said gently, "What's wrong, Ellie?"

Funny how much easier it is to talk when you aren't facing someone. "Nothing is wrong exactly, just everything is changing, and I'd like to stop the world and get off."

"You haven't seemed quite right since Pen had the baby."

My eyes widened in surprise. I thought I was hiding how I felt quite well, how many other people had noticed?

"I'm OK. It's not Lottie per se, she's lovely." I didn't want everyone thinking I didn't like my Goddaughter. "It's because suddenly everyone thinks Mark and I should have a baby as well. He'd like one soon. Well, he'd like one straight away, but I don't know if I'm ready. I wish people would stop hinting about it because I feel like they're harassing me."

She nodded, "They don't mean anything by it, Ellie, people speak without thinking, they want to see you happy. It's the next step in people's minds, I guess."

I looked at her in the mirror. "Well, not for everyone! I look at what Pen went through, and I'm not sure I could cope. She has so much on her plate. I know she's still there, but I miss the old Pen. And now you're going too. I'm feeling a bit sorry for myself."

There was a pause as Vale scooped up another section of hair into a clasp and started to dry the other side.

She hesitated, then said, "I know how you feel. I'm going to miss you too, Ellie. I love the gang here and all we do together. It's so relaxing to come over, do fun stuff and hang out. I can relax and let my guard down." She looked sad, "Corporate life can be tough for anyone, but it's even worse as a woman, it's very competitive. Working so hard means I haven't got many girlfriends, mainly colleagues. You and Pen are my besties."

I wasn't quite sure what to say. I'd always seen Vale as so high-powered and sophisticated, I sometimes wondered if she found Pen and me a bit ordinary. I'd never imagined she could be lonely.

I swivelled round and put a hand out to her. "Oh, Vale, don't feel lonely. It's only miles, we won't lose touch, and it won't be forever."

She bent forward to press her cheek against mine. I saw her eyes for the first time in the mirror. Like me, she had been crying recently, and their blue was shadowed by a sombre tone as if a summer sky was clouding over. "I'm holding onto the thought that it won't be forever," she said.

"It won't. I'm sure you and Dom will sort something out." I glanced at the clock and realised with a gasp that I'd been upstairs for way longer than an hour. "Come on, we'd better go and sort lunch, or it will be teatime. Alessandra and Peter will be here in a minute." I glanced back at myself in the mirror. "You've done a much better job of my hair than I would have done. Are you sure you won't stay on as my stylist? I can show you how to look like you've been dragged through a hedge backwards in exchange. Come on, it's a tempting offer!"

We laughed despite the underlying tensions. For different reasons, both of us were clinging to a life-raft in stormy emotional seas.

We'd just about finished peeling the vegetables, and the potatoes were boiling, ready to be tossed into sizzling fat and join the chickens in the oven, when Alessandra arrived with Peter. A hubbub ensued as she bestowed lavish kisses all around, and we rearranged the fridge to accommodate a huge Tiramisu, which was Alessandra's contribution to the meal.

"We're running a bit late," I confessed.

"Wonderful, more time for us to enjoy the cocktails. Peter, darling!"

He stepped forward in his quiet way and produced chilled champagne and orange Armagnac out of a cool bag.

Alessandra looked at me expectantly. "Glasses, Ellie? Then we'll leave him to do magic," I obediently pointed Peter towards the cupboard with the glasses. She held out a bangled wrist to Vale and me. "Come on, girls, let's go and dig those boys out of the office."

Narrowing her eyes as she hustled us out of the kitchen, Alessandra said more quietly, "You could both do with a cocktail by the look of you." She didn't miss a trick.

Feigning tragedy as she saw Dom, she said, "Leaving me for another woman and leaving the country, I am heartbroken."

"Guilty as accused, but what a woman," he said, pulling Vale into him with an arm around her waist.

Alessandra opened her arms and hugged them both. "Of course, she's wonderful, and you must never let her go." Then she looked at Vale. "Any man who wouldn't follow you to the ends of the earth, doesn't truly love you."

Bending to kiss her hello, Mark said, "Mamma, you'll make us all cry. Thank goodness Peter's here with the drinks. Oh, and Pen with Lottie."

More hugs and more greetings followed. Lottie looked very stylish in the pink jeans Vale had bought her when she was born. She was smiling properly now, all the better to entrance the assembled adults, and she giggled as Dom blew raspberries on her hand. Alessandra took her from Pen and sat her on one hip. "Peter, give these girls a drink." It was difficult to resist Alessandra's charm and vivacity as she drew us all into her warm, embracing net.

"To all of us, happy times. We can never be apart because we love each other." She raised her glass of wonderfully potent orange cocktail.

"To us," we raised our glasses in return.

I was happy to let her sweep us along. My sleepless night, and all the emotions that had gone with it, made me tired. I felt floaty as if I wasn't quite there. What Alessandra had said to Vale, "*Any man who wouldn't follow you to the ends of the earth, doesn't truly love you,*" had brought Brett back to mind and felt like a stab in my heart. He hadn't chosen to follow me.

Lottie passed from Alessandra to Mark because he couldn't keep away, and I slipped back into the kitchen while the conversation turned to the things to do and enjoy in London and New York.

To the casual observer, we were an unlikely group of friends: Pen and me, the country girls with Angus; Dom and Peter city people; Mark in the middle, and Vale and Alessandra, so elegant and sophisticated. But appearances were deceptive, and for me, our connection was about unspoken respect and loyalty. We were all survivors, regardless of the clothes we wore or the places we'd visited.

Part of being a physio is to find common ground with all sorts of different people. Suffering can strike anywhere, anytime, regardless of wealth or beauty. I doubted I'd ever see Alessandra in wellies, up to her ears in mud, and she'd probably never see me wear Givenchy. We may all have come from different backgrounds, but we liked each other, supported, and loved each other just the same.

Pen followed me, "There are plenty of arms to hold, Lottie, I thought I'd come and lend a hand."

"Thanks, Hun, it's only the vegetables to do, then we can serve up. Sorry lunch is late. I expect you want to get away to see Angus."

She shook her head, "No rush, his mum and dad have gone in first. He needs to chat to his dad about the farm; they'll have to decide what they can do and who can come in to help them run it in the short term. We'll sort it out somehow. I got the impression he'd be out of action for a while."

I gave her a sympathetic look. "I think he will, Pen, he'll be in a splint for at least six weeks."

She rolled her eyes. "He has terrible timing! I keep telling myself you managed last year when you were out of action with your knee. Look what came out of it, you ended up with Robin, who was brilliant for the clinic. Nothing is all bad."

I remembered it well, and she was right, it had all turned out for the best, but it had still been worrying for me at the time. I guessed until Angus had a plan and some help in place, he would continue to fret about the farm. Like me, he pitched in and worked hard to get through difficult times. I felt for him, it came as a shock when that coping strategy got taken away.

Pen sighed, then shrugged. "I'll have to drive the tractor if necessary, I've done it before. There's room in the cab for Lottie's car seat."

"*Three wheels on my wagon*," came to mind, and as I began to sing, she shoved me on the arm, feigning outrage, "Don't mock!"

"I'm only teasing you, I know you're struggling."

She looked at me with a mixture of despair and frustration. "He can't even help me much with Lottie because of the hand. At least if he'd injured something else, he could have been a stay-at-home dad. Just our luck, it's typical!"

"You've had a tough time, you poor thing. At least you'll get to spend a bit more time together." Judging by her look, she wasn't convinced.

Their worries were only reinforcing my fears. If we had a baby, I could see myself running about like a mad thing trying to juggle work and home without having time to do anything properly while Mark swanned off on business trips with Dom. Before I agreed to have a baby, I needed to have a proper think about how or if I could manage. I felt for Pen and Angus, they were in a real predicament, and none of this was making me feel like having a baby.

Mark had been right about Dom leaving with Vale. Dom told us over dessert that he'd booked tickets on the same flight. I glanced across at Mark, a small crease between his brows was all that suggested any concern. Vale's radiant face as she kissed him and Dom's confident smile were proof that Mark deserved a medal for stepping in. I just hoped I hadn't encouraged him to take on something that would be too much work for him.

Pen was first to leave to get to the hospital, and she promised to give me an update as soon as she knew more about Angus. As Vale held Lottie for a last cuddle, she said, "It's you who will have changed the most when I see you again. What will you be doing, huh? Walking, getting into mischief. You won't remember your Auntie Vale." She hugged her close and breathed in. "I'd like to bottle that baby smell. She's a beauty, Pen."

Dom and Alessandra hugged and swayed. Their bond was evident, they adored each other. Dom had been a lonely little boy, away from home, at boarding school, and he had shared some of Mark's home life. It struck me that Mark's loving generosity came from his mother.

Mark was seeing Dom in six weeks when he travelled to America, and I went to Sydney. They would also speak most days, so beyond a firm handshake and a clap on the shoulder, they insisted this wasn't saying goodbye.

As Vale and I hung on to each other, she whispered, "Be brave, Ellie, you'll sort it all out. You're amazing." I looked at her, startled, and she mouthed, "You are."

I didn't feel amazing, I felt confused and restless.

After everyone finally left, the barn seemed quiet. Mark squeezed me to him. "That was a lovely day, but I've barely seen you this weekend. Are you alright?"

I nodded, "Yes, I'm sad to see Dom and Vale go. I hope they'll be back soon."

"Don't worry, they will. They both want to bring up their family here and not in the States. Dom was talking about it the other day."

I froze slightly, there it was again. If it wasn't the 'B' word it was the 'F' word. I tried to hide my reluctance with a joke. "You've got it bad, Mark Roxbury, not just you. Everybody seems to have babies on the brain."

He stiffened for a moment and looked serious. "No, I haven't, Ellie, but I would like to know where you stand. You keep fobbing me off, with sometime-never and reasons why a baby would be difficult, but I don't buy it. None of the reasons you've given would make insurmountable problems if you genuinely want a family."

I sighed, we'd had a lovely day, but I was tired. "Do we have to do this now? I'm feeling drained, and so are you. Can't we talk about this another time?"

He looked cross. "There you go, fobbing me off. There's never a good time."

He tried to pull me closer, but I wriggled free and started to collect up some dirty glasses. I didn't want him to corner me like this because I didn't have an answer.

He caught my hand. "Ellie, what now?"

I raised my eyebrows. "Nothing, nothing, I just want to get cleared up and chill for a bit before the weekend's over." To emphasise my point, I clattered a few plates together and scooped up a handful of cutlery.

He let the subject drop, but our conversation left a frosty atmosphere between us that I had never felt before. After some half-hearted clearing, he said, "I need to finish some work in the office." He bent and picked up a tiny sock of Lottie's that was half under the sofa. He straightened it and tossed it on the table, glancing at me with a closed expression on his face.

I watched him shut the office door with something akin to a snap and thought, *Ellie Rose, you have got to talk to him!*

"I know, I know, I will!"

The dogs watched me, and I imagined reproach in their eyes too. “What?” I said to Jeeves, “What does everyone want from me?”

Mark came to bed late, well after I’d fallen asleep, and I only barely registered his warmth beside me. I slept fitfully and had terrible dreams. I was back in the flat in Sydney, but it was all in black and white. I could hear crying from our bedroom, and I rushed in. I walked towards a lace-covered crib in the corner and reached to rock it, but the crying had stopped. The crib was empty. I turned to run, but someone was preventing me. I fought and pushed, screaming, panic-stricken, needing to break away.

“Ellie, Ellie, it’s alright, it’s me. You’ve had a bad dream. It’s okay.”

I looked at Mark’s face, full of concern, despite our earlier disagreement, and I tried to drag myself awake and leave the dream behind. My heart was pounding, and I could feel a trickle of cold sweat between my shoulder blades as he stroked my hair. “Alright now?”

I nodded shakily. I hadn’t had a nightmare since soon after Brett had died. I settled into the crook of Mark’s shoulder as my heart rate returned to normal, and my breathing slowed to match his. *What was happening to me?*

Chapter Fourteen

Work in Progress

I woke to the sound of water pattering on the shower tray. Half asleep, I initially thought it was raining, but then realised that the noise came from inside. The duvet was thrown back on Mark's side, the empty bed, and his absence indicated he was already showering in the en-suite. As yesterday's stalemate flooded back with a sickening lurch in my stomach, I remembered that things weren't right between us for the first time since we'd lived together.

I realised that my internal dilemma about having a baby was still no closer to being resolved, and the thought turned the lurch into a vague sensation of nausea. That we loved each other, I was sure, he had comforted me so gently last night when I was scared. But would that love survive me not wanting a baby? I was less sure about this. I sat up, the uncomfortable anxiety making me restless, and busied myself pulling clothes from the chest of drawers.

The shower stopped, and Mark came through to the bedroom with a towel knotted around his hips and his curly hair wild from being towelled. Pretending to be busy allowed me to chat with Mark in a would-be normal way without looking at him directly.

He seemed no more anxious to engage with me. All our usual half-glances, eye contact and smiles were absent as he moved around the room dressing for work. Unable to bear the atmosphere and nervous about the tension, I scuttled off downstairs to make coffee and hid behind the whoosh and bubble of the percolator.

I was desperate to avoid any more questions to which I had no answers, so I ran back upstairs, kissed Mark and said, “Have a good week, your coffee is on the table, I’m going to get the dogs out and head off a bit early myself.”

Other than a slight tightening around the mouth, Mark didn’t say anything other than, “Fine, Ellie, I’ll see you on Friday.”

I tried to pretend to myself that I was walking off in my typical relaxed fashion, but with adrenaline pumping around my body, it was hard not to take off after the dogs and run down the track as fast as I possibly could. I forced myself to turn and wave as usual, but Mark was not watching from any of the windows. I continued to walk with tears pricking my eyes but dashed them away. There was no point crying. I felt how I felt, and Mark had a different agenda.

Sometimes lately, I’d almost felt like I was outside my body, watching myself struggle. Yesterday for part of the meal, I’d felt utterly detached from the conversation. It was an odd sensation.

I longed to go and sit in the crook of Grandmother Willow in the garden of my cottage. All through my grieving for Brett, it had been my safe place. I had found comfort and calmed myself there. However, I could hardly burst in on Robin, who was currently letting the cottage from me, to go and sit in a tree. Turning left and ducking through a barbed wire fence, I did the next best thing and walked up to the farm's highest point to an old oak tree. Naked of its leaves, the oak branches snaked away like the arms on the statue of Vishnu, which sat on a window ledge in the barn, a relic of Brett's travels in India. As I looked up through the bare canopy, the tiny twigs looked like a cracked glaze on the pottery blue sky above.

Calming myself with deep breaths, I walked to and fro, gradually slowing the frantic pace and forcing myself to notice the wind on my face and take in the details of the view down to the Crouch to still my thoughts.

The dogs, worried by my odd behaviour, came around me, nuzzling and walking alongside. As a reflex, I dropped a hand onto each shiny black head to reassure them and found the familiar gesture steadied me too.

As the rising panic subsided and my mind stopped racing, I began to wonder what on earth the matter was with me. *Just do it, have a baby, everyone else does!* But the resistance was still there, and I had no idea why these fears had surfaced now. I was pushing Mark away, but I couldn't see my way through the maze.

I thought about Annie and Max in Sydney. I was so disappointed that Mark's rotten meeting in America was going to spoil everything. A holiday together would have done us good. I played back the moment he'd announced the American trip and felt more and more irritated. I wished I'd never suggested he help Dom out, and I had no one to blame but myself.

Alessandra's idea of me going to Australia alone and Mark coming later to join me popped back into my brain as if a light bulb had switched on. Suddenly, I knew what I needed to do. I didn't have to cancel because Mark couldn't come, planning the trip would take my mind off things and seeing Annie and Max was the tonic I needed

Relieved and excited, I realised being away from here would help me clear my head and get my fear under control.

Annie and Max in Australia were my last links to Brett and my old life. Maybe I needed to go back to move forward. I could talk to Annie about anything, she'd give me some much-needed baby perspective. Quickening my pace and eager to action my new plan, I would go away to Australia if it killed me.

I started to make a 'to do' list in my head, and ideas came tumbling into my mind of what I needed to organise before I went away: See Robin this morning to ask if he would cover me leading up to Christmas; look in at the travel agent to check on flights; ring Annie.

My mood swung back up. I had been stuck in a rut, that was all, and I felt sure that this was the solution. I was pleased with myself for making a half-decent plan and felt more in control already. Mainly relieved, I was also excited at the prospect of going away. I strode off down the field because I wanted to get to the clinic as fast as possible to see Robin.

Luckily, he was in the office as I arrived, and he received the long-lost friend treatment from both dogs as he sat at the desk.

"Hey, Ellie, you're early."

Plonking my bag on the desk and wriggling out of my coat, I said, "I was hoping to catch you before you started. I've got a favour to ask."

"Should I be worried?" he asked, raising his eyebrows.

"No! Nothing like that. I've just heard that my friend's getting married in Aus next month. I'm going to be her bridesmaid, and I thought if you're alright to cover me, I'd take a few weeks off and have a holiday at the same time."

He looked at me with a slight crease between his brows, "That should be fine, except it doesn't give us long to sort out a locum. It's not like you to be taking time off at short notice. We normally push you to take enough holiday."

I grinned, feeling light-hearted. "You mentioned a girl called Maisie a couple of weeks ago. She was looking for locum work. Would she still be available?"

Robin pursed his lips thoughtfully. "I'd ruled her out because Louise and I aren't going away until the Spring, and she'll be travelling again by then." He shrugged both shoulders. "It's possible some work now may suit her, but you'll still need someone when I go away. Do you want two different locums at the clinic in such a short time?"

I took a deep breath. "I was thinking, could you and Louise pull your trip forward? Maybe go after Christmas when I'm back, then Maisie could cover us both?"

Robin swivelled back and forwards in the chair, thinking. "It could work out. I'd have to discuss it with Louise."

Maisie was the kid sister of one of Robin's friends. Nice girl, apparently, who'd qualified about four years ago. From Robin's description, she'd fit in well here. The only snag was her boyfriend, who needed work too. He wasn't a physio, but perhaps we could help him find something.

Excitement bubbled inside; things were falling into place, which seemed like a good omen that I was on the right track.

As I returned to my desk during a coffee break, Sarah said, "James called, left his number, and he was very keen you call back. He's the chap from the Small Business Association…" She gave me a long, slightly disapproving look which I pretended not to see as she handed me the slip of paper. I could feel I'd coloured up slightly.

"Probably wants me to do another talk." I endeavoured to turn her off the scent lightly.

As I dialled his number, my heart was beating a little faster. "James? Hi, it's Ellie. You left a message for me."

"Hi, Ellie, how lovely to hear from you… yes, I rang to see if you'd like to come to a wine tasting on Thursday. I've got a couple of spare spaces."

"Thursday? Mark will still be in London, unfortunately."

"Well, never mind, in fact, even better, come alone if you'd like to, you can sit with me, and I can introduce you to people."

I could imagine the twinkle in his eye. He knew he'd said something outrageous as if it were quite acceptable. I had to smile at his barefaced cheek. "Um, well, thank you, I'd enjoy that." Something to look forward to, I thought, as I put the phone down.

I had barely rung off when it rang again. "Hello again," I said, assuming it was James calling back.

"Sorry?" said Pen's slightly flustered voice.

"Oh, hi Pen, I thought you were James. I've just put the phone down from chatting with him."

"Oh, really?" She said, "He makes a habit of a little chat mid-morning, does he? Are you sure it's a good idea to encourage him? Why does he keep phoning?"

"Pen! He just rang to ask Mark and me to a wine tasting."

She tutted, "He's up to something; I don't trust him."

I omitted to mention I was going alone. There was nothing in it, and I deserved a bit of relaxation but sensed that Pen would think I should find my fun elsewhere. I wasn't sure where, my usual social circle were all busy with their own issues.

I switched the conversation back to her. "Anyway, everything alright?"

"Yes and no. I've just collected Angus from the hospital, please, will you see him, Ellie? Knock some sense into his head, he's already talking about doing stuff on the farm, and we've had a row about me driving the tractor."

I paused, thinking about all I wanted to get done today and said slightly reluctantly, "I could fit him in at the start of my afternoon list."

"Do you mind? I'm sorry to be a nuisance."

For once, I did mind. I wanted to get everything underway for my trip, but I didn't feel I could say no to Pen. I could hear she was worried, so I swallowed my irritation. "Wheel him down about two o'clock, and I'll do my best." That should still give me time to find out about my plane ticket, I thought.

My search was very helpful at lunchtime, I had flight times and dates now, so as soon as I'd spoken to Maisie and confirmed she could work for me, I could book my holiday. So far, so good, and I still had time to eat my sandwiches.

I couldn't wait. Direct flight to Sydney with a quick change in Hong Kong. I was going back. In my mind's eye, I could see the terraces of pastel-coloured houses with wrought-iron balconies festooned with bright bougainvillea and feel the dry heat kicking back off the pavement.

All that was left to do was tell Mark. I would phone him tonight and let him know; surely, he'd be pleased. I was finally getting my head on straight.

With that optimistic thought in mind, I turned my attention back to work as Angus arrived sporting a splint and a large compression bandage over his hand which he was protectively holding across his body.

I smiled in welcome, my earlier irritation forgotten. "Hi, come on through, let's take a look at you."

"Hi Ellie, thanks for seeing me. I'm not sure why I'm here, Pen is having a complete wobbly about me doing anything, and suddenly she thinks she's superwoman and can do everything! Can you tell her, please?"

I looked at him with a rueful smile. "Ah, well, I can tell you why you're here, it's for me to tell you to behave yourself."

He looked at me with something approaching a scowl and then had to laugh. "Feeling like a bad third in this fight at all, Ellie?"

"Piggy in the middle, maybe."

"All I wanted to do was check a few bits on the farm, and she went nuts."

I tried to be reasonable. "Well, look at it from her point of view, you nearly lost the use of your hand, and you've been lucky, so she doesn't want you to muck it up."

"Pen's just had a baby! I can't have her doing a load of heavy work on the farm, and I know my dad will also try to get involved, which he shouldn't. It's a mess."

I gestured to him to sit down. "Look, you're right she oughtn't to overdo it, but you don't need to wrap her in cotton wool either. Pen's recovered well. I know she was poorly, and I was worried about her straight afterwards, but it might do her good to help, she's an outdoorsy girl."

Angus didn't look particularly convinced, so I ploughed on. "Pen is right about you being on the farm. This next couple of weeks are crucial for your tendon repair, and you mustn't overstrain it or get an infection in the wound."

Angus started to protest, but I cut him short. "Before you eat my head off, if you start working, it'd be so easy to do something without thinking that could set you back. The ends of the tendon will have retracted back when they were cut and had to be stretched back together and fixed. The repair will be fragile until your body has produced enough collagen to bridge the gap. Even then, the repair will need lots of refining before it's anything like as good as before. If you fell on it or forgot and gripped something hard, the repair could rip apart again."

He looked shocked. "What are we talking about here? The hospital said twelve weeks, but that's nearly the Spring."

"They're right, twelve weeks in total, but things do progress during that time. For the first four weeks, you can only do gentle exercises to keep the swelling down and the tissues mobile. That's why you have the splint to stop you from over-stretching. After that, for four weeks, the splint comes off, and you start using your hand for light activities and a bit more vigorous rehab. Then the last four weeks is building up to normal strength."

His shoulders drooped. "They weren't joking then. I don't know how I'm going to cope on the farm."

"What you need is someone to help with the heavy stuff, and I have half an idea. I'll let you know." Maisie's boyfriend was looking for work, it was a possible fit.

He looked at me expectantly, but I wasn't telling until I'd checked this out. I was on fire today.

I grinned, "Hop up on the bed and let me take a look at your hand."

I removed the splint carefully, leaving the wound cover in place and gently moved the fingers asking Angus to join in, slowly flexing and extending without putting any tension on the repair. We moved the elbow, shoulder, and neck as well to keep everything supple and encourage good blood flow through the arm.

"It doesn't feel like my hand. I can't believe it seems so clumsy."

"It will for a while, just keep moving little and often through the day. Two or three out of ten discomfort is acceptable but no more for a few days. The real suffering starts later when the full rehab starts!"

As I bandaged again to keep the splint in place, Angus coughed in a slightly embarrassed way, then said, "Ellie, is everything alright with you and Mark? Pen thinks you're in a rough patch."

I paused in what I was doing and looked at him, remembering the awkward parting with Mark this morning. "Things are a bit strained, that's all, Angus. Mark wants a baby, but I'm not sure about it. I love my job, I still have a business loan to pay off, and I'm self-employed, so no one is giving me paid maternity leave. Mark doesn't seem to realise how difficult it could be for me to juggle a family and a business."

Angus looked puzzled. "It wouldn't be just you, though, would it? Mark would be there, and Pen and me. Alessandra and Peter, your mum and dad. Loads of mums who work have an au pair or a childminder."

I looked at him stubbornly. "I'm not used to relying on other people. Sometimes they disappear just when you need them the most and if you think the prospect of having my mum taking my life over is a comfort, think on, she calls in her debts big time!"

"Ellie, that's not very fair." Angus interrupted. "None of us would knowingly let you down, and anyway, sometimes it's good to be a bit gracious about accepting help, it gives other people a chance to shine."

"Well, I'll remind you of that when you're grumpy about your hand," I replied tartly, thinking *the cheek of him!*

About six o'clock, I was writing up notes, my list completed, when Robin popped his head around the office door. "Ellie, is tomorrow or Thursday evening any good to meet Maisie?"

Thinking of my wine tasting with James, I said, "Can't do Thursday, but tomorrow is fine."

"Okay, I'll call her. I've still got to talk it through with Louise, but I've checked on travel prices for us to leave after Christmas, and I think it might be alright, a bit cheaper to travel, and we'd catch the Summer there too."

"When you speak to Maisie, will you ask if her boyfriend has any farm experience, please? Angus and Pen are going to need someone, and I wondered if he might be able to help."

"No idea, but no harm in asking."

My mood, which had taken a nose-dive after my chat with Angus, began to pick up again.

Chapter Fifteen

The Tipping Point

I popped in to see Pen on the way home for a cup of tea and a chat. I was so excited about the upcoming trip I wanted to tell her all about it. The kitchen was warm and cosy as usual, and as Pen boiled the kettle, I looked at the scatter of baby clothes on the table and began absent-mindedly folding them.

"Oh here, give me those, don't worry about that," she said, trying to collect them up..

I stopped her. "I'll do it while you make the tea. Some of these are cute," I said as I held up an all-in-one with pink, stripey legs and a motif of Winnie the Pooh on the front.

"I know, she's so spoilt, she'll grow up to be a monster! Thank you for seeing Angus earlier, he certainly seems to have taken what you said on board. He's even saying he'll ask around for someone to come and help him."

"I wanted to talk to you about that, I've had an idea." I explained about my trip and told her about Maisie and her boyfriend.

Pen looked thoughtful. "He could be just what we need. But is it a good time for you to go away? I mean, with Mark commuting now, you don't see much of each other. I don't mean to pry, but you two seem to be having a difficult time."

I looked away, Pen was right, we had hit a glitch, but I thought some distance might help. I looked back at her worried face, "We're alright, really, but he's baby-mad at the moment, and I need time to think."

Pen hesitated, then said doubtfully, "Well, if you're sure it will help, but don't go off on self-destruct, Ellie. You do over-think stuff sometimes. There isn't only one type of mum, you can be the type of mother you want to be. If that's a busy working one, well, so be it. You'll still be great."

I turned my palms up and shrugged, taking a break was the best plan I'd come up with. "Maybe, I don't know. It'll do me good to get away, and Mark's so busy anyway, I reckon he'll be glad to have a bit of peace and to let me get my head straight."

She frowned, "Hmm, you know him best. I know Angus would hate it if I did that. Australia must be sensitive for Mark as well, your life there seemed so perfect. It must make him feel a bit insecure sometimes trying to live up to a dead saint."

I gasped, "Brett was not a saint. I've never said he was."

Pen seemed conflicted. "Look, Ellie, I'm not getting at you, just saying maybe play down the Aussie perfection a bit, give Mark a break. Brett died when everything was still wonderful and romantic, it hadn't had time for the gloss to wear off and reality to set in."

Feeling a flicker of impatience, I nodded but steered the conversation away, and we got talking about safer topics. Eventually, it felt like old times, chatting about the dogs and laughing together in the kitchen.

We were interrupted by a wail from Lottie through the baby monitor. Pen said, "Will you go and grab her? I'll sort out some food. I'm glad she's awake. I want to show you something. She may need a quick change before you bring her down."

I grinned, "No worries, as long as she doesn't mind her nappy on back to front."

Pen raised her eyebrows. "Get on with you. You and Mark were pros when Angus went into hospital."

"Beginner's luck, and mainly Mark," I laughed and went to rescue the crying baby. Tears turned to hiccups, then smiles, as I picked her out of the cot. "Come on, you wee rascal," I said as I swung her high above my head. "Let's get you changed, see if your wicked godmother can remember how." I popped her onto the changing table. As I changed her, Lottie kicked with chubby and surprisingly strong legs. She had a delicious chuckle, which was very endearing. I tried to imagine she was mine and wondered if I could devote myself to child-care all day, every day? I didn't know. "Come on, let's find Mummy, she has food for you."

I handed her to Pen when we got to the kitchen. She put Lottie on the floor on a mat with a toy beside her and said, "Watch."

Lottie turned to look at the toy, reached across and, with a slightly undignified plop, rolled onto her tummy and tried to lift her head. "Clever girl!" said Pen delightedly and clapped her hands.

"Wow, she's on the move already, beware your ears and tails, dogs," I said, looking across the kitchen at Belle and Daisy.

Now settled on Pen's lap, supported in the crook of her arm, Lottie drank her bottle with great efficiency. The rapt concentration of daughter, the loving attention of her mum, their eye contact, the trust, and bond was beautiful to see. I shivered. It was beautiful but rendered them both vulnerable.

"I'll leave you to it," I said, unable to watch any more. "I need to walk the hounds, and I want to tell Mark about Australia."

Pen flicked me an anxious glance. "Leave a small space to change your mind Hun, if… well, if you think it may be better to stay,"

"It'll be fine. I don't think it's a big deal."

I couldn't have been more wrong.

"If you've already decided, and that's what you want, Ellie, then I suppose I have no say." Mark's voice over the phone sounded grave. He wasn't happy about my plans.

"Well, you could sound a bit more enthusiastic. I think it would help me to get away for a bit, to make some decisions."

He sounded exasperated, "Of course, I'm not enthusiastic, Ellie. I hardly ever see you, now, when we have some big issues to resolve, you're telling me you want to disappear! It isn't just you that has to come to a decision, we need to decide things together surely."

I began to feel irritated. "It's hardly my fault we don't see each other. I didn't know Dom was going to swan off early and dump so much in your lap."

Mark sighed, "Neither did I, but now it's happened, I must see it through for a while. I thought the extra money behind us would be a safety net if we have a baby. So hopefully, you feel less pressured about having to work long hours in the clinic. Ellie, this trip idea makes me feel as if you're running away from me."

I shook my head and flicked at my thumbnail. "That's unfair, just because I want some space to think doesn't mean I'm running away. Anyway, you'll be in America for your meeting most of the time, so I might as well be in Australia as sitting in the barn on my own."

"You could come to America with me and fly to Australia for the wedding together. You'd get a break, but we could do our thinking together."

My heart sank, I could see it was another option and perfectly reasonable, but right now, it wasn't what I needed. Having had the idea to go, I now longed to be back in Australia. I wanted to talk to Annie again, and I needed to be away from Mark to decide what was right for me. I could feel tears welling up from nowhere as Mark continued, "Ellie, why can't you talk to me about this? I feel like you've disappeared behind a brick wall."

"I am talking to you," I burst out, "but you aren't listening. You've decided what you want and are trying to coerce me into doing that. You Pen, Angus, Sarah, everyone, all pressuring me! I'm not a brood-mare, here to produce a child just because that's what you all want me to do. We aren't living in The Handmaid's Tale! I need some space, Mark."

There was a silence on the other end of the line, and tears rolled down my cheeks.

"I'm sorry you feel like that, Ellie, because I don't think it's true. I think you're over-reacting. And you're right, I don't fully understand. You wanted a baby with Brett, you trusted him and were prepared for the compromises. Now having a baby with me seems to be a major issue for you. You don't seem to trust me the same way."

His words stung like a whiplash. "Don't you dare bring Brett into this, it's not about Brett. You are not going to make me feel guilty about who I trust the most. Trusting him made no difference, he still left me alone. And right back at you, Mark, I'm not having a baby to smooth your insecurities about whether I love you as much as him."

There was a long pause, and I imagined him running agitated hands through his hair. "Ellie, I'm sorry I shouldn't have said that. I don't feel insecure, well, not in that way, but I do want you to believe in me and how strong we are to face life together. I want to be sure that our life is the life you want."

Completely triggered now, I said, "And what if I say I don't want a family at all or what if I can't have a baby? What then?"

I could picture his devastated expression.

"Ellie, if we can't have a baby, we'll sort it out between us, we'll cope. I don't know, adopt, IVF, something. If you don't want a family at all, that's different. I honestly don't know if I can handle that because I do want kids, I honestly do."

I couldn't bear the hurt in his voice and could feel a massive knot in my chest.

I whispered quietly, "Let me go, Mark, just let me go to Australia. I will get my head around this, but I need some time on my own."

His voice sounded weary, "I'm not going to stop you, Ellie, I couldn't anyway, but I wish you'd chosen America, that's all."

"I don't want to hurt you, but try to understand, I need some time on my own. It's about me, not about you."

There was nothing more to say except our goodbyes. I replaced the phone in its cradle, and the silence in the house pressed around me. I stared out the window at the grey clouds scudding over the moon. I was frightened and wondered if this was the beginning of the end for us. I wrapped my arms tightly around my knees and let a wave of misery wash over me. Why was everything so hard?

I needed comfort, so I padded down to the kitchen, where the dogs were gently snoring in their beds. The dull thump, thump of both tails against the cushions, told me they knew I was there, and I said, "I'm in a mess, guys."

Thump-thump came their agreement in stereo. As they watched me with their soft eyes, they also managed to add, but we still love you.

I made myself a hot chocolate and suddenly felt exhausted. I broke the usual house rules and invited the two dogs up to bed with me. Unable to believe their luck, they settled, curled up in the small of my back, and I drew the comfort I needed from their steady warmth beside me.

I woke with the rushing clouds of the day before still dulling my brain, and set off with the dogs. As I plodded through the autumn fields with heavy feet, my heart wasn't in it, so I cut the walk short.

As we re-entered the barn, I snatched up the ringing phone. I hoped it was Mark. Instead, Robin's cheerful voice hailed me. Maisie had agreed to meet us later that day, and

Louise was happy to change travel plans. The wheels I'd set in motion the day before were turning. I couldn't change my plans now.

Maisie turned out to be a bubbly, energetic girl, full of enthusiasm to take on the locum position. I thought Robin was right; she'd do well here, so I offered her the post. Her boyfriend Adam was also a lovely chap, quieter and more reserved than Maisie but with an air of dependability.

"If you're still looking for work as well, Adam, there could be an opening on my friend's farm."

He looked delighted. "Oh, really? That would be great, Ellie. My uncle's a farmer back home. I spent most of my holidays as a kid helping there, you couldn't keep me away. Do they know we're only here until the Spring, though?"

I nodded, "Yes, they only need you temporarily, Angus is getting over a hand injury."

Adam looked at Maisie, and they both beamed. "Perfect. If you can put us in contact, that would be great."

No time like the present. "I can do better than that. If you have time, I can drive you up there to meet them and drop you back at the station afterwards."

He looked surprised but said, "Sure, if you don't mind."

As we drove to the farm, I explained a bit about Pen and Angus. We piled into the kitchen and chatted together with them over a cup of tea. It was good to see they all seemed to get on. Angus took Adam off for a walk around the farm leaving Pen, Maisie, and me in the kitchen with Lottie. Maisie was a great hit with Lottie and had her giggling with peep-boo games and loud raspberry noises.

Looking up from the happy baby, Maisie said, "If you ever need a babysitter while I'm here, I love kids."

Oh, brilliant, I thought. *Someone else who dotes on kids.* Was I the only person in the world who had reservations? I was beginning to feel like an alien on Planet Baby.

I said as much the next evening to James. After a round of expertly led wine tasting, he came to join the table. The group he'd put me with were now enjoying the wines we'd tasted, paired with some delicious food. He threw back his head and roared with laughter. "I'm with you. I've never really seen myself with a family. I love my life too much. My nephews and nieces are great, but much better now they're a bit more grown-up, and anyway, I can always give them back."

I gave him an indignant glance. "It's alright for you to laugh, you haven't got the biological clock ticking and everyone breathing down your neck."

His eyes crinkled in sympathy, "You poor thing. Here, have another glass of this excellent red wine and let's plan your escape. Now, where will it be, Mexico? The Bahamas?"

I laughed, "Oh, I'm already escaping. I have a trip to Australia coming up. I'm fleeing the country and leaving the clinic in Maisie and Robin's capable hands."

He made a celebratory drum roll on the table. "That's my girl. Life's too short. Where are you staying down-under?"

"I'll be visiting my old flat-mates Annie and Max in Sydney. I was going to their wedding mid-December anyway, but I'm extending the trip."

He looked at me with a mischievous twinkle. "I was only looking at flights myself today, I'm overdue a visit to my suppliers in the Hunter Valley and thought I'd escape the English gloom."

Astonished, I fell into the trap. “Are you kidding?”

He winked, “Well, I haven’t exactly looked at flights yet, but I am overdue a visit. You could bring your excellent nose and do some tasting with me.” His eyes were dancing with merriment, and I had to laugh back. “Say yes, Ellie, it’ll be fun.”

I don’t know if it was the wine talking or the sheer delight of finding an ally, but I said, “I’d love to.”

Chapter Sixteen

Conversations

I didn't feel anything like as scintillating the next morning, and I groaned as the alarm sounded like the entire percussion section of an orchestra. My mouth felt dry, and a dull headache battered at my temples.

"I think I may have overdone it last night, guys," I said to the dogs as I shuffled downstairs in search of an Alka-Seltzer and a big mug of hot water with honey, lemon, and ginger.

They wove around my legs affectionately, and then Jeeves moved hopefully in the direction of the door and rattled his bowl.

"Food? You want food?" I looked at them in disgust, "Walk first, you horrors. Your mum needs fresh air."

As we walked, I thought about last night. It had been such fun to be light-hearted for a change. I wasn't too sure about James including himself in the Australia trip. I concluded he was probably only flirting and felt pretty sure nothing would come of it. Still, I'd be lying if I said I wasn't just a little flattered. I couldn't think what James saw in me; he was so sophisticated. If he'd seen me this morning with my PJs tucked in my wellies and an old waxed jacket slung over the top, he'd soon change his mind. I bet his girlfriend looked more like Vale.

Thinking of Vale, I remembered that I'd promised to ring her regularly and made a mental note to check the time zone and do that today. I also had to book my plane ticket. I got a little buzz of excitement as I thought about going back to Australia. Knowing I was going to Sydney felt like a warm hug.

I just had to convince Mark…then Pen, Angus, and Sarah. I hadn't even mentioned it to my mum, she wasn't going to approve either. Perhaps I should have taken heed, but they had made me feel rebellious. Everyone could think what they liked, I needed this trip. If I was going to be in the doghouse, I would have to make mine comfortable. It looked like I'd be spending time in it for the foreseeable future.

When I spoke to Vale at lunchtime, she seemed to be settling in after her whirlwind move.

Her voice was warm as she said, "Ellie, it's good to hear your voice. I've missed you. I've missed London and the farm too."

I tried to imagine her amongst the skyscrapers. "We've missed you as well. How's New York?"

"Cold and noisy, but I'm surviving. The company have done us proud. Our suite has an amazing view of the city. I can see the Empire State so close I could touch it. We're still house-hunting and looking forward to Mark coming out for the conference. Hopefully, we may have found somewhere to rent by the time Mark arrives."

I laughed, "I'm sure he'd be just as thrilled to join you if you're still staying in a posh hotel as well."

She suddenly sounded excited, “Why don’t you take a holiday and come with him? I’d love to show you around.”

I sucked in my breath, “Ah, a sore point, I’m afraid,” I explained to Vale what I’d decided to do instead.

She sounded surprised, “Okay, wow. That’s brave.”

I’m not sure brave was a reassuring word. It implied I was risking something by going.

Vale continued, “Well, good for you. I hope it helps you to make some decisions.”

I sighed, “So do I.”

“Look, I’m so sorry you’re having a hard time. I feel terrible because it’s partly our fault. If I hadn’t had to move, none of this would have happened.”

I sat up and tried to reassure her, “You mustn’t think that! It’s not your fault, the baby thing would have still come up.”

“Listen, let me talk to Dom, he’s the man to talk Mark around. You go and take the space you need and don’t feel guilty about it. Enjoy your break, it’ll do you good. It’s tough thinking about a baby and a career. I don’t know how I’ll feel when the time comes either.”

I was touched; it felt comforting to find someone else supportive, someone, who didn’t think I was being unreasonable and understood my point of view.

Vale continued, “We’ll look after Mark when he comes to New York, don’t you worry, and I’ll keep him out of the clutches of any designing women.”

I snorted, “He’s so grumpy at the moment, I don’t think anyone would have designs on him.”

She laughed, “What? With that sexy English accent and the boy-next-door look, he rocks? You’re joking. Best I keep my eye on him.”

I knew she was only joking, but I wasn't sure how I felt about that. Mark was Mark, and I hadn't thought of him as stealable.

Angus was the first patient on my list after lunch. I removed his splint and was pleased to see that the skin around the line of neat stitches was looking pink and healthy. Not too much swelling, either. I watched the intense concentration on his face as I asked him to flex and straighten his fingers and suddenly laughed.

"You look just like Lottie when you're concentrating."

He rolled his eyes. "Who knew it could be so hard just to bend your fingers!"

I made haste to reassure him, "It will get easier, just keep at it gently, little and often."

As it was still early days for the repair, I made sure the rest of the arm and Angus's neck were all working full range and reinforced how important it was not to overdo things in this first couple of weeks.

He nodded, "I have taken heed, and I'm trying to do everything you say. Oh, by the way, change of subject, thank you for suggesting us to Adam, we've settled that he'll come to help me. He seems to know his way around a farm."

I wondered if he was trying to talk about something different to avoid any more probing questions about how much he was doing at work. However, I let myself be distracted. "It helps us both out, Maisie is going to locum for me first and for Robin later on."

He looked up, "Yes, she said she was. Will she be treating me?"

"No, I'll get Robin to do that." I didn't say so but felt Robin might rein Angus in more effectively if he started to overdo things.

Angus continued, "We've managed to sort out some accommodation for Maisie and Adam." I looked up eagerly, I'd been thinking about how to sort this out. "Mum and Dad have offered them a little annexe flat that used to be for Dad's parents. Maisie and Adam will have to tidy it up a bit, but it should be fine."

I gave him a double thumbs-up. "Brilliant, that saves me a job. I was going to start asking around for some temporary accommodation for the two of them." I mentally punched the air, one more problem solved.

"So, you're still going then?"

"Yes, I am," I said firmly. "All that's left to do is sort the dogs out, and then I'm ready to go."

He looked at me, surprised. "We'll have the dogs for you, Ellie, don't be silly."

"I think you have enough on your plate," I said, indicating his hand. "And Pen certainly has. I was going to ask if their breeder would board them for me."

Angus frowned at me. "Ellie, you would hurt Pen's feelings if you did that, she's expecting to have them. Will you give up on this independence kick you're on and accept some help! I shall make walking them part of Adam's duties if Pen can't manage. I reckon he'd be more than a match for two Gordon Setters."

"I'm not on an independence kick!" I replied hotly, but he raised an eyebrow and gave me a stern look.

"You're on something."

Everyone was clucking about me doing something by myself as if I was heading off to Outer Mongolia or something. "Angus, I need a break, that's all." He seemed unconvinced. "Look, if you're sure about the dogs, that would be a great help. It's good of you both, I know you don't think I'm doing the right thing, but I appreciate your help."

He put his good hand on my arm. "We just want you to feel settled and happy again. You were so lonely when we first knew you, and we thought that was all finished now you're with Mark. We're your friends. We worry."

I felt a twinge of impatience again. Maybe this was the new me. People change, what then? Would Pen and Angus stop loving me?

"Angus, I don't know what to say. I'm still me, I need to work through some aspects of my life, but mostly I'd like a fun holiday."

When Angus had mentioned Mark, I realised with a start that he would be home tonight. I felt absurdly nervous about seeing Mark after our conversation earlier in the week. If he so much as hinted at a criticism of me going away, there would be trouble, I thought defiantly, then deflated slightly. Mark hadn't sounded critical on the phone, more like sad. Everything was so complicated.

I turned my attention back to Angus's hand and replaced the splint and bandage.

"I can't wait to get rid of this clumsy, itchy thing," he said.

"Only a couple more weeks, then you'll only need it at night. I'll be in Australia when you come out of it, but Robin will guide you through, and I'll be back to see you to full activity again."

As he swung his legs off the bed and I watched him leave the clinic, I knew in my heart that he still thought I was wrong to go away alone.

I finished my list, and my pending reunion with Mark began to give me butterflies in my stomach. It had to be faced, but I felt like running away.

As soon as I got home, I showered and made a special effort with my hair, as if that might paper over the enormous emotional cracks. Mark was due home at about seven o'clock, and as the minutes ticked by, I busied myself preparing the meal and began to feel slightly sick. When the phone rang, I was cutting tomatoes, and as I jumped nearly sliced off my thumb. I sucked at the cut as I answered, expecting it to be Mark. Instead, it was Mum, and she went straight on the offensive.

"I spoke to Alessandra earlier. She told me you're going to Australia well before the wedding, instead of going to America with Mark. I felt very hurt that she was telling me before you had. Are you sure that's the right thing to do?"

I wanted to shout, "Mind your own business," and, "No, I'm not sure, but you giving me a hard time doesn't help." But I said neither. If my mother sees a crack, she's a great believer in hammering a wedge into it. Instead, I said, "I've only just decided, but everything fell into place with a nice locum, so I decided to take the opportunity and spend some time with Annie. I was going to call you at the weekend."

She tutted loudly, "I think you should make Mark your priority. He's very busy with that new job, you should be supporting him, not gallivanting off. It's not always good to go looking back into the past, either. Your dad and I don't want to see you upset again like you were when you came back before. It can't be easy for poor Mark living in the shadow of your old boyfriend."

I swallowed back another angry thought about the fact it would be nice if she were on my side for once but said, "Thanks Mum, I'm not going to Australia to look back, I'm having a holiday and being one of my best friend's bridesmaids."

"Well, it seems a bit odd to me when you could have gone to America with Mark. I hope you don't upset Mark, he's such a nice chap. I think you're lucky to have met him."

I wanted to say; *actually, I'm thinking of running off with a wealthy, sophisticated older man called James, who thinks I'm the best thing since sliced bread and has made up an excuse to follow me to Australia* but thought better of that too. "Sorry, Mum can't chat now, I'm just in the middle of making dinner. Mark will be back any minute. I'll call you back."

Her voice softened, "Well, at least you're cooking him a nice meal, he's been so busy. Eventually, you may have to think about cutting your work down, Ellie. Somebody has to keep the home fires burning."

As I put down the phone with smoke coming out of my ears, I kicked out at an empty bag that had fallen to the floor and shouted, "I've been bloody busy too, who's here cooking my meal? At least James would have had a wonderful restaurant booked and be whisking me out to drink fabulous wines." Both dogs looked at me but sensibly forbore to comment.

Well, if Mark was looking for a fight, I certainly felt in the mood to give him one, I thought savagely as I hunted through the first aid box for a plaster.

In the event, he wasn't. Tired and weary, he took one look at my body language, and we both retreated behind some polite conversation and left the elephant in the room sitting on its own. He stretched his arm around me as we sat on the couch to watch the news. Although I didn't pull away, I couldn't relax and snuggle into our normal head-on-shoulder or feet-on-lap easy intimacy. All those unspoken words seemed to form a barrier between us, and I could neither continue the conversation we'd had on the phone nor pretend it hadn't happened. He kissed me goodnight as we got into bed and turned away from me. We may as well have been strangers. I stared wide-eyed into the night.

Sleeping only fitfully, I woke the following day feeling headachey and dull. Mark wasn't in bed. I hadn't heard him get up, but when I went downstairs, the dogs were gone, and so were his wellies. Only a couple of months ago, he would have woken me with a teasing kiss and a coffee, then dragged me out of bed to go with him.

When they got back, he looked at me from the boot room door, hair tangled from the wind, large black bags under his eyes. Naturally lean, he looked almost angular. "Ells, put the coffee on. This is dreadful, we've got to talk."

"Forget the coffee. Put your boots back on, let's walk." I couldn't handle the intensity of a face-to-face conversation.

He shrugged and slipped his feet back into his wellies. I slipped on my tweed coat and boots. We headed off, my hands stuffed deep in my pockets.

"About Australia… Ellie, it's okay. Go. I get it, I do. You need some headspace."

"I do," I said gruffly, "I'm sorry you're so hurt."

He glanced at me briefly. "It's not the holiday that hurts, Ellie. I feel you're slipping away from me into a parallel world. I can't seem to help, and you don't seem to trust me enough to explain what you're feeling. It brings back all the pain from when I lost Katrina."

I flared, "That's not true, I'm here. It's me who feels shut out by all you Planet-Baby people. I'm not Katrina, I'm not leaving you, and I don't feel it's me who's changed."

"Not changed exactly, but withdrawn, as if you've stepped away. I know you're not her, but please don't slip away, Ellie, it makes me feel nervous."

I fiddled with the zip on my jacket. "I feel pressured, Mark."

"I know, but I don't see why. It isn't a straight choice, career, or motherhood. I'm not asking you to give up Touch to have a baby." He stopped and turned towards me, still with a haunted look. "Dom's on your side, though. He rang me and said to cut you some slack and stop being so parochial. So, here's what I thought, I'm going back to London today to get out of your hair and give you some space. I'll come to Australia before the wedding. If we've both had some time, I'm sure we can sort it out. We can speak on the phone if you like or not..."

He tailed off and, when I didn't answer, said, "Ellie, throw me a lifeline, please, I'm dying here."

The truth was, all the while he'd been resisting me, I felt adamant and justified. Now he'd given me what I asked for, I felt deflated.

"Ellie?"

I flushed and looked at him, finding it hard to meet his eye. "Yes, yes, okay, I mean, thank you."

He looked as deflated as I felt. "Don't thank me, this is what you want, isn't it?"

I nodded, "I need it, Mark. I'm so confused." Tears started to run down my cheeks and were blown back into my hair by the wind.

Mark stuffed his hands into his coat pockets and looked out over the fields for a moment with an unfocused gaze. He seemed miserable and undecided. I tried to guess what he was thinking and failed, so I let the silence hang for a while. Mark sighed, squared his shoulders, and turned to me with a more resigned expression,

"Whatever you decide, Ells, I'm going to organise with Dom to put a limit on my consultancy hours with him while I'm in America." I looked up sharply, and he put up a hand, "I won't let him down, but I don't want to be away from you, from home, all the time. The work is exciting, but the long hours and pressure are wrong for me. Going back into corporate has made me realise working like that isn't who I am. Just because I can do it doesn't mean I should. I'm not Dom."

I felt horribly guilty, the contract had been my idea. "I know, I'm sorry, I should never have suggested it."

"It's not your fault, Dom wanted my help, but I could have said no. In one way, it's been good. Without trying again, I may always have wondered about what 'might have been' in corporate land."

We walked on in silence, both sad but at least without the crackling tension of last night.

"Want a coffee?" I offered as we got back to the barn.

He shook his head sadly. "No, Ellie, my bag's in the car, I'm going to head back. I can't do this. I love you, but I can't do this, the not knowing."

I always thought Mark had coped so much better with his trauma than I had with mine. But seeing the raw pain on his face, I realised my doubts had triggered old insecurities. My sense of desolation grew, I was struggling to manage the mess in my head and felt drained, and now I felt guilty about Mark too. I was usually the one solving issues with people, not causing them. But it's always easier to see clearly when the problem belongs to someone else.

Mark came into the barn briefly, changed his boots for shoes and ruffled the dog's heads. "See you guys, and I'll see you in Australia." With a kiss on my cheek that seemed to burn there long after he'd left, I watched his car disappear down the drive.

I sat and stared into space. *What had I done?*

Chapter Seventeen

Australia Revisited

I don't know how long I would have sat there had it not been for a tap on the door. I looked up and saw Alessandra smiling outside. My heart sank. She was the last person I wanted to see today.

She scooped me into a hug. "Hello, darling girl, how are you? I wanted to catch Mark, he isn't still in bed, is he?" she said, looking around as she peeled off her coat and gloves.

"No, he's just left," I answered dully.

Her large brown eyes swivelled towards me, looking closely for the first time. "What on earth has happened? Is that naughty Dominic overworking Mark? I will be cross, it was always the same. Dom doesn't know when to stop!"

"No," I replied, "Well, in part, but it's not that. Mark and I can't seem to agree on the future, and we both need some space to think things through. I'm going to Australia for a longer trip, and Mark has gone back to London before his trip to America."

I tried to speak lightly, but Alessandra was no fool and quickly said, "So you've quarrelled! What a piece of work over nothing, I'm surprised at you both."

"Sorry?" I couldn't believe my ears.

"Well, here you both are, running away from each other. I don't think your real issue is having a baby at all. I think in different ways, you're both scared in case you get hurt again. I know Mark, he can be like his father. I bet he's being very serious and very noble about it all. Being dignified when he needs to laugh away your fears and give you a shake. And now, the whole baby debate has turned into such a big issue, that neither of you can see your way out of it."

I looked at her aghast, "I'm not running away!"

"Oh, I think if you're honest with yourself, you are, even if you haven't realised it yet. No, don't eat me, I'm not going to fall out with you as well," Alessandra said, laughing. "You couldn't get much further away now, could you? Australia! I know I suggested you go on your own, but I didn't realise then what a pickle you two were in. Well, go and have your holiday, but don't make it too much of a drama, the two of you. You both want everything under control, planned out, because it's safe that way, but you have to live a little, enjoy the chaos, that's where the best bits of life are."

I couldn't believe it. She was almost making fun of us, as if we were a pair of squabbling kids.

"If he isn't here, I shall have to call him. I wanted him to help Peter with some heavy lifting, but it will have to wait now. I don't suppose he'll be back until you go. What a nuisance, even Angus is injured." She smoothed her gloves back on and slipped into her coat. Even in my misery, I marvelled at how she could make an anorak and gloves look stylish. "Have a good trip. Laugh, have fun, scare him a bit, but not too much, then come back and get on with your lives."

With a waft of her usual Chanel perfume, she headed back outside, and I wasn't sure whether to be offended or to laugh. She made life sound so simple.

I wanted to ring Mark and tell him what she'd said, but in the circumstances, I thought not. Instead, I took out my frustration and despair on a big pile of ironing and watched a video of Friends episodes back-to-back, then went upstairs and laid my summer clothes on the bed in the spare room. Apart from random desultory thoughts which threatened to de-rail me, I was all ready to head for Australia in only a few days.

On Sunday, I spent most of the day at Touch writing hand-over notes and generally "fussing", as Robin would have said. I was sure the team would be fine without me but wondered if I would be fine without them. Work usually saved me when things were going badly; I simply put my head down and didn't take time to think. In Australia, I would have nothing but time to think. But it was no good worrying about it now, I was going, and that was that.

James offered to drop me at the airport, but I politely declined. I would struggle to explain that one to Pen or Sarah, both of whom had offered me a lift as well.

He was, true to his word, going to visit his Hunter Valley suppliers and promised he'd be in touch when he arrived in Sydney. I hadn't expected him to make the trip, and his persistence was beginning to concern me. The last thing I needed was another complication. Or, as he put it, a little light relief.

I shrugged off the concern, he had never even made a move to kiss me, not that I wanted him to. He was just being friendly. I loaded my case in the back of Pen's car and slipped in beside her. "Got everything?" She asked, "Passport, tickets, money?"

I grinned, "Yes, Mum, all organised."

"Just checking. Normally when we head off on a road trip together, we've got a car full of dog gear, and we're heading up to the moors. It seems strange to be dropping you at the airport for a city break."

Pen didn't quite understand what an amazing, varied city Sydney was. "There'll be plenty of beach walks and trips into the bush, but I do love the city too. It's beautiful the way it sits right on the harbour. You see glints of water all over the place where there are creeks and inlets, and some of the beaches are stunning."

She shrugged, "Well, you know me, I'm a country mouse, too many people everywhere in cities. Give me the moors any day."

We chatted about the first time we went up to Yorkshire when I'd injured my knee and Mark had come to rescue me. It was nice to talk about something safe, but I felt a pang as I remembered how good it had been when Mark and I got together, and he looked after me following my injury.

My internal struggles now were real. I had to be sure that I wasn't settling for comfortable and going with the flow. Neither Mark nor I deserved that.

Pen parked in the drop-off zone and got out to give me a huge bear hug. "Ellie Rose, rest up, relax, come back with your head on straight, and don't you dare decide to stay out there for good."

"No chance of that happening," I said, hugging her back. "I've left the dogs with you."

Pen gasped, "Charming! Nice to know where I stand in the pecking order! Write me a postcard, enjoy yourself." Only the tiny, worried frown gave her away, but she seemed determined to keep things light.

I checked in my bag and sailed through the boarding protocols, feeling that at every stage, I was shedding another skin: physio, godmother, friend, lover. By the time I boarded the plane, I felt a sense of freedom, like a weight had been lifted off me. Just for today, I could think about nothing at all.

Apart from the dreadful flights after Brett died, I've always loved flying. The air hostesses look after everyone so well. I read, listened to music, binge-watched movies, slept, and was constrained to do absolutely nothing for as long as the flight lasted. The whole journey was bliss, no responsibility, no hassle, and no phone calls. Despite the background roar of jet engines, I drifted in limbo and enjoyed every minute of it.

As we flew over Australia and near Sydney, I watched as thousands of tiny turquoise dots got larger, revealing swimming pools in almost every garden. The cultivated vegetation looked more lush as we flew over the suburbs, leaving the arid bush behind. We bumped once or twice on landing, then the reverse thrust of the jet engines slowed us with a swooping motion and the aeroplane, which seemed clumsy now it was no longer airborne, taxied to a halt.

I waited until the initial commotion of everyone emptying the overhead lockers quietened down before I followed the stream of people to the baggage carousels. My suitcase arrived in acrobatic style, tumbling over and over down the slide and careering off the side of the carousel with a thud. I looked in dismay and hoped against hope that my perfume and wedding gift, a delicate porcelain figure of an embracing couple, had not shattered into a million pieces. Thank goodness it wasn't one of my dogs in a travel crate arriving that way. I had seen small dogs on the luggage carousel before now.

Lifting the seemingly stunned case, now immobile on the floor, I hauled it through customs, got my visa stamp and walked into the Arrivals Hall. Annie was waiting; she scanned the faces of the steady stream of arrivals looking for me. Our eyes met, and her face broke into a beaming smile. She waved and came running towards me, enfolding me in a tight hug. As she did, I noticed she felt different. There was a tiny hard bump where there would normally be a concave stomach. I pushed her back to arm's length and looked, taking in her rounded face and, wonder of wonders, a bust! "Annie, are you?"

She smiled sheepishly. "Four months, Eagle Eyes. I wanted to surprise you."

"You have," I said, "Annie, congratulations! Well, I mean, I hope you're happy?"

"Ecstatic," she said, linking her arm through mine. "I am blooming, as the saying goes. I have never felt so well and couldn't be happier."

Should have bought the family figurine as my wedding gift, not the couple, I thought fleetingly. *Well, Ellie Rose, you can run, but you can't hide, the universe is determined to rub your nose in pregnancy and families. Planet-Baby it is.* I laughed.

"What are you laughing about?"

"I'll tell you later. Right now, I'm so happy to see you."

She squeezed my arm. "I'm glad you've come. Now when does your hunky man arrive? We're dying to meet him."

"He's gone to America first, Annie. Mark has been working for Dom looking after the London office while Dom is away with Vale, so he'll get here about a week before the wedding. He's flying in direct from the States."

She looked disappointed but then smiled. "You'll miss him, but that means we get you to ourselves."

"I will miss him, but it'll be good to have some thinking time to myself as well. Truth is, Annie, we're a bit stuck. Mark wants us to have a family as soon as possible, and I don't know if I want a baby now. I like my life the way it is." I gave her a playful push. "You're no help being pregnant either. I thought you'd be a working girl ally!"

She held up her hands. "Sorry to disappoint, I can't say we planned the pregnancy, we didn't, but I think it's the best way. We got thrown in at the deep end with no choice. What's the problem for you? I thought you wanted kids. You and Brett always talked about having a big family."

"That was before, though, Annie. It took me a long time to get over losing Brett, and if anything happened, I don't know if I could go through that again. My work, the clinic, it got me through, and I don't think I can give it up to have a baby."

She frowned, "Sweetie, that's life. We can't hide in corners hoping it won't happen. You must be big-hearted and trust you have the strength to get through. Just because you lost Brett doesn't mean anything else awful will happen. And you have Mark now, he doesn't expect you to give up work, does he?"

I sighed, "No, he doesn't in theory, but when it comes to it, would that change? What if I didn't have Mark for some reason, or worse, what if the baby died? I don't think I could cope. I've been having terrible nightmares about empty cots."

"Ellie! Oh, my goodness." She looked distressed and glanced at me in surprise before turning her eyes back to the road.

I clapped my hand to my mouth. "I'm so sorry, I shouldn't have said that. It was thoughtless."

Annie glanced away from the road. "You don't have to hold back with me. I won't lie, I've thought about something dreadful happening. I expect everyone does in a dark moment, but if you worked on the principle of not going ahead with things because something might happen, you'd never do anything. Life's a risk so is love. None of it comes with guarantees."

I looked out of the window at the life going on in the city. "I know you're right; I never used to be afraid like this."

"What does Mark say?"

I blushed, "We haven't talked about it, well, apart from a horrible row the other day. He thinks I don't trust him the same way I did Brett. I told you about Katrina, didn't I? I think that whole trauma has left him very sensitive about trust issues, so he's taking this hard."

Straight for the jugular, Annie flashed back, "And do you? I mean, trust him? Why aren't you talking? You and Brett talked about everything."

I hesitated, "I don't know, I do trust him, maybe it's me I don't trust." I stared at the familiar scenery as we sped towards the flat. I sounded lame, even to myself. "Anyway, enough about me, I've come here to clear my head. What are the plans?"

We drew into the car park of the flats, and it was achingly familiar; the frangipani tree at the entrance and the thick succulents in the beds along the walkway - all part of another life.

"Dump your bags. I've put you in our old room. Max and I use, um," she hesitated, then rushed on, "The other one now, with your box room as a dressing room. We haven't decided which bedroom we'll use when the baby comes. I'll make us a cold drink; it's getting hot already."

Somehow in my mind, the flat had remained unchanged, and Brett's room, our room, would still be as it was. But of course, the interior looked completely different, new décor, new furniture. Max and Annie were not enshrined in the past.

"So, tell me about the wedding," I said as I joined her on the balcony.

I seemed to have diverted her attention, although knowing Annie, she'd be back after me about Mark again later. She never was one for letting anything drop and was a fierce believer in talking issues through, however painful. I suppose that was, in part, why I was here. Annie knew me inside out, nothing I could say would phase her.

She told me about the wedding. A fitting appointment was booked tomorrow at the bridal shop for her dress and mine. I'd only seen the photograph she'd sent me so far and was curious to see how I'd look in my dress. The style was different to anything I'd worn before.

"And do you have any special plans?" she asked, explaining that she couldn't be with me every day as she was still working.

"I want to visit Brett's grave to leave something and to say hello. I never saw it on the day of the funeral. I fancy some long walks on the North Head, and I might go out to the Hunter Valley while I'm here, just for a few days. A friend is out here, and we said we might hook up."

"Oh well, she's welcome to stay at the flat if she would like a base to see Sydney. She'd have to bunk in with you."

"Um, he; and that's very kind of you, Annie, but I think he's tied up visiting wine suppliers." I felt a blush creeping up my neck.

"Ellie Rose, you're blushing; who's this mystery man? Are you up to no good?"

I cut in hastily, "No, it's not like that. I've done some talks for James' business association, and we get on very well. He's a wine importer, a bit older than me, but good fun, and he comes over here regularly and just happened to book a trip at the same time."

Annie looked unconvinced. "Oh, really? What an amazing coincidence! Ellie Rose, you're so naive. I bet he's utterly smitten if he's following you around the world."

Alessandra's words came back to me again, about men following their loves to the ends of the earth, but I ignored them.

"He isn't smitten, and I may not even hear from him."

This prediction proved not to be accurate, as, later that evening, when she answered the phone, Annie said, "I'll just get her," and handed me the phone with a slight frown. "It's James for you."

I took the receiver. "Ellie! Hi, hope you had a good journey over?"

Aware of Annie's scrutiny, I said, "Um, yes, fine."

"Look, I'll be arriving at the weekend. If you're free, we could do our Hunter Valley trip from Monday to Wednesday. I can pick you up."

I put my hand over the mouthpiece and said to Annie, "Is the first part of next week free, no dress fittings or anything?"

"No, nothing booked." Then she mouthed, "Is this a good idea?"

"That's fine," I said to James, looking at Annie and shrugging an unspoken, "What's the problem?"

"I'll book us in at the Neath Hotel; it's a lovely old place, a proper traditional country pub. I've stayed there before, and I think you'll like it."

I ignored Annie making exaggerated slicing movements across her throat. "That sounds great, James, I'll look forward to it."

"Bring your nose. I've got your address in Drummoyne, so I'll aim to be with you about ten." He rang off, and I turned to face Annie's objections.

"Ellie, aren't you playing with fire a bit here?"

I tried to look bewildered even though I'd had the virtually identical conversation with Pen. "He's just a friend, honestly."

She gave me a hard stare. "I bet Mark wouldn't like you going off together."

That was like a red rag to a bull. Annie couldn't have said anything that would make me more determined to go. According to Vale, Mark could be chest-deep in glamourous American women, all drooling over his accent by now. Well, we'd see about that.

"He's got no reason not to like it. James is a friend, nothing more."

"All I'm saying is if things aren't the best between you and Mark, Ellie, don't go making things more complicated. It's tempting to make a change rather than sort things out, but in the end, I know you, you'd hate yourself."

I looked up exasperated. "Annie! I'm not making a change, and I'm not going to cheat on Mark."

"Well, don't fool yourself about what this is or how it may end up, that's all."

We put all thoughts of complicated decisions aside as we arrived at the bridal shop the next day and stepped between the pages of a glossy magazine world. The main shop, carpeted in deep navy with cream furniture and lined with full-length mirrors, was softened by gauze drapes and gentle lighting. Rows of dresses hung lovingly encased in silk bags on rails fitted around the walls, and a central plinth allowed for dress fittings and a panoramic view of whoever stood upon it. Bernice, the owner, greeted us with the sort of reverence reserved for visiting royalty, and a young assistant brought two glasses of sparkling wine and tiny almond biscuits. While we sipped our drinks, Bernice brought our dresses to the robing rooms.

Talk within that hallowed hall was only of the wedding and the intricacies of matching the right shade of white to compliment skin tone, bugle beads versus crystals and the merits of roses over fuchsias to create the right texture in a bouquet. Bernice patiently turned me this way and that as her skilful fingers made tiny adjustments with pins to the hang of my dress and deliberated with her assistant about the hemline. Up an inch? Slightly lower? More edging or lace?

I was slightly cynical at first, but Bernice drew me into the soft focus and fun of it all with consummate professionalism. When we left, I looked at Annie, and we both laughed, "What was that?"

"I know," she said, "It's totally outrageous, but every time I go there, I feel cleansed of all life's impurities."

I giggled, "I hope my patients feel half that good when they leave Touch."

Annie linked her arm through mine. "It's good to have you here for a few weeks. We're going to spoil you rotten, and we're both looking forward to meeting your Mark."

Thinking of Touch later that day, a call to Sarah reassured me that Maisie and Robin were managing well together in the clinic. Another to Pen brought me up to speed with Jeeves and Birdie, who were by all accounts being good dogs. They doted on Adam whenever he took them onto the farm and had accepted life with a small but vociferous baby like old hands. Angus was adhering to his instructions, albeit with bad grace. I thought Pen sounded more upbeat than she had for a long time.

Ellie who? I thought as, from all sides, people reassured me that they were fine without me.

Chapter Eighteen

Closure

The following morning, I borrowed Annie's car and set out for the Rookwood Necropolis, Sydney's enormous graveyard. I stopped to find the Catholic area and realised this place was like a small town. It seemed to have a mixture of graves, from simple modern slabs to ornate Victorian edifices. I shivered as I passed the Circle of Love, a shrine to infant deaths. I thought of Pen with Lottie and now Annie and the bump; no one deserved the pain of losing a child.

The cemetery was full of beautiful plants and shady trees, neatly tended. In places, happily, nature had run riot and spilt out, gloriously alive, which almost seemed an act of rebellion. As a place to rest for eternity, I'd seen worse.

I finally found Brett's grave. The inscription, "He was not ours; he was not mine," chosen by his mother Elsa, was apt at every level. The neat grey oblong containing white quartz chips that lay in front of the headstone bore no resemblance to the larger than life, laughing, abundantly gesticulating boy I loved. I resented its neat containment of a life that had been so creative, and I whispered, "You're not here, are you?"

There was no reply. I drew a tissue-wrapped stone from my pocket and freed it lovingly. In my palm sat a large chunk of deep purple amethyst that Brett had given me when we were in Japan. I placed it amongst the uniform white and looked at the stark contrast – my small act of rebellion on his behalf.

Suddenly I couldn't wait to leave this neatly incongruous memorial and turned, half-running, half-walking to the car and drove away.

Returning to the flat, without going in, I left the car and walked to the small jetty at the end of the road and took a ferry across to Circular Quay. I smiled; I had taken this boat across the harbour most days when I'd been studying here. Jostling with the crowds of tourists in flowered board shorts and flip-flops, some of whom were burned fifty shades of red under their sunblock, I checked the departure boards and boarded a ferry to Manly. Most of my fellow passengers were heading for the beach and carried an assortment of brightly coloured beach bags, cool boxes and body-boards. I did not follow them onto the sand, instead, I walked along the sand-strewn promenade under the palm trees and candy-striped awnings of the beachfront shops.

As the trappings of beach culture thinned, I left the beachfront and walked up the steep hill to the North Head. Even when I had a stitch, I pushed myself to keep striding out; I was desperate to re-connect with Brett somehow, and we'd spent many happy hours walking on the North Head. I almost collapsed when I reached the top, my breathing ragged. I found a secluded bench overlooking the sea and took in the breathtaking view. The cloudless blue of the sky was reflected in the water, and its restless motion showed in the white tips of the waves as they broke on the rocks. I could see the ferries, small dots on the water with dark wake trails behind them, and the white sails of dinghies that bobbed and danced over the sea. Brett and I had come to the same spot for a picnic the day we got together.

After several minutes of stillness, feeling intently for some sign of his energy, I came up blank. "You're not here either, are you? Are you?" Suddenly a surge of anger shook me. "You're off adventuring somewhere for eternity, laughing and taking photos or climbing some rock face."

It seemed the top had come off a tightly capped bottle, and my impotent rage spilt out like over-shaken champagne. "Do you know how much you hurt me, everyone, you idiot? Killed out in a plane taking photos, who does that? I hate you! I hate you; I've come all this way to see you one last time, and you aren't even here."

I thought furiously about how I'd hung on to the memory of the good times and the fun, all the little challenges that had made me feel adventurous and my certainty that I'd found my soulmate. But a terrible thought was eating me up. That was all me doing his stuff. The one time I'd needed him to do something with me, he'd let me down. And then he'd bloody-well died, so I would never know if all the good stuff was an illusion. When we'd quarrelled, had he been entirely self-interested, or had it been me being needy and selfish?

I sobbed uncontrollably, wiping tears and snot on the back of my hand and gulping in air. "I can't even get on with having a new life and a baby because I'm scared of going through all the pain again."

I cried until I'd cried myself to a standstill. Empty and exhausted, I was ashamed of myself for being so completely out of control.

The waves continued to crash at the bottom of the rocks, the sun shone in a blue sky, and none of that changed one iota because of my grief. As the wind blew in from the sea, a small white feather swirled and danced in front of me, it brushed across my face with the lightest caress and caught in my hair. I threaded it out carefully and looked for a moment, then opened my hands, let the wind take it and watched it dance away. "I didn't mean it," I whispered, "I don't hate you; I've always loved you. But you're right, I've got to get myself sorted. It's time to let you and that dream go and move on into a future that's real."

I walked back down the hill calmly and more thoughtfully. The sense of urgency that drove me relentlessly up the slope earlier had faded, replaced by an unfamiliar void at my core. Until a moment ago, that space had been occupied by Brett's presence which I'd clung to all these years. I had walled off the finality of his death and avoided facing it, lied to myself that I had found closure, until today. With a soft sadness, I finally acknowledged that we had said our goodbyes in this life, imperfect though they were. I needed to resolve some of my anger before my thoughts could turn to the future.

I meandered back to the flat via several coffee stops. My mind worried at the new space inside my soul, the way the tongue incessantly fidgets with the hole left by an extracted tooth. The physical sense of Brett had entirely left me. What remained was the memory of love, short, intense, and well-lived, alongside a new doubt that I'd previously denied. A photograph album in my mind of snapshot moments in time, all from the past. Now I had to exorcise my fear and the pain his death had caused.

As I walked into the flat, I was glad to find it empty. Annie and Max were still working. I felt overcome by exhaustion and curled up on my bed, grateful for its soft, unquestioning welcome and drifted into sleep with barely a pause.

I awoke to feel thirsty and found the room in complete darkness. I tilted my travel alarm clock towards me, and the tiny phosphorescent dots told me four-thirty. I had slept the evening away and most of the night. I wondered what Mark was doing in America. It was only lunchtime there, and suddenly he felt like my safe place, and I was desperate to hear his voice. I looked at my mobile phone. It would cost a fortune to phone him, but then I decided I owed us that much. I punched in the numbers and waited; two rings, three, four - come on, please answer.

"Mark Roxbury."

Relief flooded through me, and I sat on the bed, feeling like my legs wouldn't hold me as I heard his voice.

"Hello, hello?"

"Mark, it's Ellie."

"Ellie, oh my goodness, Ellie, hello. Look, give me a moment."

I heard muffled voices and footsteps, and then Mark's voice returned with less background noise but more echo.

"I was in the office, and I've just stepped into the stairwell if I sound like I'm in a goldfish bowl. How are you, Ellie? I've missed you so much."

"I've missed you too, Mark."

There was the sound of a deep exhalation, and I imagined him leaning against the stairwell wall, phone to his ear.

"Are you alright? It must be the middle of the night there."

"Yes, I am. I was exhausted yesterday and slept through from the afternoon, I've only just woken up."

"Are you horribly jet-lagged?"

"No, I don't think so. I went to see Brett's grave yesterday and walked to the cliffs where we met."

"Oh, I see." His voice, so hopeful a minute earlier, sounded reserved and dull. "Ellie, you needed to do this, I know you disagree with me, but you don't seem ever to have got over Brett properly. Sometimes I feel like I'm a poor second to this perfect person you have in your memory, and he's dead, so he never puts a foot wrong. You only remember all the good bits. I just don't know if I can ever compete."

I sniffed, "I'm so sorry, that's a terrible thing, I never meant you to feel like that. Brett wasn't perfect, I loved him, and we had a good relationship, a magical year together. But we never got put to the test, not really. There was a time just before he died when I needed him to be with me, but he chose his work instead. We never got the chance to repair that breach of trust. I guess it's easier to remember the good things."

He exhaled slowly. "Brett died five years ago. Is he going to stand between us forever? I know I'm not perfect either, but I'm not going to walk away when you need me. How can I make you trust me?"

I started to explain quietly, haltingly, "Mark, yesterday I was angry, so angry with him and with life, and I've never felt that way before. I screamed like a banshee at thin air and cried ugly tears. I frightened myself and felt completely out of control. I don't know where all this has come from and why now. I thought I'd let Brett go. I was sure I had, but some awful thoughts are coming up. I feel a bit disorientated now."

He gave a mirthless laugh. "You and me both. If it's any help at all, my counsellor told me delayed emotions can be part of the grieving process. They can come up at any time after a trauma; we don't know what triggers them. I knew you weren't yourself, but I couldn't seem to talk to you about it without you being angry or upset. Ellie, we've got to be able to talk to each other. I wish I were there with you now." His voice sounded sad and frustrated.

"I wish you were too, but you will be soon. I'm sorry for being distant. I'm so confused about what's a problem now and what's from the past."

His voice softened, "Don't be sorry. At least we have something to work on, even if it's painful. It beats feeling rejected. I can't wait to see you, Ellie. I thought I'd lost you."

"No," I replied quietly, "I'm confused, not lost."

I must've made more noise than I thought because as I hung up, I heard the sound of padding feet and a light tap at the door. "Ellie, you alright? I've got a cup of tea for you."

Annie peeped around the door, swathed in a towelling robe that looked way too big for her. She looked like a little girl in dressing-up clothes. I wondered how many people had been deceived by her apparent frailty. Annie was one of the most put-together people I know, grounded and honest. She seemed fearless in the face of most things.

"Come in. I'm sorry I woke you. I came to, and when I saw the time, I thought I'd call Mark."

She nodded, "We thought we'd let you sleep yesterday,

you looked exhausted. Don't worry about waking me, you weren't noisy. I've been sleeping lightly recently. Sometimes I wake up early with wedding and baby plans whirring through my brain. I heard your voice when I got up to get a drink."

We sat on the bed and pushed our feet under the covers. Despite being summer here, the early morning felt fresh, and all the emotion had made me shivery. I hugged the mug of tea with both hands.

"So, how was it yesterday?"

I looked at her. "Honestly? Pretty gruelling. I couldn't connect with Brett at all, and I suddenly felt so angry that he'd up and died and left me to cope with the pain. I lost my rag big-time, scared myself because I felt so out of control."

Annie put her arm around me. "Oh no, Ellie, I shouldn't have let you go out there alone."

"It's not your fault. Something happened. I can't explain, but I feel like being angry somehow made me realise I hadn't processed all my emotions. Annie, you remember before Brett died, we'd had a big argument, so as well as the pain of him dying, that mess was unresolved. It's all just going around in my head along with the baby debate."

"Did you tell Mark?" I nodded. "What did he say?"

"I think he understands because he had a bad reaction and went off the rails when Katrina left. He has tried to talk to me about not being over the bereavement, but I took it badly because I thought he was wrong. Much as I hate to admit it, I think he may have been right."

Annie smiled, "I like this man already, when's he coming to join you?"

"Just before the wedding."

Annie nudged me with her elbow. "So, what's this baby hang-up all about Ellie? It doesn't seem like you…tell your Auntie Annie."

"Don't you dare say I'd make a great mum, Annie. I feel like it's a stick everyone is beating me with."

"Sorry, it's just, don't let your silly pride about having to be independent get in the way or the idea that you have to carry on working so hard because you'll fall apart if you don't. Sometimes you have to be afraid and get on and do things anyway. I'm sure you and Mark could work it out."

I looked at her feeling all my insecurities again. "I'm terrified, Annie. You didn't see me straight after the funeral, I thought I was going mad, putting one foot in front of the other, pretending to be normal and all the time screaming in pain on the inside. I didn't even want to risk going out with Mark in case I got hurt again."

She pulled me into her and squeezed me tight. "I watched Max go through it."

"I know you did. I'm sorry, it's selfish to think this has only happened to me."

"No, you're not selfish. What happened to Brett was a massive trauma Ellie, but it would be a second tragedy if you let it wreck a happy future as well. You need to talk to Mark, and I think maybe you need to see a counsellor, try to get some perspective before you make a decision you regret. It helped Max a lot."

I began to feel anxious again. The prospect of admitting I couldn't cope felt like a failure.

"Not having a baby because it may die doesn't sound like a good reason to me. Being a working mum takes organisation, but you're not stupid, you can do that, I'm going to. I doubt any set-up with kids is perfect, and there are times it'll be tough, but we get through those times. It sounds like you're transferring the trauma of Brett's death onto this new situation, which has nothing to do with it. What would you tell one of your clients to do if they told you they felt like this?"

I smiled, she had me. "I'd refer them for counselling. I'm great at giving other people advice, but I don't always take it myself."

"Curse of the medical profession. Max is the same, always on the 'caring for' side, doesn't like needing help himself."

I leant against Annie. "Feeling like this now, so long after Brett died, has knocked me sideways, Hun. The pain I've felt for a long time, the anger, just welled up out of nowhere. I thought I was over Brett, and everything was good with Mark. But when Pen was so ill during her pregnancy, I started to think she was going to die, which is when the anxiety started. Then when I saw how much she loved Lottie, I was having nightmares about empty cots, and I was scared for Pen in case something happened to Lottie. Scared too that if I had a baby, it might die."

Annie looked shocked. "Ellie, this is not normal, why haven't you talked to anyone about this?"

"Well, because I thought it seemed a bit melodramatic, and I thought I could cope. But then everyone started pressuring me about having a baby, how Mark and I were next, and what a good mum I'd be. Mark said if I didn't want children, he didn't know if he could handle it. All the pain came back about losing Brett, and I just knew I couldn't cope with losing someone else I loved that much. I had to get away, Annie, and I just ran, really."

"It's alright, Hun, it's okay," she carried on comforting, "You ran to the right place, we can get it sorted."

She enveloped me in a hug, rocking me gently and the tears that had been threatening again began to pour down my face.

"And the James thing? Whatever you say, I don't think he's come half-way around the world just because he wants you to help him taste wine. What's going on with him?"

I wiped my hand across my face spreading tears, "He's not 'a thing' Annie, nothing has happened. It was just so nice to get out of all the mess and be with someone light-hearted and fun. He's older and doesn't want kids, so he made me feel like it was alright to think about a different life. And it is; not everyone wants children, but I felt terrible deep down because I knew I should be sorting things out with Mark."

Annie looked stern. "I think you could do without the distraction, Hun. Why don't you call him and cancel this trip on Monday?"

"No, I'm going to go. I'd like to see the vineyards. James hasn't only come to Australia for me, even if he enjoys flirting a bit. He was coming to see his suppliers anyway, me being here just gave him an excuse to come now. He knows I'm with Mark."

"Hmm, well, have it your way, but I'm not sure I trust his motives. He's probably a trophy hunter, the kind of guy who loves a challenge and then loses interest. I think you're too vulnerable for this now."

I nudged her. "To be honest, there was a spark when we first met, but I would never do that to Mark. I'm going to make it clear that I'm only interested in friendship when we travel down."

Annie shook her head, unconvinced. "If you get into trouble down there, you can call me, and I'll drive down to get you."

"I won't get into trouble, Annie, honestly. We've become friendly over the last couple of months, and I enjoy his company, that's all. He's a nice guy."

Annie was about to carry on protesting when another tap at the bedroom door made us both look around. I realised that while we'd been talking, dawn had broken, and the rising sun now bathed the bedroom in a bright glow.

Max poked his head around the door. "You girls talking secrets, or can I come in?"

He was curiously attired in shorts with a pink robe that was way too small, stretched across his broad chest. "Annie stole my dressing gown," he offered by way of explanation.

"Come in and talk to Ellie. She needs to see someone, talk to her, you're a doctor. I'm going to make more tea."

He looked at Annie and said firmly, "I'm not her doctor, though, and Ellie may not want to blurt out her confidences to me."

I smiled at Annie's impulsiveness and his diffidence. "It's alright, Max, I'll tell you as a friend, I don't need you to treat me. Annie is going to tell you anyway, the minute I'm not here."

He acknowledged that likelihood with a smile. "So, what's all this about?"

I explained again what had been happening, and Max listened calmly and thoughtfully, in doctor mode, despite his pink robe. Annie brought more tea and chipped in with bits she thought I'd left out.

When I'd finished, Max said, "I think you may have had a mild flare-up of Post-Traumatic Stress Disorder, Ellie. It's what my counsellor said I had after Brett died. Classic symptoms; the nightmares, anxiety, trauma-triggered avoidance behaviour and fight/flight response. In your case, flight – right to the other side of the world!"

"I thought PTSD was after battle stress or physical traumas like abuse or rape?"

"Well, it is, but for some people, other traumas can trigger the symptoms, and it can come back to bite you on the butt at different times."

I looked down, embarrassed. "I've been a bit of an idiot, not talking to anyone. I felt pressured but thought I was coping."

He smiled, "I don't think you're an idiot. It sounds like all the people who know you well have had other things on their plate, and as things slip gradually sometimes, we don't or won't see we're in a mess. Don't start beating yourself up about that as well."

I gave him a rueful grin.

"Ells, would you like to see someone in my practice? I can't treat you, you're too close a friend, and it isn't my field."

"No, I think I'd rather just relax while I'm here, talk to Mark, then maybe see someone when I get home."

He agreed, "Well, that sounds like a plan, but if you don't feel better, then you must say. It might help to have some medication, but I think talking therapy is the recommended treatment."

I leant in to kiss him on the cheek. "I will, I promise. I already feel better for having a bit of a crisis yesterday and talking to both of you guys, thank you."

Chapter Nineteen

Mis-communication

We had a quiet weekend, bought tiger prawns and swordfish steaks from the fish market, barbecued them in the garden and lazed by the pool. Apart from Annie trying to enrol Max to persuade me to cancel my trip with James, everything was harmonious.

Eventually, he exploded, "Annie, will you leave me in peace, woman! Ellie is a grown-up. If she wants to spend a couple of days in the Hunter Valley wine tasting with her friend, James, I'm sure she knows what she's doing!"

Undeterred, Annie poked him in the ribs with her finger, "You're just too idle to stop her."

He jumped and looked outraged. "How can you say that?"

"Because I know you. I don't think Ellie should go. She isn't well, and some rest would do her good."

Ignoring Annie's protests, I packed a small bag on Sunday evening and promised her that she could vet James before we left.

True to his word, James arrived punctually at ten o'clock on the following Monday. Despite the already mounting heat, he looked crisp in a white polo shirt, beige chinos, and navy boat shoes. He greeted Annie with his usual effortless charm, presented her with a bottle of champagne as a wedding gift, and offered to take my bag. Determined not to like him, she said to me, "So, if Mark rings, I'll get him to call you on your mobile?"

I frowned at her. "Yes, of course."

James raised his eyebrows but said, "I'll wait for you by the car."

Annie made a silent gagging gesture and whispered, "Too slick, I don't trust him!"

"Annie! I'll see you on Wednesday. Stop it!"

She walked down the path towards the car to see me off and said, "Get you," as she saw James waiting in a Mercedes convertible.

"You're jealous, that's all," I whispered as I bent to kiss her goodbye.

I lowered myself into the leather seat, and as we pulled away, James said, laughing, "I sense your friend doesn't approve."

"Oh, she's just naturally grumpy with people she doesn't know."

The journey down was glorious. We took the Pacific highway towards Gosford and took a detour east to enjoy the coast road. It was worth the extra miles as the sun jewelled the ocean with the sparkle of a bright, faceted sapphire. The beauty of it began to lift my spirits. I felt sure a couple of days away would do wonders for how I felt. We stopped for lunch in Forrester's Beach and, avoiding the noisy fun park, we ate on the waterfront at Forrie's café to watch the surfers.

We stretched our legs as we walked down to the beach and along the sand. James kept up his usual flow of light banter, and as I turned to laugh at something he said, he stopped mid-sentence. Suddenly serious, he said, "You don't know how enchanting you are, Ellie Rose, do you? I may be falling in love with you."

I looked at him, dawning horror on my face and said, "Oh no, James, no, you can't, you're my friend. I mean, I never meant… I'm in love with Mark. I thought you understood."

"Ellie, are you sure? Things have been rocky for you both with the family issue, I know that, and with Mark going away and you coming here, I thought… I thought we get on so well, Ellie. Why don't you think about it?"

His urbane mask had slipped, and I saw the raw longing in his eyes. He stepped toward me, but I stepped back.

"Don't, James, don't. I've made a terrible mistake. I had no idea you were serious about me. I should never have come, I'm so, so sorry."

I turned to run up the beach.

"Ellie, where are you going?"

"I don't know. I'm going back. I can't… I shouldn't be here." I felt panic-stricken, I should have listened to Annie.

"Hey, hey," he said, catching my hand, "Hey, it's okay, you don't have to run. I'll take you back if you want to go. I'm not Bluebeard."

"No, no, please don't." I pulled my hand from his and started to restlessly twist them. "I've caused enough trouble already. I'll ring Annie or get a train. You go on, you've got business meetings."

"Ellie, will you calm down? There are no business meetings until tomorrow. I'm not leaving you upset like this. I'll ring Annie if you don't want to come with me."

I nodded gratefully and slumped down on the sand. I knew I was over-reacting, but I couldn't deal with any of this right now. I just wanted to be back with Annie and Max, and I wanted to see Mark.

James had a hurried conversation with Annie, anxiously glancing towards me now and then. I listened vaguely and then tuned out to the roar of the surf and the warm sun on my face. What had I been thinking? I imagined we were friends; he reminded me of how I felt when I was with Brett and was flattered by what I thought was harmless flirting. Now I had hurt Mark, James, and embarrassed myself as well. I was hopeless.

James came to sit on the sand beside me. "Annie's on her way. Ellie, look, I'm sorry. I oughtn't to have blurted that out. I didn't mean to upset you. I didn't realise how much things have been getting on top of you."

I shook my head miserably. "Don't say that. It's all my fault. I haven't been quite myself recently, but I hadn't realised how bad I was until I got here. I'm afraid I've been giving out mixed messages. I'm embarrassed, I felt a bit panicky and over-reacted."

"Mis-communication on both sides, Ellie, but truly, you can trust me." He smiled kindly. "Still friends?"

Recovering his poise and back to being my elegant friend, James was making this easy for me, and I was grateful. I was struggling to string two words together as my brain darted in every direction. "Friends, yes."

"Shall we walk for a bit, or would you like a drink? Annie will be a little while getting here."

I was grateful to have something to do. "Let's get a drink, my shout. I owe you that much."

"Ellie, you don't owe me anything." He took my arm, and we walked back up the beach, feet slipping on the soft sand with a warm breeze from the sea pushing us from behind. "I don't want to pry, but from what Annie has just told me, you've been overdoing it a bit recently and not taking care of yourself enough."

I shrugged, "I always work hard. You know what it's like, James, you run a business too. I think without realising, I've been using work to push down the grief after losing Brett without giving myself time to process it properly. With the extra pressure on me recently and being back here for the first time, all the trauma resurfaced with a vengeance a couple of days ago."

"Listen, Ellie, a word to the wise. I do work hard, but I set boundaries. You could work twenty-four/seven, but someone would always want the twenty-fifth hour or the eighth day. You must take care of yourself."

"I was happy to be working hard, it helped me to start with."

He looked understanding. "You have to adapt and review all the time. Don't just keep running on the hamster wheel. What was right for you a couple of years ago may not be right now. The thing is, you can't look after anyone if you aren't well yourself."

I huffed out, "I'm learning that the hard way. I don't feel too clever right now."

"Listen, the world won't stop turning if you need a break. Get yourself right again before you push too hard. Come on, what do you fancy, a hot drink, or shall we have a glass of wine? That's if we can find anything worth drinking."

James pushed open the door to the café once more and stood back to let me in. I chose a table in the window, and he looked at the wine list. "Pretty much as I feared," he said, scanning down the list. "Oh, except, this one may be drinkable."

"Such a snob," I managed a small laugh.

"Not at all, this one should be lovely. Peaches and cream with just a hint of oak and perhaps honey. It's one my supplier produces."

As the waiter poured a glass each and James asked for a selection of bread to nibble, he looked at me over his glass, and I detected a trace of sadness quickly shielded. He seemed about to say something, then changed his mind and instead said, "Here's looking at you, kid."

I gasped. "That's what Brett used to say."

About half an hour later, the door to the café pushed open again, and Annie's familiar face looked around the tables, fixing on the two of us. Her expression of pinched worry relaxed into one of relief as she saw me. She looked behind her, and as I followed her gaze, a familiar figure filled the doorway and came across the room in long strides. I was only half out of my chair when he swooped down on me and enveloped me in his arms, lifting me the rest of the way out of my chair. "Mark, I don't understand. How did you get here?"

"Long story. After we spoke, I couldn't wait to see you, so I flipped a few switches and jumped on the first available flight from New York. I wanted to surprise you. Luckily, I phoned Annie from the airport and got to the flat just as James called."

I looked at his familiar face, currently etched with worry and noticed a muscle twitching with tension and fatigue in his cheek. He could have arrived in sackcloth and ashes and he would still have looked like heaven to me.

He turned to James with a trace of stiffness in his voice and stance. “Thank you for ringing and for looking after Ellie.” He held out his hand formally, and James stood to return the greeting, meeting Mark’s look with a level gaze.

“My pleasure, of course. But if you no longer need me, I’ll hit the road. Ellie, look after yourself. I’ll be in touch.”

I stood and kissed him lightly on the cheek. “Thanks for everything, James.”

He turned to Annie. “Nice to see you again. I’m sorry you’ve had to come so far. I could have brought her back, but she insisted I call.” He shook her hand, and I saw an understanding nod pass between them. I was glad she wasn’t hostile. As he left, James turned back and waved. In the circumstances, he had been a real gentleman. I was ashamed; he had been one of my recent catalogue of mistakes.

“Ellie, what on earth happened?” Annie said as soon as he’d left.

“Nothing,” I said, “My fault, I felt better after the weekend, but I shouldn’t have tried to travel. I had a panic attack after we had lunch. James offered to bring me home, but I didn’t want him to miss his meeting.”

“If that smarmy git upset you…” Mark began with unusual vehemence.

“He didn’t. He wouldn’t. He’s been very kind. I made the wrong call, and it’s my fault.” I wasn’t going to give James away. He didn’t deserve that.

Mark looked at me as if trying to be sure I was telling the truth.

"Mark," said Annie resting a hand on his arm. "Why don't we just get Ellie home."

He nodded, we settled the bill and walked back towards the car which was in the shade of a netted car park but still hot inside.

I slid into the back of the car beside Mark, grateful for his reassuring presence and lent against him, inhaling his Mark smell. His arm came around my shoulder, and I rested my head down against him. I felt safe for the first time in weeks.

The rocking motion of the car and the heat felt soothing, and the whir of the air-con hypnotic. Overcome with weariness, I closed my eyes and drifted asleep.

I slept fitfully and heard snatches of their conversation, "Fragile,", "May need to talk to someone,", "Medication," drifted into my consciousness. Still, I felt unable to drag myself awake to say anything. The afternoon sun felt hot through the window against the side of my face. There was time to sort this out tomorrow; for now, I wanted to drift on in my pleasant, sleepy haze.

I woke as we arrived at the flat and stretched, a slight crick in my neck.

"You alright?" said Mark, "You slept well."

"I'm feeling better. What about you? Are you shattered?"

"Wired on too much coffee, but I'm going to sleep well tonight."

"What about you?" I said to Annie, "I imagine you're tired too with all that driving. I'm sorry I dragged you out. Can I tell Mark your secret?"

She nodded, "Mark, Annie's pregnant. I know you'd never know because she's so slender still. But she is."

"Annie, that's wonderful, congratulations. When's the baby due?"

She smiled, "End of April, Autumn baby. If all goes according to the due date."

Mark raised his eyebrows. "Beware with that, our friend Pen's baby gave us all a big shock. Don't let Max out of your sight after March!"

Annie took Mark's arm. "Come on in and meet him. Max is dying to see you, and you must be desperate for a shower and tidy up."

He assumed a mortified expression. "Oh dear, I was hoping no one had noticed."

Annie looked around in dismay until she realised he was joking and narrowed her eyes. "I can see we're going to have trouble with you."

Chapter Twenty

Talk to me

We didn't make love that night; we were both emotionally and physically exhausted. For me, it was enough to feel Mark's body curled around me, the yawning gulf between us bridged, although there was much still to discuss.

Taking everyone's advice, we took it slow over the next few days, allowing the sun to seep into our dark corners and the fresh breeze to blow away the cobwebs of fear and misunderstanding. We talked of cabbages and kings and let the serious discussions wait their turn until we were more rested and resilient. My impatience went, and I was happy to drift to the pace of these slow summer days. We spent some time on the beach at Bronte, swimming, reading, and lazing. In the evening, we brought in simple, fresh ingredients to cook together and ate with Max and Annie late in the cool of the evening.

Max and Mark got along well, finding common interests in sport and having in-depth discussions about health business management. The pinched look on Mark's face smoothed, and his tired sallow skin took on a healthy, tanned glow. My English-Winter skin remained pale, but freckles multiplied into a band across my cheeks and nose, which gave the illusion of Summer.

On the third day of being together, Mark and I packed a picnic and headed for the botanical gardens by way of a change. The plaza around the opera house was busy, and it was pleasant to walk on the grass in the park until we found a shady spot under a blue gum tree.

The mid-day heat made me drowsy, and I tilted my sun hat over my eyes, allowing myself to drift into sleep. A light tickle along my forearm roused me. I swatted at it, only to have it persist until, eventually, I was wide awake. I sat up to see what the offending insect was, only to find Mark, propped up on one elbow, tickling my arm lightly with a long blade of grass. I scowled, pretending to be cross, but it warmed my heart that we had re-found those teasing intimacies between us.

He pulled me towards him until I lay with my head in his lap, looking up at the sky through the canopy of leaves. His fingers combed idly through my hair, and he said, "Ellie, talk to me. Tell me what's been happening?"

I paused. I knew this conversation was long overdue, but I wasn't sure how much to say.

"I got spooked, I guess. Something triggered off a whole cascade of panic. Maybe, when I saw that Pen was so ill through her pregnancy, I subconsciously thought we were going to lose her. It didn't occur to me that my fear was triggering old feelings. I was busy being the health professional coping with it, absorbing the trauma. Then more and more, I began to feel uncomfortable about the whole baby thing and pressured by everyone, until the whole situation seemed to close in on me, and I had to run."

"Why didn't you tell me you were scared?"

I knitted my brows together, then said, "I didn't know. I hadn't analysed it that well. Everyone close to me either seemed completely invested in us having a family or was busy with their own lives, and I felt isolated and as if I'd lost my anchor points."

Mark looked distraught. "Oh no, Ellie, I'm so sorry, you can always talk to me."

"Well, you say that but I couldn't. You seemed determined about the way our future lay, and you were worried that I had loved Brett more than you. I didn't feel I could talk to you."

He nodded, "I was struggling myself, Ellie, I didn't know you were scared. I read it wrong because you didn't seem frightened. Quite the opposite, you suddenly seemed turbocharged. I was panicked because I felt I almost didn't know you anymore. I've been tired and distracted as well. The contract with Dom has been more work than I expected."

I reached up to touch his face. "We're both as bad as each other."

He nodded, "It shows how quickly things can get off balance, though. I'm not going to let work get between us. I've spoken to Dom. Much as I love him, I don't owe him my future happiness. He knows it's more work than I want, so we've agreed that I will pull back gradually as we run up to Christmas until I'm only in London two days a week, which is what we originally agreed. He is going to look for someone permanent in the New Year."

I hesitated to bring up the main difficulty but knew we had to discuss it.

"And the baby thing?"

"What about it?"

"I'm going to speak to someone about my fear of loss, and I'm also going to look at this dependency I have on working hard. Max and Annie think it's become a way of putting a plaster over wounds and not facing how I feel.

I think they may be right, but even so, I will always want to have a career, I'm sure. I'm not saying 'no' to a baby forever, but I am saying 'no' until I feel a bit clearer about those things. Is that enough for you?"

He paused and looked at me with a slight clouding in his eyes. "Yes, Ellie, it's enough. Most of all, I want you to feel well again. But don't shut me out, however bad things are. You can tell me anything. Honestly, I'm tougher than I look. When, *if,* we have a family, I want to be hands-on, I'd be happy to cut my work down as well and be involved in the childcare. I promise you won't have to bring up our baby alone."

I looked at him and felt a sinking feeling that I couldn't hide.

"Mark, don't promise things you can't control. You can't tell me it won't happen because losing a life-long partner has already happened to both of us. It probably won't happen again. I know that, and I'm not morbid, but I need to be real about this. I have to be sure I can cope with the worst scenario."

Mark's shoulders slumped. "Oh, Ellie, I feel sad when you say those things. I think that's the trauma talking. Even if something happened to me, God forbid, you wouldn't be alone. We have amazing friends and family so that you would be supported. So many people love you, and you don't seem to realise."

I looked at him, desperate to make him see. "I do. I know we're lucky that way, but it's not about them. It's about me feeling safe. I know it's complicated, but can you understand?"

He shrugged, "Ellie, I don't want to live our lives being afraid of the past. It would be tragic to deny ourselves the joy of a child because something may happen."

"That's exactly what Annie said. I don't normally feel pessimistic like this, so I hope it's just a passing phase. I'm going to take part in talking therapy when we get back, but for now, can you accept that this feels real to me right now?"

He pulled me in closer. "We can work through this. I'm sure we can. I'm so sorry you are feeling the grief all over again. It's horrible."

I blinked, unable to open my eyes for a moment. "I can see that it's making you sad as well."

"Ellie, I love you. I can't see you like this without feeling anything. But I'm fine, better than when I thought you were leaving."

I looked at him for a long moment, unsure what to say, then he smiled and pulled me to my feet.

"Come on, enough talking, I want a huge ice cream with mango and lime sorbet." He set off with a purposeful stride.

I laughed, catching his mood shift, and ran after him. "Are you sure you aren't expecting? The other day I had Annie combing the shops for Cherryade, now you want lime and mango."

Both puffing slightly, we arrived outside the gelato shop that he'd noticed on the way past this morning.

"What flavour for you, Miss Ellie?"

"Make mine lemon and lime," I said.

Clutching our cornets, we walked and ate, catching the fast-melting drips with our tongues. One giant blob eluded

Mark and ended up on the front of his t-shirt. He promptly sucked it off, making the stain much worse. He shrugged and poured some water over it and rubbed it with a tissue. Half the front of the shirt was a dark stain now, with fibres of the paper hanky stuck to it.

"Classy!" I said, but I had to laugh. I couldn't imagine James doing that, and the familiarity made Mark seem dear.

"Come on," he said, taking my hand, "I want to walk over to the Rocks."

We cut across the back of Circular Quay and into the Rocks, leaving modern Sydney behind as we entered the narrow, cobbled streets lined with tiny shops and restaurants. Although very busy and with a holiday atmosphere today, it was easy to imagine its nefarious past.

"Where are we going?"

Mark consulted his street map and said, "Not far."

We stopped outside a small jeweller, the shop front barely wider than the entrance door.

"This is it," he said. "I saw a video about this woman on the plane, and I want to treat you to something. She does amazing work."

"Mark, I…"

"Don't be silly, come on. I'd like to treat you because this holiday has turned into a celebration, and I'd like to give you something beautiful to wear to the wedding. A keepsake."

The tiny shop had beautifully displayed jewellery, all of it in fluid shapes as if the molten metal had been captured and frozen mid-flow. Some of the pieces had embedded precious stones, and others had a satin finish.

The designer, Jannali, explained that each piece had unique energy and that I should choose by how each one felt as I wore it, as well as how it looked. “It will carry your energy too, even when you aren’t wearing it. You need to find the piece that speaks to your soul,” she said. “Take your time.”

An unusual concept, but she was right. I tried on so many beautiful necklaces and bracelets, but in the end, I slipped on a bangle that felt like it belonged to me. As it sat on my wrist, I met her eyes and said, “This is the one.” A simple rose gold band, slightly uneven in design, with flowing curves, the metal brushed to a satin finish. It was stunning in its simplicity.

I didn’t want it packed, I wore it there and then.

As Mark paid for the bracelet, Jannali said, “When you two get married, I’ll design a wedding band to match.”

Mark and I looked at each other, and I started to say, “We haven’t planned…”

But Mark butted in and said, “I’d like that.”

Jannali smiled, “Give me your hand.” She slipped a ring sizer over my finger and said, “What’s your name?”

She wrote my name and ring size on a small card and placed it into a filing box under ‘R’. “You’ll be back,” she said with a smile, “I get a feeling about these things.”

As we left the shop, I glanced at Mark. “She was fascinating,”

“I thought that when I watched the video on the plane. It said she believes in second sight and healing. She inherited gifts from her grandmother, who was a shaman.”

I nodded, “I can believe that healing and energy medicine are amazing, and some people seem to have wonderful gifts.”

"She certainly had something about her, you could almost feel it, but I don't claim to understand how any of that works."

I laughed, "I think the scientific proof is a bit thin on the ground, but there are a few different theories. Most healers feel they channel energy through prayer, or they try to link to a 'universal' energy in some way. There's a form of healing in most cultures and religions, so I wouldn't discount what they do."

He pointed at me, and I frowned questioningly. "Several of your patients have said that you have 'healing hands' or 'magic fingers", so you must do something a bit extra that they feel."

I smiled, "I'm going to go on a course one day. It's amazing what you feel when you're working with someone. When I'm using acupressure, I sometimes pick up a sort of energy signal as I'm feeling for pulses or when I palpate to find the acupuncture points. Maybe it's my electromagnetic field or the heat field around me that interacts with the patient's field. We use electrotherapy and sound waves all the time to influence tissues, why not our natural energy field?"

He looked at me, interested but a bit unsure. "I've never really thought about it. I've nothing against healing, provided no one trades on the vulnerable."

I tilted my head to the side, considering. "I guess there are bad eggs in every barrel, but it doesn't mean all healers are unscrupulous. Most of the practitioners I've met are very caring and competent. The best deal is if we all work to complement each other and have respect for each other's scope and limitations."

Mark saluted, "Yes, ma'am, very proper," he said.

"Oh, shut up," I laughed, "You brought the subject up."

"Guilty as charged," he replied.

"I might investigate a course when we get back to see if I do have any skills and to hone them. I think I'd enjoy adding that holistic dimension to what I already do with acupuncture and massage. When Pam – you know, Peter's wife – was terminally ill, there was a lady who used to give her Reiki, and she found it a real comfort. I'd like to be able to offer that in the clinic."

Mark now looked worried. "Isn't that a bit gloomy for you, working with the dying, with what you've been through?"

"No. You know it isn't, death is part of life, so maybe I'm exactly the right person to do it because of what I know. Anyway, healing isn't just for palliative care. It can be used to help everyone. I'm going to think about it seriously, meeting Jannali has really got me thinking."

As we continued to stroll around The Rocks, we enjoyed the amazing views across to the Opera House. It was truly majestic, with the three white roofs like unfurled sails gracing the harbourside. I kept looking at the band around my wrist as it glowed in the afternoon sun. Simple, strong, and beautiful, it gave me courage. Would we ever be back for that ring? I didn't know. For today, it was enough to be together and talking without any constraint.

That was the last full day we had alone before the wedding. Suddenly, we were in the final run-up to the big day, and the flat became a hive of activity. Annie and Max were busy with last-minute arrangements and phone calls, and we made ourselves useful sorting out practical things like buying the day-to-day food and running small errands for them. Annie and I went to collect our dresses, and they were hung carefully in the little box room that had been my original bedroom all those years ago. We went for an all-girls lunch afterwards and left Mark and Max to check the cars and the venue.

"Are you nervous?" I asked Annie.

"About the wedding or about getting married?"

"Either, both?"

"A bit about the day. I keep having panics that I'll tip something down my dress before I get to church or that no one will come."

I laughed, "I'll keep everything but water away from you, I promise, and wrap you in a sheet until you leave the flat."

Annie giggled, "Bernice at the bridal shop looked like she half didn't trust us to take the dresses away from her sanctuary."

"Probably right," I added.

Annie continued, "About getting married, not at all. I'm quite sure. We've been together for over seven years, and I can't imagine being with anyone else."

I looked at her and knew she was being honest. "You've always been so right together."

"What about you and Mark? I know you've had a bit of a tough time recently, but do you think you'll get married?"

"I don't know, Annie. He hasn't asked me yet for one thing. I need to sort out my issues about loss first. You know he wants a family more than anything, and I'm not going to tie him down if I decide I don't."

She gave me a nudge. "Ellie, he's crazy about you, that much is obvious. I couldn't imagine you with anyone but Brett to start with, and Mark's very different. When you first came, and you seemed so confused, I wondered if you'd made a mistake with Mark, but we like him for what it's worth. You're good together, and he seems very caring and supportive. That's a big positive."

I agreed with her. "It's a steadier kind of relationship. With Brett, it was all breathless and crazy, but how long could we have carried on like that? I suppose I was a different person by the time I met Mark. You're right. He is very caring. He can be a moody git too…"

"He's hot, though."

I looked at her in fake shock. "Annie! You're getting married in a few days."

"Doesn't mean I don't recognise hot when I see it."

"Shame on you." I couldn't help smiling inside, though, she was right. I just needed to be sure that he understood fully about me loving my work and that I still wanted to have space to develop because I liked new ideas and learning.

Talk turned away from Mark to the wedding, and lunch ran late, well into the afternoon, before we guiltily realised the time and made our way back to the flat. I had been right to come to Australia. Annie was as good as any therapist.

Chapter Twenty-One

Max and Annie's Wedding

On the day of the wedding, I had never wished harder that I'd paid more attention to hair, makeup and sewing. I felt a bit under-qualified to support Annie on her big day. Vale would have been able to answer all her questions so much better than I could.

"More mascara? What do you think?"

"You look beautiful, Annie. I don't like very heavy make-up."

She looked at herself in the mirror appraisingly. "But do you think my eyes will show up in the photos?"

I pulled a face. "Honestly? Not a clue, shall I call Vale?"

"No! I'm just nervous," she giggled. "Max doesn't like too much make-up either. He says it's my work face, and it scares him."

I nodded, "Mark doesn't either."

"Ellie, I do like Mark. He's a keeper, Hun, I'm sure of it. You weren't really tempted by James, were you?"

I thought about it briefly. "I like James, he's fun, and he said all the right things to make me feel good about myself when I was feeling misunderstood. I didn't realise it was getting out of hand."

Annie shrugged dismissively, "He's far too old for you, anyway."

"I never thought of him as old, but I think you're right, he was more part of the problem than part of the solution. Stop talking about me, today is about you. Come on, we'd better get going, we need to stop chatting and get dressed."

Annie stood in front of the huge, mirrored wardrobes in their bedroom, which had been Brett's and mine back in the day. There were no ghosts in the room today, though. I watched in awe as I slipped the creamy white dress over her head and watched it fall into place, transforming my friend into a beautiful fairy creature. The dress fitted loosely to the hips and caught the light with tiny crystal beads. It had a many-layered handkerchief skirt in gossamer-fine lace, and her tiny feet peeped out from underneath, not in her habitual running trainers but in delicate ballet pumps, embroidered with pearl beads in different sizes.

Annie's long blond hair looped inside a fine snood which was embroidered with the same crystals and pearls. It settled heavily in the nape of her neck. A simple posy of pink and cream roses completed the outfit.

The beautiful blooms were currently nestled in a lace surround also studded with pearls. Resting on the stand beside them was a matching wrist corsage for me. The florist from a contemporary shop close to the city had issued strict instructions about caring for the flowers here and those that would be left at the reception venue. Annie said the florist made her feel like she was back at school.

"Beautiful, Annie, just beautiful." I sighed as I gently coaxed the folds of lace into place on her dress as I'd seen Bernice do, then stepped back.

"I don't look, you know, pregnant, do I?"

"No, you look absolutely amazing. You're Titania."

My bridesmaid's dress was a simpler version of Annie's dress in a pale 'ashes of roses' pink, and my hair fell loose, clasped at the sides with pearl combs.

In the absence of her mother, who had left when Annie was a tiny baby, I tried to take my role as bridesmaid seriously and make this morning very special for her. I had laid out Annie's lingerie earlier, fine silk stockings and garter, while the hairdresser finished her hair. Now I double-checked I had pins, grips, needle and thread, and spare make-up in my bag. Also, a plentiful supply of tissues; if Annie and I didn't need them, I was pretty sure Max would. Annie was going to bowl him over, and he was prone to tears as well as laughter.

Doug, her father, was pacing in the other room. He was muttering intermittently, which I suspected was him rehearsing his speech. He had been sternly warned to say nothing to make her cry and mess up her make-up before we left.

The car was due any minute, and he shouted that he was going downstairs to watch for its arrival. Annie walked through into the lounge, but I lingered, looking around the familiar bedroom that had been mine and Brett's when we all lived together. Out of the window was a stunning view over the garden and down to Sydney Harbour. I had taken its beauty for granted when I lived here but I fully appreciated it now and felt its comforting familiarity soothe my nerves.

I knew I'd been lucky; I had always been loved here. I had found the strength to carry on after Brett had died, and now I was blessed again with love from Mark, who would be waiting at the church for me. My loneliness of earlier when I'd left England had lessened, and the acute symptoms of anxiety I'd felt had faded. I still had issues to resolve, but they seemed more approachable now they had been named. I gathered up my delicate wrap, placed the armour of all that love around me and responded to Annie's call of, "The car is here," with, "Coming!"

Doug looked smart in his pale grey suit, if a little uncomfortable. He was more at home in shorts and flip-flops. As he turned to take his daughter's arm, he looked at Annie in wonder.

"You look like a fairy-tale princess, took my breath away for a minute there, girl. I love you so much, and I'm proud of you too."

"Well, so much for not saying anything to make me cry, Dad!" Annie said.

He guiltily offered his big handkerchief. I took it and blotted Annie's face. Mascara left black smudges on the white cotton. A quick patch-up was achieved with the emergency kit stowed in my tiny clutch bag. Annie took a deep breath and said, "Ready, everyone? I'm ready."

I held her bouquet, and Doug helped Annie into the car, which swept along the road to the modern church near the shops. It seemed that everyone shopping stopped to see the bride. Ladies with net shopping bags over their arms beamed and pointed. Mums with kids lifted them up to get a better view, and many called out greetings and good luck as Annie stepped out of the car. A peal of bells rang from the bell tower, and the sun shone over the church as they chimed gaily. I straightened both our dresses again, and Doug took Annie's arm.

The parish priest, resplendent in a cream, lavishly embroidered cope, waited at the door.

"Annie, my dear, I will go in first to announce you and then Doug. Will you, please, bring Annie into the church?"

The organ music swelled around the church, and Annie walked, step, pause, step, pause, with Doug towards Max at the front. There was a distinctive smell of incense in the building, and the whole scene was highlighted with dancing, coloured lights as the sun shone through stained glass windows. Annie walked towards Max, and I saw his eyes locked onto her face, full of love. I knew this wasn't just an event to them, this was the acknowledgement of the qualities they'd found in each other.

I was walking towards Mark, too, and he turned in the pew and watched me all the way down the aisle. A small smile played around his lips, and he mouthed, "beautiful" to me as I drew level. Annie stood beside Max, glowing with happiness. She turned to pass me her bouquet, and I stepped back to take my place beside Mark.

"Dearly beloved, we are gathered together…"

The service lovingly consolidated all that they felt for each other now, but also prepared the path for life's difficulties that may come. I listened to them promise to support each other come what may. The words had never seemed so beautiful or meaningful as I listened and heard my two friends make their vows. Mark and I were working towards a point where I could also say those things. I realised it was an enormous undertaking.

We adjourned to a nearby restaurant for the reception. When the photos were taken and the meal began, Annie whispered to me that her jaw was aching. All those teeth, all those smiles. She looked glad to take her place beside Max to listen to the speeches.

Doug was nervous; his speech was short, simple, and heartfelt. It ended beautifully. "I love my girl so very much. I couldn't love her more. I give her to Max to look after, and I trust him to do that always. I'm proud to stand and ask you to raise your glasses to Annie, the most beautiful bride."

"Annie, the most beautiful bride," echoed around the room.

The evening passed in a whirl of dancing, congratulations and snatches of conversation between good-natured interruptions, cake cutting and more photographs.

"Miss Ellie?" Mark tapped me gently on the shoulder, "Would you care to dance?"

I looked down and simpered. "I'd love to, but are you on my dance card?"

He laughed and pulled me into him gently as we joined the other dancers. "Good day?"

"The best. I'm so happy for Annie and Max."

"They're very special to you, aren't they?"

I nodded without hesitation. "Yes, it doesn't matter that we live so far away, as soon as we're together, everything just clicks back as if we've never been apart. A bit like you and Dom, I guess."

"Do you remember the wedding reception in London when he introduced us to Vale? I think that's the last time we danced together; we should go dancing more often."

I leant into his hold. "It feels good."

As we were dancing, I saw Max touch Annie on the shoulder, and he smiled into her eyes as he nodded towards the door. Their honeymoon car had arrived.

Together they walked through the avenue formed by their guests. Annie hugged Max's parents, Mark, and lingered with her arms tightly around me.

"Be happy, Ellie, find your way together."

I kissed her. "I'll try. Thank you. For everything."

Finally, she came to her dad. He held her at arm's length as if fixing the picture in his mind, then pulled her in close. I heard Doug say, "You look after my girl," to Max. Then the doors closed, and their car pulled away, whisking them off to the hotel on the harbour that was their wedding night destination before they flew to Bali for their honeymoon.

The party began to break up. The lights in the restaurant were turned up, and the DJ began to pack his kit away. Clusters of people chatted while others scouted around for their belongings, and a queue began to form at the cloakroom.

"How are your feet faring in those shoes?" Mark slipped his arm around my waist.

"I'm eternally grateful to Annie for choosing flats."

Mark slipped a wrap around my shoulders. "Walk with me a while?"

I nodded. We crossed the road in front of the restaurant and strolled over the short, dense grass of the park opposite, hand in hand. We were heading back towards the flat where we would stay while Max and Annie were on honeymoon until it was time for us to head back to England.

"Happy?"

I nodded, it had been a glorious day, and I felt at peace here with Mark, the dilemmas of the last few months beginning to be resolved. Turning into the entrance of the flat, we wandered down to the harbour wall and sat to watch the moonlight play across the dark water and the stars shine in an inky sky. I leaned against Mark, our fingers intertwined, and he played gently, rubbing his thumb lightly across my hand. Each sweep of his thumb made my skin tingle, and I looked up at him in the darkness. We kissed slowly, and I revelled in our closeness after feeling estranged for months. He gently tugged at my bottom lip with his teeth and kissed me again. As if carved from the same stone, our bodies moulded together. My arms snaked around the curve of his muscles under the formal suit, and his arms encircled me. I suddenly longed to be free of formal restraints and drew him to his feet. We retraced our steps across the lawn and contained our passion only until the door to the apartment closed behind us.

I slowly loosened Mark's cravat and let it fall to the floor as I kissed the open 'v' at his throat left by the open shirt collar. Hearing a small groan, I pushed both hands into his jacket, eased it off his shoulders, and unbuttoned his shirt, stopping to kiss his chest as I moved lower. Shirt removed; I traced the curve of his arms with trailing fingers.

"Enough," he whispered and spun me round to release my hair from the pearl combs and kissed the side of my neck. He slowly undid the chain of my gold necklace with the pearl cross and whispered, "I don't want God to see what we are going to do tonight…"

I shivered slightly as he nipped my neck and traced the contours of my arms, breasts, and belly as he slowly peeled off my bridesmaid's dress. I stepped out of it and into his arms. He scooped me up and placed me gently on the bed, looking at my pale body with his dark eyes. We made love, entwined, two bodies, one flesh.

As we lay together afterwards, Mark ran his finger slowly around my wrist, following the curves of the rose-gold bracelet.

"Ellie, about that ring to match the bracelet?"

My heart started to thump in my chest. "Yes?"

"Ellie, I'd like to contact Jannali and ask her to make it for you."

"Oh?"

"Ellie, will you marry me, baby or no, baby? I don't ever want to live without you."

I shook my head slowly, a scalding tear running down my cheek. "No, Mark; the answer is 'no' right now. It's only fair to you. Ask me again when I have had my therapy."

He ran his hands through his hair. "You are the most maddening, stubborn, infuriating woman, Ellie Rose."

Chapter Twenty-Two

Back home

Our holiday was almost over. Mark's flight was scheduled for tomorrow and mine for the following day. We planned to be home for Christmas. It seemed hard to believe, with the temperature in Sydney reaching thirty degrees most days, that we would soon be plunged back into the cold and dark. Decorated for the season, the shop windows here were beautiful. Very different to the English window displays, despite the same use of baubles and lights, the tone here was more Santa on surfboards and Christmas barbeques than sleigh bells and mulled wine.

Mark was quiet. He slipped out of bed that morning and went for a long swim, returning with beads of water glistening over his chest and back above the towel wrapped tightly around his waist. I made coffee and placed two mugs on the counter, then reached out my hand to him.

"Thank you for last night. You are so generous and trusting, but I'm right to say 'no' this time, Mark. I love you, I have no doubts about that, but I have to be sure what else I'm offering in return for your proposal, and you need to know too. A lot has happened this year, and I don't think this is the right time for either of us to make a big decision."

"I've made mine. I can't do any more. You have my promise, and I'll wait until you know how you feel about a family, but I won't change my mind."

"Thank you."

As we sat in slightly subdued silence, Mark's mobile phone rang, and he padded over to answer. "If that's London, they can make whatever decision they are calling about without me. I'm not back until at least Wednesday."

I nodded, "Put your foot down. You're on holiday."

He clicked the button to answer, looking slightly mutinous, and I watched as his face changed to one of pleasure and amazement.

"What do you mean? Where are you? Well, yes, yes, of course. Hang on, let me get Ellie."

He held out the phone to me. "It's Dom. He and Vale are at Heathrow. They want to know if they can come to us for Christmas."

I looked at him slightly stupidly for a moment, so he offered me the phone a second time, waggling it slightly.

"Dom, how wonderful, what are you doing in England? Yes, of course, you can spend Christmas with us. It's a scratch affair this year, but we'll get something sorted. Head straight over to the barn if you like. Pen has keys if you haven't got yours with you. No, you didn't wake us, and you can switch off your imagination – we're both dressed! Well, Mark isn't, he's in his swimmies, but decent I assure you."

I rang off and turned to Mark, who now had a broad grin on his face, "I only saw him ten days ago, and they were spending Christmas in the States. You wait, he'll be up to something."

"I think they're mad. Dom says he'll explain why they've come back when we get there. It will be great to see them. I know you only saw them a short while ago, but it feels like a long time for me. I think you may be right about Dom being up to something. He was very excited."

"Unbelievable. I'd better get dressed."

His mood had lifted; both of us were grinning like Cheshire cats. Christmas with Dom and Vale was an unexpected treat and something to look forward to at the end of the holiday.

While Mark got dressed, I phoned to confirm both our flights. Thinking of Dom and Vale at the barn made me think of the dogs, Pen, and the clinic. I still didn't feel quite as calm and steady as usual, but at least now I had a plan. I felt ready to go back and face everyone again.

"What do you want to do today?" I said to Mark.

"I don't want to be touristy, let's walk up to the Italian café and have a lazy coffee. We can do the crossword and chill out. I bet I get more clues right than you do! Then a little siesta…" He threw me a slow wink, "Perhaps dinner somewhere overlooking the harbour."

"Sounds good to me." After all the emotional upheaval, a simple day together was what we both needed. "That's a proud boast about the crossword, by the way. Ten dollars says you're wrong."

Mark was indeed wrong; two of the clues were medical terms which were quickly mine, and I was better than him at the three-word sayings too. He handed over his ten dollars, laughing, "You can buy a coffee at the airport on me unless you fancy re-betting it on the Sudoku? Double or quits."

"Oh no, I know when to stop! You'd fleece me," I said and pocketed my dollars while I was ahead.

As Mark's flight was late afternoon, and mine early the next day, we travelled to the airport together, and I decided to stay overnight in a hotel nearby.

I closed the door to the flat without the twinge of sadness I'd been expecting. It was Annie and Max's home now, the ghosts of younger Ellie and Brett weren't there, and my life now lay in the future, whatever that held.

"I wish we were flying together."

"I won't be long behind you, Mark, and you can organise a lift for me when you get back. Because you love me."

"Hmm," he said, looking at me through narrowed eyes, "I'll think about it."

When I arrived at Heathrow, a cold sparkly morning greeted me. Although it was picture-postcard pretty to fly in over frosted fields, I pulled on extra layers before I left the plane and still shivered as I crossed the tarmac and boarded the bus for the terminus. Queues of weary-looking travellers filed through passport control, and after the usual scrummage at the baggage carousel, I was happy to wheel my case into the Arrivals Hall.

Waiting for me on the other side was Pen, grinning from ear to ear with Lottie sporting a 'Welcome home Auntie Ellie' placard on the front of her buggy.

"Pen!" I wrapped her in a warm hug. "Aww, it's good to see you and you, little munchkin," I leaned down to wag one chubby hand that was reaching out to me. The toothy grin with two little pickle chasers at the front of her mouth was sweet. "Oh, my goodness, she's sprouted teeth!"

"Yes, keep well out of range — Lottie's experimenting on anyone unwary enough to get close. Poor Belle had her tail chomped the other day when Lottie was in the buggy; it was wagging just at the right height."

I laughed, "Poor girl, it's a good job she's so good-natured. Thank you for coming to collect me. I was expecting Mark or Dom."

"I said I'd come because Mark's still tired, and Dom and Vale are out buying supplies for Christmas. I was so surprised to see them. I wanted you to myself for a while anyway. How are you?"

I thought about it for a moment and said honestly, "I'm doing OK, Pen. I wasn't when I left, well, you knew better than I did."

She heaved a deep sigh of relief. "I've been thinking about you."

"It's been a roller coaster ride emotionally. I had a bit of a meltdown while I was there, but I got a few things straight. There's more to do, but I feel so much better."

Pen nodded and looked at me to gauge my response. "I heard about it from Mark and some from Vale. Bless you, Hun, no wonder you're tired, Mark too. And James? Did he turn up?"

I looked shamefaced. "James is a casualty Pen. Don't tell anyone because I'm not proud of this, but I was wrong about him. He wasn't just flirting with me; he was looking for something serious and thought Mark and I were breaking up."

"Was he very hurt?"

"I don't know, but he was very kind to me. I'll write to him once things have settled down."

"And you and Mark?"

"We're feeling our way, Pen. He's asked me to marry him, but I said 'No'."

She gaped at me. "What? Why? Because of Brett?"

I shook my head. "I've stopped grieving for Brett. That's one good thing that happened in Australia." I looked at Pen, "When I left England, I thought he'd be there somehow, that he'd guide me. But, he wasn't, he didn't, he's gone. When I realised that, it triggered all the anger I'd been blocking out for years. More like rage when it started to spill out, but I think perhaps I've finally got closure."

I paused, "Trauma seems indelible, we learn to cope with it as time passes. So not everything is sorted, perhaps it never will be, I need to talk that over with someone before I accept Mark."

She touched my arm. "Ellie, you sound like you've been through the mill. How awful."

Pen looked haunted for a moment, and I said, "It wasn't all bad, there were fun bits too. The wedding was awesome, and Summer in Sydney is glorious."

"It beats Winter in Essex, I bet."

Feeling the cold, damp air, I hesitated, pretending to give the matter thought. "I think you may be right, Mrs Drayton. Now, tell me about the dogs and the farm and everything."

"I don't know where to start… the dogs are fine and back with Mark. They are so going to flatten you when you get back. Remind me to kiss you for sending us, Adam and Maisie. They are great, and I wish we could persuade them to stay."

"Talking of which, how is Angus' hand?"

"You know what? He's doing well. The hospital is pleased with him. He's cutting down splint time and starting to get the movements back well. He listens to Robin, wonders will never cease, and with Adam being so good on the farm, he hasn't fretted much at all. It's been lovely to spend time together with Lottie, and we've even done some date nights courtesy of Maisie and Adam volunteering to babysit."

"Fantastic, I must go away more often," I said.

She shook her head. "Oh no, you don't! I love your dogs, but the amount of mud washing I've had to do because of their long coats isn't funny. You are only allowed to go away in the summer from now on."

"I have something beautiful for you to make amends," I glanced at her. "Some of those posh rubber gloves and hand cream." She shot me a dagger look, and I held up both hands. "No, only joking, wait and see."

As we pulled up on the drive, everyone piled out of the barn. The dogs got to me first, and for a couple of minutes, they kept me fully occupied as they wove through my legs and bumped against my hands, asking for cuddles, emitting squeaks and grunts of delight. Mark came next for a kiss when he could get near, and then I turned, his arm around my shoulders, to greet Dom and Vale.

Vale held both hands out and said, "Ellie, look at you with freckles across your nose. You look properly sun-kissed and summery."

As I took her hands, I felt an unfamiliar ring on her left hand and pulled her hand forward to look more closely. Vale was wearing a band of gold which glinted in the morning sunlight. I looked up at her, incredulous. "Is this what I think it is? When did this happen?"

She nodded excitedly and said, "Last week."

I looked from Vale to Dom, who was grinning broadly, "Congratulations!" I looked at Mark, "Did you know?"

"Not until I got home, it wasn't mentioned before I left the States. Although I've had my suspicions that this would happen."

Dom said, "Come inside. The champagne's chilled. Come and have a glass, and we'll tell you all about it."

"I'm bowing out of this one," said Pen regretfully. "I need to get back. We'll catch up before Christmas."

"Oh, wait, wait, let me give you this." I rummaged in the top of my hand luggage and drew out two small parcels. One for Lottie, a flat sheepskin koala that I'd been unable to resist, and a small square box for Pen, which contained a silver lapel pin of a pointer's head. "With my love," I said.

We waved her off, and the four of us trooped into the kitchen to take up seats around the breakfast bar while Dom poured the champagne.

"Cheers! Here's to the married couple. So, tell all…"

"We were married in Vegas, by Elvis, on a marriage license issued by the State of Nevada that we collected from the County Clerk's office the day before."

"No! You're kidding me."

"I am not. I wore a dress I bought the day before and carried a bouquet that the chapel lent us, and I couldn't be happier." Vale beamed as she told us, and she and Dom exchanged glances and grinned.

I looked from one to the other. "But what brought this on?"

"Well, in part, you."

"Me?" I looked at her in amazement.

"Perhaps that isn't quite fair. You two were the final straw. The truth is, we never settled in New York. When we realised that you and Mark were miserable too, we felt like we were partly to blame for your problems because Mark was so busy with the work for Dom. You know what Dom's like, he said, 'Why are we messing about when the solution's simple? Let's get married and go back'."

"What just like that?"

"Sure thing. Dom hustled me into a taxi with just my toothbrush, we got a standby flight, and the rest is history."

"Oh, my goodness, Vale, I can't believe you did that."

"Dom's a force of nature." She looked at him, and I saw the love that flowed between them in that glance. "So we're back, I'm likely out of a job, and we're homeless." Then they both laughed, "It feels pretty good."

"You aren't homeless," I said firmly, "Are they, Mark?" I looked at them both straight-faced. "We can get a caravan for you in the garden, no problem."

Vale looked at me, her eyes widening for a moment, and then we all laughed. "Had you going," I said.

I trundled my cases up to our bedroom and pushed them into a corner. Champagne and jetlag were a lethal combination. I felt odd, awake, but rather vague, like I was floating. I'd sort the bags out later, right now, if I didn't get some fresh air, I'd fall asleep, and I wanted to stay awake at least until early evening.

Mark said he'd come with me for a walk. We piled on yet more layers to ward off the sharp wind blowing, and he and I set off with the dogs. Away from the fizz and bubble of our arrival, Mark was quiet, and I thought I knew why.

"Are you wondering why it's so hard for me when everyone else seems to get married without hesitation?"

"No!" He turned his dark eyes towards me, and I could see the hurt he was trying to mask.

"Liar!"

"I wish it were easier, Ells, for you and me."

I squeezed his hand. "I'm sorry."

We walked in silence for a while, which was broken only by the sound of our feet crunching in the frosted grass and then suddenly by the thrumming reverberation of a flock of geese, whose wings created a low sound as they wheeled overhead, disturbed by the running dogs.

"Does this mean you're out of a job too?" I asked cautiously.

"No, not immediately. Dom will only take back over gradually. He still has to liaise with the American office. He said we could be flexible and has asked me to stay working part-time, but I will probably step out as soon as I can. I prefer working with my small businesses."

"Well, that sounds like a good compromise."

"Yeah," he said with little enthusiasm, then paused and said, "Ellie, will you talk to someone soon?"

"I'm on it, I promise. I'm going to ask a psychotherapist I know to recommend someone. I want to go to a therapist who doesn't know me professionally and to whom I don't refer my patients to. I think that's best."

He wrapped his arm around me and squeezed, placing a kiss on the side of my temple.

Chapter Twenty-Three

Christmas and a New Year

The next day, I decided to pop into Touch. Determined not to indulge in my drug of choice and begin to work too hard, I decided not to pick up my caseload again until after Christmas, when Robin and Louise left on their travels. Maisie and Robin were doing a perfectly good job without me, proving that no one was indispensable. It was hard for me not to rush straight back, and I felt restless. I kidded myself that popping in to say 'Hello' was only polite and that if I spoke to everyone and organised the hand-over as seamlessly as possible, I wasn't breaking the pact with myself.

I pushed the clinic door and felt a rush of pride as the tendrils of its calm atmosphere wrapped themselves around me. Whatever else I'd failed at, I was proud of what I'd built here. Sarah looked up from the new computer screen, and her face broke into a big smile.

"Ellie, you're back, how lovely to see you. Would you like a cuppa'?"

"I'd love one, Sarah. How has everything been while I was away?"

She pulled a face. “We’ve been super-busy, Ellie. You know how it is coming up to Christmas. Luckily, Maisie’s a little dynamo. She’s been working very hard and is so popular with the patients too.”

That was an excellent sign. If Sarah approved, Maisie must be doing something right. I glanced at their lists. Maisie and Robin were both fully booked, so I wouldn’t be able to talk to them today anyway.

“I only popped in to say ‘hi’ and to plan the hand-over for when Robin leaves.”

“We were talking about this yesterday, Ellie. Robin leaves on the sixth of January. He suggested that Maisie keep her current list and that he hands his patients to you when he leaves. So, there’s no need for you to rush back, you can relax and enjoy Christmas.”

Everything at the clinic was organised, and it seemed I wasn’t needed. As I left, I felt mixed emotions. I was pleased that they were so efficient and didn’t have to rely on me, but at the same time, I felt a little bereft. I was uncomfortably aware that some of my reasons for not having a baby, like worrying that the practice couldn’t manage without me, were being cut away from under my feet.

With no immediate need to rush back to work, I had to face up to my promise and phone the counsellor. It made me feel absurdly nervous. Greta, who was my go-to referral for any of my patients, had rooms on the other side of town. I walked over to see her, and after a brief conversation, she recommended a colleague of hers in Chelmsford and said she would ring to introduce me.

“You’re doing the right thing, Ellie. It’ll be hard work but exciting. Keep an open mind.”

When I got home, there was a note to say Dom and Mark were still in London and Vale was out buying a Christmas tree.

I looked at the business card that Greta had given me. Christine O'Hara. I put it down and decided to make tea before phoning. Mocking myself for procrastinating, I picked up the phone and dialled the number on the card.

"Christine O'Hara, how can I help?"

Her soft Irish lilt was pretty, and I stammered, "Ellie Rose here, Christine. Greta suggested I call."

"Yes, Ellie. You're Greta's physio colleague. We've just spoken. When would you like to come in?"

I took a deep breath. "As soon as possible."

"How about we meet on the twenty-seventh, at ten o'clock?"

"Um, right, yes, of course, that's fine." That was only a couple of days away. I was expecting her to offer something in the New Year. Oh, well, things were in motion, for better or worse.

I was still looking at the card and wondering about my appointment when Vale came in, very flushed and dragging a small Christmas tree behind her. I pocketed the card and got up to help her, as did the dogs, who seemed to like the idea of a tree indoors.

"If I hang onto this, can you get the stand from the car, please, Ellie?"

Together we wrestled the tree into its stand and, after a couple of attempts which resulted in it looking very drunken, managed to get it standing straight.

"I've got some tree decorations from last year in the spare-room cupboard."

She handed me a small box. "Here's one from me to add to them. Mom used to add a new one every year when we were kids. It's a family tradition."

She handed me a beautiful hand-painted glass bauble that said, 'love and friendship'. I looked up at her, touched by her thoughtfulness, and she said, "Here's to us."

"My family tradition is that Mum always has a glass of Madeira, and we watch Meet Me in St. Louis while we decorate the tree. We always cry when Judy Garland sings 'Have Yourself a Merry Little Christmas'. You up for it?"

"Hand me a glass and a tissue," she replied.

When Mark and Dom got back from London, the tree looked beautiful. There was no dinner, and we girls had indeed been shedding sentimental tears over the film. As I looked at Mark, I wondered if our troubles would be long gone by next year. Who knew! For now, fish and chips were the order of the night, and he and I were both trying hard.

Dom's idea of getting in supplies for Christmas was to raid the local deli for every delicious thing he could see and have it delivered with copious quantities of wine to go with it. It was just the four of us this year, Peter and Alessandra were with friends in Kent, and Mum and Dad were with my godparents.

I didn't have the energy to rustle up culinary miracles, so I decided to relax and go with the flow. There would be plenty of years to eat turkey and Christmas pudding, and it seemed quite fitting that this strange year should be different.

After a long walk with the dogs in the morning, we stopped off at Pen and Angus' house to add yet more presents to Lottie's pile and consume mince pies with coffee. From then on, back at the barn, Christmas day became a running buffet, with lots of laughter and increasingly silly games in the evening.

One of my Christmas presents to Mark was Christine O'Hara's business card with my appointment time scribbled on the back. I left it in a little box on his pillow with a note which said, 'Time for the future to begin'.

Christine's address turned out to be an annexe attached to her house.

The smell of fresh paint and new carpet assailed me as I pushed open the door. I realised my heart was racing, perhaps this was how new patients felt when they came to Touch as well. The small waiting area had smooth walls decorated in neutral tones with colourful abstract paintings that drew the eye, and gentle background music was playing. I perched on one of the leather chairs, a mixture of apprehension and relief that I'd come to get some help warring in my brain.

The treatment room door opened, and a young man in sweats lounged out. He turned to an older lady, who I assumed to be Christine. As he said goodbye, I took in her navy-blue pinafore over a flowered cotton shirt and her salt and pepper hair caught back in a ponytail. She looked unthreatening, and I willed myself to calm down.

"Thanks, Christine, see you next month." He grinned at me with a sort of 'you'll be alright' look and headed off.

"Ellie? Hello, welcome, come on in."

The treatment room was like a small lounge with two modern armchairs and a wooden coffee table sporting a carafe of water, some glasses, a box of tissues and a glossy-leafed succulent of some kind. That plant must thrive on tears, I thought, then wondered why that had popped into my head – it was just a decoration.

"Do sit down." She smiled, indicating one of the chairs, while she settled back into the other. "I wondered, first of all, if you could tell me what you hope to get from today's session?"

The question took me by surprise. Of all the questions I'd imagined Christine asking, I didn't have an answer prepared for that one.

"Take your time."

After a moment's hesitation, I said, "I had a bit of a melt-down while I was away on holiday, well, maybe it started before that, and I need to get things sorted because it's affecting my relationship."

"Could you explain what you mean by melt-down?"

I explained about how Pen having Lottie had triggered my fear of loss, the pressure-cooker feeling as I felt more and more isolated from everyone, and then the escape to Australia. Once I started talking, everything came tumbling out, prompted by Christine's quietly spoken questions. I almost felt breathless with relief as I let go of all the pain I felt inside; my anger with Brett, my terror of loving someone as much as Pen did Lottie, my fear of losing my anchor if I couldn't work.

"What makes you think that love always leads to loss and pain?"

"I don't, I mean I know it doesn't, but I don't think I could cope if what happened to Brett happened again. It was awful, terrible and…" I gulped. "I'm sorry, I'm sorry."

I couldn't speak anymore. Tears entirely suspended my voice, and the pit I'd fallen into when Brett had died opened again.

"Ellie, this is very painful for you to remember." I nodded and sniffed. "Can you take a few deep breaths with me?" I nodded again, reached for a tissue to blow my nose, and then joined in with her until I felt calmer.

"I'm sorry, I feel steadier again, thank you."

"Don't apologise; it's normal to cry when we're hurt. You don't have to be braver or better than anyone else. When we grieve, it's usual to try to avoid triggers initially, which helps us to cope in the early stages. But we do need to grieve. If we suppress sadness and inhibit expressions of loss completely, the grief can become distorted, so when it does resurface, it seems illogical. Distorted grief may be part of what has happened to you recently."

I nodded again.

"I'd like you to write down as many of the good things as you can remember that came from loving Brett, and from losing him, for example, how you developed as a person."

She handed me a piece of paper on a clipboard and a pen. "Would you like a drink while you do that?"

"Thank you." I took the glass she offered and began to write.

In the end, it was a long list, amazingly long on the good things that came from Brett's death. It included my skills, confidence, and the new people around me.

I went to hand her the list, but she said, "No, the list is for you, Ellie, I want you to see that although you would not have chosen for Brett to die, some good has nonetheless come from it, and you have the resources to develop coping skills. I would also like you to see that Brett wasn't your whole life, even though it felt that way at the time. Remembering these things is very important when you assess the more mature model of love that you are living now. To love someone, you do not have to give yourself away entirely."

I looked at her for a moment. "That is a lot to take in."

"Then I think that's enough for today. Why don't we meet next week, Ellie?"

I shook her hand and walked back out into the street with a burgeoning hope that the maze my mind had become was not impenetrable.

The hope rapidly turned to exhaustion, and I was happy to return to the barn, close the blinds and snuggle under the duvet, which was where Mark found me when he returned from London. Dom and Vale were staying in town to start looking for a flat, so mercifully it was just the two of us.

He slipped in beside me and said, "How was it?"

"Painful but good. Today we've been looking at love and fear. Love has become inextricably linked with pain and loss at a subliminal level for me somehow. We looked at the possibility that sometimes we can emerge not destroyed, but stronger for loss."

"I've always thought you were incredibly strong, but I sometimes wonder if you miss the point that you're even stronger if you share problems and confront life with your support team rather than alone."

"You're right, losing Brett made me wary about depending on people."

"But Ellie, I don't think it's about depending. Depending on someone is passive, I'm talking about trusting, which is about choosing to accept help. Why do you find it so hard to trust people?"

I paused for a moment, then said, "When I was a little girl, I used to confide in Mum all the time. I trusted that she wanted what was best for me. But even when I was quite young, I realised that sometimes she used my confidences to try to get me to comply with what she thought I should do or be."

He frowned, "Aren't all parents a little guilty of having hopes and dreams for their kids?"

"This was a bit more extreme. Mum is obsessed with what people think and with conforming. She chipped away at my self-esteem, so she could mould me to be 'good'. Or what other people thought was good."

"Don't you think she just wanted what she thought was right for you?"

"I don't think she thought about what was right for me because I'm not sure she knows who I am at all. Mum has this picture of who she wants me to be. It's sad. I don't think she's a bad person, just very insecure, but it had a big impact on me. I began to stop telling her things, and I couldn't wait to get away by the time I went to uni. When I met Brett, he was so carefree and confident. He was like an antidote. I think you're right, I trusted him, but perhaps I depended on him too much. He lived on the other side of the world to my mother too – very convenient!"

"I know you and your mum aren't that close, but I didn't realise you felt like this. Not everyone who loves you is trying to control you, though, Ellie."

"I know, I just lost sight of it for a while in the panic last year. Gut reactions are primitive instincts, not rational reactions. I got caught up in my instincts."

As January wore on, it seemed like a long time ago that we waved Louise and Robin off on their travels. Dom and

Vale found a flat and moved back to London. The barn seemed empty at first without them, but I liked the peace too. Mark and I needed time together to work out our issues and find a new rhythm together. Mark continued to work with Dom in London two days a week and saw his clients for the rest of the time. He said it was the right mix for him, and he was certainly less stressed.

Sarah was right about Maisie. She was an absolute dynamo, which helped me to put into practice my good intentions about working sensible hours. My return to work felt good. Once again, helping others was helping me heal, but I was determined I wouldn't use it as an excuse not to face issues in my life anymore. I think Mark and I had both learned over the last few months that we preferred a simpler life.

I had three more sessions with Christine during January. She worked me hard, and together we painfully teased out reality from illusions. She was quick to spot an excuse and challenge it with a carefully weighted question. The onus for change lay firmly with me and how I chose to react to life events, but she helped me set workable parameters.

One thing she was very keen on was that I vary my work environment more, to loosen my dependency on Touch. We discussed not just my professional qualifications but how to value my personal qualities and how they could develop my professional life outside the clinic.

I explained how interested I was in energy medicine, and we agreed that I could look at taking a course when Robin came back. She suggested I might look into more lecturing as I'd enjoyed the challenge with James. We also discussed taking my intellectual property and making it into online courses so that if we chose to have a family, I would have a passive income from this, even when I wasn't available to teach in person.

Mark and I did a lot of our talking on foot, walking the dogs. Somehow things felt less highly charged than when we were inside, perhaps the wide spread of fields and sky that the estuary terrain offered gave us perspective.

"I need you to acknowledge something about me and think about it carefully. I think I've only just come to terms with it myself, and it may be a problem for us. I love you, I love my work and our home, but there is also a part of a restless free spirit in me. I will need to be able to take up new challenges and break the routine. Otherwise, I'll get claustrophobic again and end up running."

He raised his eyebrows. "To Australia, I saw it!"

I watched an egret lift gracefully off the riverbank, circle over the field to our left and land on the edge of a small lake caused by flooding in the water meadow.

"I love Pen to bits, and it's great that she finds her satisfaction at home, but I'm never going to be that woman. I'm not sure I would have been right to lead the sort of roaming existence that Brett craved either.

What I'm saying is, that I'll need you to support me to get a good balance. I don't want an open relationship, I'm not talking about that, but if we have a family, I'm still going to need those things, and that may not be what you have in mind."

We walked on in silence as I waited for his reply. Silence can mean so many things; this one wasn't charged or awkward, it was merely a pause for thought. One of the many positive things to come from my sessions with Christine, I had become comfortable with pauses and less eager to fill them. They had beauty and purpose all of their own.

"I meant it when I said I'm happy to take my share of the parenting, Ellie. I'm not Dom, I'm not driven by work, even though I enjoy what I do. Look, we may need some childcare help as well, I'm OK about that, and I guess nobody gets all of what they want all the time, we'll both have to make some sacrifices."

"So, if I need to go away for some headspace or to take a course?"

"Look, I'm not saying I won't feel grumpy about it sometimes, and I know I'm more of a homebody than you, but I'm happy to give and take. I don't want to squash you into a mould. I want you to be yourself."

I nodded, "Thank you." I tucked my hand into the crook of his arm, "Hungry?"

"Starving."

I whistled up the dogs, and we retraced our steps back towards home. I was gradually feeling much more secure again.

"Ellie, I think our next session may be the last one we need. How do you feel about that?"

"A bit frightened, it's been good to touch base with you regularly. It makes me feel safe." It had been comforting to have Christine's calm guidance.

She smiled kindly, "I think you have enough to work with. You need to go out and put things into practice."

I swallowed hard. "Okay, if you think so."

"In this last session, we'll look at keeping up with good intentions." Christine explained, "What I'd like you to do for the first couple of months is to commit to writing a diary of hazards, intentions, and strategies for feeling well, then check it daily against what you are actually doing. It would be a good idea to elect a diary buddy to make sure you're sticking to your plans or to help you adjust them if you've been overambitious."

I thought for a moment. "I think Mark is an obvious one, and perhaps Pen too. I know they will keep me honest."

"Go with Pen if she has time to work with you. Changing habits isn't easy, Ellie. If it were, we'd all be perfect. So initially, expect to fail and to need to adjust regularly. After a while, though, you'll only need to check in with your diary buddy occasionally because you'll be self-regulating. If she tells you things are slipping, listen! This kind of thing can crop up again at different phases of your life."

She smiled, "You'll be fine, trust yourself. You're insightful."

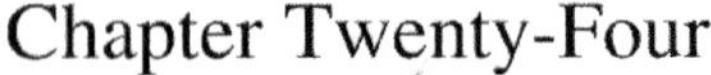

Chapter Twenty-Four

Second time lucky

One of my patients that I'd been pleased to see again was Angus. He'd been working with Robin while I was away and had been doing very well.

It barely seemed possible, the time had slipped away fast, but he was in the final stages of his rehab. The clumsy hand with the bright red scar was barely recognisable as he showed me a full closed fist and a wide-open hand. Robin had adapted Angus' old splint to make a mini gym to strengthen his fingers with different elastic bands making the resistance. With his return to farm work beckoning, I decided it was time to look at his functional fitness.

We adapted a soft-grip handle, and I showed him a series of strength exercises that involved whole-body twists against elastics and some lower limb conditioning and lifts too. We worked out a circuit that would improve his cardiovascular fitness as well. I don't think he realised how much of the form he usually took for granted had slipped away during his imposed break. Breathless after a session of exercise, he said, "I can see that I've been slacking!"

"Well, that's what Adam was here for, to let you take a break. It won't take long to get your fitness back, but we need to prepare the hand and the rest of your body gradually, or you'll end up with another injury."

He looked at me gratefully. "Adam's been fantastic, he's a natural farmer. He's got some excellent ideas too. He was looking at a couple of old barns that had fallen into disrepair. We're thinking of converting them when he and Maisie come back from their travels as holiday lets, and he's been talking to me about making a fishing lake and stocking it too. It would make the farm income less vulnerable by being diverse. I'm going to consider it."

I smiled, "You and he get on well then?"

He nodded, "We do, and he and Maisie like it here. I didn't realise how lonely it gets sometimes working on my own all day. Mum and Dad have enjoyed having them in the annexe, the house is too big for them, really, but they're not ready to give it up yet."

"Maisie will find it easy enough to get other physio work if they want to stay. I'm not sure I have enough work for three."

The intentions diary was a good idea. Christine was right; I needed the accountability of the journal because I kept failing. I couldn't believe how easy it was to keep saying 'yes' to things and end up getting overloaded. Also, how much I sacrificed time to myself to fit in other commitments.

I was sitting in Pen's kitchen with a cup of tea after work as she read my plan in the diary, and then looked at my actual time management.

"Aha!" She said, stabbing her finger at Tuesday's page. "You were supposed to finish at six o'clock and go to a yoga class. What happened? It says here you finished at seven-thirty."

I grimaced, "I know, I know, one of my old patients rang in and needed an appointment before they went on holiday."

"Yes, and the emergency slot we blocked out every day for, well, emergencies? Or for you to do paperwork and reading? What happened to using that?"

I looked guilty, "The patient couldn't make that time, and she only wanted to see me."

Pen looked cross, "So not much of an emergency then! Ellie, you have got to toughen up."

"I know, but look, I did stick to plan on Monday and Wednesday."

"Okay, two out of three, you're getting better. Right, let's do some role play, give me your polite saying 'no' speech."

"Pen!"

She got a steely glint in her eye. "No, go on, do it!"

I rolled my eyes and chanted, "I'm sorry, those are the only spaces available, the rest of my diary is full. Would you prefer to see one of my colleagues?"

"Exactly. You are only telling the truth. You do have an appointment, except it's to do a regular yoga class as part of your work/life balance. Remember what you agreed with Christine, you can't look after other people if you aren't well yourself – equal importance, you, and them."

I chucked a tea towel at her, which she caught. "No need to get violent. I'm just doing my diary buddy job."

I sighed, "I know, I am getting there. Christine was right. It's hard to break old habits."

She glanced at me and came to sit beside me. "You're doing really well, and you seem more relaxed, happier."

"I am, I don't feel restless like I did."

"Have you heard any more from James?"

"No," I said, looking down. I still felt guilty about him. "I wrote to apologise and thank him. He sent a half-case of wine back to the clinic with a note saying, 'My new wines from the Hunter Valley. Hope you approve'. He tagged me in on the next small business association meeting invite too, but I think I'll just let that settle for a while."

"Probably best," she said, sounding relieved.

Lottie was sitting up now and had been playing with some toys on her highchair table while we chatted. Suddenly frustrated, she banged a wooden pig hard on the top several times and shouted, "Da, Da, Da."

Pen picked up the toy and patiently said, "Mum, Mum, Mum."

I laughed and said, "I'd better let you get on."

When I arrived home, Mark's car was in the drive, and I could see him in the kitchen, moving from the fridge to the island. That boded well. I was hungry, and I hoped he was rustling up food and a glass of wine.

"Hey," I called as I slipped off my shoes.

"Hi, Ellie, come and get a glass. I'll put a couple of steaks on."

"Oh, wonderful, that sounds good." I kissed him lightly on the cheek, "I love you even more. The dogs do too." They were watching with interest as he prepared the meat.

"They aren't getting any of this. It's far too good."

He was right, the steak was delicious, and as we settled on the sofa afterwards, I groaned and said, "I've eaten too much."

"We can walk it off tomorrow, no work to worry about."

"True." I sighed with satisfaction. The weekend was ahead.

He suddenly looked a little shifty. "Ellie, this arrived today from Australia. What do you think?"

I opened the white cardboard "Auspost" box, and from in amongst a mess of packaging puffs lifted a small green bag with 'Jannali' embossed in white script on the outside. I looked up at Mark, but he just smiled and said, "Go on, open it."

Inside was a small ring box. My fingers faltered slightly as I opened the sprung catch. Glowing with a satin sheen were two rings in rose gold that fit perfectly together. Similar in form to my bracelet, the etching on them made them appear like tree bark, and one had coloured stones embedded – carnelian, citrine and peridot – to form leaves coming off the circle.

"Oh, they're beautiful."

Jannali had produced a work of art, and the energy coming from the colours she'd chosen was powerful.

Suddenly, Mark looked vulnerable. "Ellie, I hope this isn't too soon. Please say 'yes' this time."

I looked at Mark; his dark eyes fixed steadily on mine, waiting. It had been a long road to here, but filled with newfound confidence and security, I leant forward to kiss him and whispered, "Yes."

Mark took the engagement ring out of the box, leaving the simpler wedding band inside. He slid it onto my finger and said, "I love you."

"I love you too."

I settled back against him happily as he held my hand, his fingers playing over the ring on my left hand. "When shall we get married?"

I knew without hesitation. "This Spring, May, when the hawthorn blossom is out. I don't want to wait too long, but I would like Robin and Louise to be home."

He looked relieved. "Sounds good to me, May it is. Will that give us time to get everything planned?"

I turned to look at him in surprise. "How big were you thinking?"

"Not big, if that's alright with you, just our best friends and family."

I nodded, "That sounds perfect to me. Do you think we could have the reception here, maybe?"

"No, I want you to have the perfect day and not worry about anything. But I know where we could have it – Wisteria Cottage. Mum would be in her element. She and your mum could organise it together, and there is room for a marquee behind the cottage."

I puffed out my cheeks and let the breath go with a pop, "I'm not sure Peter will want all those people tramping on his lawn." I imagined the hours he spent tending to it and the possible carnage.

"You wait and see. Mum will persuade him."

I giggled, "Shall we start to ring people?"

"Not tonight, Ellie. Tonight, I have other plans for how to celebrate. Wait there." His eyes sparkled as he flashed a grin at me and disappeared into the kitchen. He returned with a bottle of champagne, frosted with condensation and a glass. As he twisted the bottle slowly, I couldn't take my eyes off his slender-fingered hands. The cork emerged with a whisper and a small puff of vapour. He poured a glass, handing it to me. As I reached out to take it, he said, "Uh, uh," and pulled it away, "Come here."

I edged across the sofa, and as I got within range, he tilted the glass to my lips and then kissed me. He took a sip himself and traced a lazy line with his fingers, cool from the bottle, down my cheek and to my neck, making me shiver. He stopped at my collar bone and said, "Tilt your head back." He tipped a tiny drop of the liquid in the hollow there and bent to drink it with a kiss.

I took the glass and put it aside, never taking my eyes from his, and watched the changes of expression as I moved forward to kiss him more deeply.

As I began to unbutton his shirt, Mark said, "Here?" Raising his eyebrows.

I looked around our sitting room, then back to him. "I think so…"

"Conduct unbecoming in my future wife!"

"Get used to it."

I woke with a lazy stretch the following morning and felt the unfamiliar ring on my finger. I looked at it in the half-light. It had rich, subtle colours and a glowing polished brightness. Something unique to me, to us. Mark slumbered beside me, and as I looked at his face, I thanked goodness for his steady persistence in the face of my fear. Last year had been terrifying, and I never wanted to feel like that again.

He was beginning to stir, so I bent over to kiss him, my hair brushing his face. "Good morning."

"Good morning to you, what time is it?"

"It's nearly eight o'clock."

"I remember now," he said slowly. "You kept me up late and plied me with drink and other things. You're a witch."

"Well, that's hardly fair, you plied me with jewels first, and the champagne was your idea, as I recall."

He looked at the ring. "Jannali did an amazing job."

"She did, it's stunning. Now she genuinely might be a witch."

He laughed, "Shall we walk over to Angus and Pen to tell them the news? I'm sure they've been up since the crack of dawn with that little monster."

An overnight frost had hardened the mud in the field, and we walked across with the dogs ranging about us. For once, they stayed clean.

Pen was still in her pyjamas, a streak of pureed something drying on the lapel and her hair flat on one side where she'd slept on it.

"Good look," I said as she opened the door. "We're too early, I'm sorry. We'll come back."

"No, don't worry, come in. The place is a tip, but you won't mind that."

Lottie seemed to have the remainder of the puree all around her chops and over the highchair table but seemed very happy about it. Her face lit up when she saw us, and she waved her plastic spoon with some enthusiasm. The dogs seeing an opportunity, tracked the blobs as they fell and did a clean-up job on the floor.

"Is everything alright?" Pen asked.

I stretched out my hand for her to see the ring, and she looked from my hand to Mark and back.

"You finally said 'yes'! I can't believe it, woohoo!" She pushed her hair behind her ears, smudging in more puree. "Look at the state of me. Keep an eye on Lottie, I'll go and get Angus and get dressed, then you can tell me all about it. I won't take long." Her footsteps sounded on the stairs as she called, "Angus, Angus, Ellie and Mark are engaged."

Mark looked from me to the mess and said, "Mad, completely mad."

He extricated Lottie from the chair and, much to her delight, held her at arm's length as he walked to the sink, saying, "Yukky, yukky, yukky." He grabbed a clean cloth from a pile on the side, passed it under the tap and cleaned her face and hands, then removed the bib, which was plastered and gave her to me. "I think she's safe."

As I jiggled her gently on my knee and blew kisses on the back of her neck to make her giggle, Mark wiped the high chair and put the kettle on. He was just putting four steaming mugs of tea on the table when Pen re-appeared looking more her usual self in dungarees and a striped tee-shirt with Angus behind her. Pen hugged me and jumped up and down, Angus shook Mark's hand and said, "That's great news, couldn't be more delighted."

"When's the wedding then?" Pen asked.

"We'd like it to be May."

Pen smiled at Angus, "I'm going to be a bridesmaid."

Angus looked up to the heavens. "Matron of Honour, and Ellie hasn't asked you yet."

Pen shrugged, "I don't care; she has no choice! What did Dom and Vale say?"

"We haven't told them yet."

"Well, ring them now," she handed me the phone. "Here, put it on speaker."

The ringtones sounded, and as they droned on, I began to think that Dom and Vale might be out, when a bleary voice said, "Hello, Dominic Lancaster."

"Ellie and Mark are getting married," Pen shouted over my shoulder before I had a chance to speak.

"What? Pen is that you?"

"No, it's me, Ellie, I'll pass you to Mark."

Mark took the phone. "Dom, sorry, did we wake you up? We wanted to tell you that congratulations are in order, Ellie said yes."

"Oh, man, congratulations! Vale's with me, she's crying and blowing kisses. Look, we'll come down later, book a table somewhere. We need to celebrate."

Mark said, "I'm on it. Be good to see you."

We eventually left the chaos of the farm kitchen close to lunchtime and walked home hand in hand. "That went well!" Mark started to laugh. I had to laugh too. The joy was infectious.

News of the engagement spread like wildfire, and it seemed we had only just spoken to my parents and Alessandra and Peter when the phone started to ring. Congratulations came pouring in from my godparents, Sarah and Jem, and Angus' parents, amongst others. My call to Australia was emotional. Annie and Max were thrilled, but when I told Annie about our plans for a May date, she said, "Oh, Ellie, we won't be with you, the baby will still be tiny."

Baby, oh my goodness, I couldn't believe that the next time we were together, they would have a child, and for that matter, so might we.

Chapter Twenty-Five

The Wedding

Everyone's enthusiasm threatened to hi-jack our plans for a simple occasion, and I quickly realised that my mother had been dreaming of something little short of a royal wedding since I'd been born.

"Dad, you have to talk to her, we want something simple and quiet, just family and close friends. She's already talking about half the W.I. and a load of people I haven't seen since school. Apart from anything else, we haven't got time to organise anything that big. We nearly fell out again last time she rang."

He sighed, "It's alright, Ellie, don't get cross, leave it to me, you two never did know how to get along. I'll head her off at the pass. Just let her be part of it all, you're her only daughter, this is special for her too."

I sighed, "I know it is Dad. It's been a tough few months, and I want this to be a happy day for all of us to share, not a Hollywood production."

"Look, why don't we come up for a few days to see you both, meet Alessandra again, I don't think we've seen her since we had that Christmas together two years ago. Oh no, wait, we did see her at the fete where we all helped. But we barely know Peter. Give your mum a call and suggest it, you'd make her day."

"That's a good idea, Dad, let's do that and see if we can sort something out."

'The wedding summit', as Mark had dubbed it went off better than I'd expected. When Mum saw Peter's beautiful garden at Wisteria Cottage, she could see it would make a unique venue. Alessandra showed her some photos of a small country wedding in one of the bridal magazines which went some way to mollify her. When I heard them discussing the relative merits of white or oyster hangings for the marquee, I knew that she'd become reconciled to the idea.

Dom was to be Mark's best man, and along with Angus, who was groomsman, my Dad, and Peter, they decided that they would go the whole hog and wear top hats and grey morning suits.

"I can tell you now, we are handsome devils when suited and booted, so I hope you ladies will fully appreciate us on the day," said Dom, after they had been for the fitting of their suits.

Mark raised his eyebrows. "Let's hope they aren't disappointed now you've given us the big build-up." He knew Dom loved a bit of a swagger and couldn't resist teasing him.

My dress was more of an issue. It seemed that these things were ordered well in advance, not bought off the peg. It was easy for the lads, they just had to hire suits for the day.

In the end, Vale came up with a workable solution inspired by one of my mum's ideas.

"I didn't have all these problems. My aunty made my dress. We copied the design from a picture in a magazine, but then, that's what we did in those days."

There was a silence around the table, and Vale said, "The daughter of a lady who works for Dom is a fashion design student. She is part of his young talent programme. She must know someone who could do the same for you."

And that's how it happened. We bought the fabric from Liberty's, and Hannah, the design student, found a 1950s pattern that looked very close in design to my favourite red vintage dress, the one I'd worn on my first night out with Mark. She enrolled two of her friends to make matching ballerina-length dresses for Vale and Pen in vibrant emerald green silk.

As the end of March was approaching, I was due to go counting ground-nesting birds in Yorkshire as usual with the dogs and didn't want to let my friend Mike down. Despite the mutterings of my mother about all we had to get done, I decided I would still go. So much had happened so fast that a moment to reflect would be welcome. Pen was insanely jealous, as we usually went together, and she loved working the dogs as much as I did. But this year, Lottie had to take priority.

"Don't you dare injure your knee again, you can't hobble down the aisle on crutches," she said.

"That injury did bring Mark and me together, though," I pointed out. "Something good comes out of everything bad that happens. Christine says so; it must be true."

It was good to be out in the fresh air, wearing plain field wear and walking boots. I was enjoying the preparation for the wedding but being out on the moor grounded me. However much you dressed me in silk and lace, the dog-walking, outdoor-loving Ellie was still at the heart of me. After all the work I'd done with Christine, it was good to acknowledge that and be able to take this break that I felt I needed without feeling guilty or torn about trying to please everyone.

The Yorkshire Dales are stunning in March, all of life is waking up there. Swathes of daffodils border every lane, the fields are dotted white with sheep, and the air reverberates with the cries of newborn lambs and the reassuring calls of their mothers. On the moor, although the heather still appears brown from winter, bright green shoots are sprouting, and the grouse call to partners in the mating game. There was a risk here too, and death because that is part of life, but for the first time since Brett died, I sensed more hope and trust than fear. I could also feel the joy of new life and the thought that maybe I was ready to think about Mark and me bringing a new life into the world together.

"Come with me next year, Mark," I said over a late-night call, "It's a special thing to be part of."

Alessandra had organised an alternative hen-night as I had resolutely refused the usual party.

Pen, Vale, Alessandra, Mum, and I had a hilarious evening at Wisteria cottage making wedding favours. Alessandra had small, embroidered material circles sent from Italy, which had to be filled with five sugared almonds and tied with a length of raffia and a bright green ribbon through which we looped a small cross.

"It has to be five," she warned, "It's tradition. They stand for children, happiness, health, longevity and wealth."

"Why sugared almonds?" said Vale, "We don't do this in America".

"I know this one," said Pen, "I read about it - to show that life can be both bitter and sweet."

I laughed, "Well, if I've got health, happiness, wealth and longevity, it sounds fine to me."

"Yes, but the children one," said Pen in a gloomy voice. "Lottie has had me up every night this week."

I put my finger to my lips. "Don't start putting me off again; I've only just started to warm up to the idea of having a baby."

"Give that woman another glass of Prosecco," said Vale, and we all chinked and drank to health, wealth, and happiness.

Mum got slightly tiddly on the unaccustomed quantities of Prosecco and started telling stories of when she and Dad were courting, which raised my eyebrows. They had sneaked off to Brighton before their wedding and signed into a hotel as Mr and Mrs Kent, Dad's favourite hero from the comic strips.

"We weren't allowed to live together like you young people do," she said, "Your grandfather used to watch for me coming down the road if I was so much as ten minutes late home. We were lucky to snatch a goodnight kiss."

She hadn't been quite as strait-laced as she would have me believe. I'd never seen her so relaxed.

All very different from each other, I was lucky to have my girlfriends, and Alessandra was a mother-in-law in a million. Mum, well, Mum had probably taught me more about who I didn't want to be over the years than who I did, but as Pen had said, you get the parents you get. That was one relationship that needed more work, and thank goodness for my dad. But I suppose it's all part of a full life, having people around you who are complementary. They don't need to be carbon copies of each other to make a tight-knit group who loves each other.

On the morning of my wedding, I stood in front of the mirror with Hannah, making final adjustments to the hang of the dress and steaming out tiny creases that only she could see. My reflection showed a pale-skinned young woman in a cream dress, tightly fitted to the waist with a circular full-length skirt which fanned out over petticoats. The dress was perfectly plain, except at the waist, where it was cinched in with a large bow that sat at the front of the skirt. The scooped neckline was circled by large fabric roses. Vale had dressed my hair in a loose bun from which a few tendrils escaped.

Although everyone threw horrified looks and uttered dire warnings about dirt on my dress, I had insisted that my first photo of the day was to be of me with my two dogs. It wouldn't be a celebration without them.

They had been brushed within an inch of their lives by Adam and Maisie earlier and kept clean in coats. No outfit is complete without a few dog hairs.

Mark, Dom, and Angus were leaving for the church from the farm. Maisie and Adam had charge of Lottie until after the service. Mum, Alessandra, and Peter were at Wisteria Cottage, where I understood caterers had taken over the kitchen, and the florist was decorating the marquee with flowers.

My Dad arrived looking more elegant than I had ever seen him. The tailored suit made him look taller. "Gosh, you look like a film star," I gasped.

"And you, look stunning, like a young Rita Hayworth." The compliment was praise indeed because Dad had had a crush on her forever.

Vale and Pen left in the first of the hired cars while Dad and I waited for the wedding car to pull up.

"All ready?" said Dad. "There's still time to change your mind…"

I looked at him and saw he was smiling, the corners of his eyes crinkled. He knew the answer.

I had lain the past to rest. The future was beyond anyone's guess, but in the present, I felt ready to make the promises that I'd struggled for so long to reconcile.

As I saw Mark waiting for me at the altar, everyone else faded away. This tall, dark, slender man, with the mass of tangled curls, was my love, my best friend, and the person I had come to trust above all others. He knew my fears and foibles, yet he was waiting there for me, just the same. No one could ask for more.

I was rich beyond measure as I walked into my future, surrounded by so much love.

The End

Chapter One

The barn had been in this small corner of Essex for nearly two hundred years. It looked mellow as I drove up the chase, seeming to smile against the backdrop of a dusky pink summer evening sky.

There were no lights on in the kitchen, just two black and tan faces at the French doors, their feathered tails waving in unison. Jeeves and Bird, my Gordon Setters, had recognised the car. They never stinted on their welcome, and I felt the day's tiredness melt away as I ran silky fur through my fingers and enjoyed their enthusiastic tails beating against my legs.

A chink of light escaped from under the study door, and I made my way through the sitting room with its polished beams and warm-toned wooden floor to the study. All the while, I was followed by the gentle click of eight sets of claws.

"Hello, Mr Roxbury," I slipped a large bag off my shoulder and heaved it onto my desk, which sat at right angles to his.

"Mrs Roxbury." Mark looked up from within the pool of light cast by his desk lamp, and his eyes softened. He frowned slightly, stood up from the mess of papers on his desk, and paused only to gently run his fingers under my eyes. He traced the blue shadows there and drew me into a tender hug. My face pressed against the textured cotton of his polo, and I relaxed into his chest.

"You look tired. Was the clinic busy?"

"Manic! Neither Robin nor I have any spaces left this week, and it's only Tuesday. Sarah is tutting already. I oughtn't complain. Do you remember the early days of Touch when I was never sure if I'd make it to the end of the month?"

"I do, either physiotherapy became very popular, or you're victims of your own success."

I shrugged, "Whichever, I can't wait until Maisie and Adam get back from their travels, I know she only came as a locum last year, but we need her permanently."

"Are they both staying in England? I wondered if they would head back to New Zealand."

I grinned, "Yep, I got an email today. They've nearly run out of funds and would like to come back here to work."

Mark smiled and gave me a thumbs-up. "That's great news; I know Angus would like Adam back to help with the harvest. I've got a feeling the two of them had discussed some new ventures for the farm too. Nice for Angus to have some help."

I nodded, "It was a relief to hear from them. I've been constantly terrified that Robin will resign if we have to keep working at this pace."

"I don't think Robin minds being busy, Ells. He's trying to get a deposit together to buy your cottage. Have you thought any more about selling?"

Pausing for just a moment, I said, "Yes, I think Robin and Louise can have it."

I sighed. Along with Touch, my cottage had been a tangible symbol that I'd had survived after my soulmate, Brett, died. To sell would be a wrench. After he died, the cottage had been my bolthole when I came back from Australia.

"Maybe it's time to move on," Mark said gently, "You could invest the money in something new for the future. If you keep it, you'd have to rent it to someone different."

"I know, and if I'm selling, I'd like Robin and Louise to have it," I nestled deeper into Mark. Letting go of the past had been hard for me. We'd had a difficult time last year, and I felt he needed to know I was confident to move on. As a wedding present, he had gifted me a half share in the barn that he'd worked so hard to renovate. I pulled back and looked up at his familiar face, with its tanned olive skin topped by unruly brown curls and eyes the colour of milk chocolate. "We could think about what to do with the money from the cottage, something for us both."

"That's up to you, Ells."

I smiled up at him and put my hands on his chest. "When Maisie gets back, I'll cut back in the clinic and look at doing some more training. Bring a new dimension to what I do."

He nodded, and his eyes softened as he ran a hand across my forehead, tucking a wisp of stray hair behind my ear. "You're overdue a break. You've worked hard enough since you set up Touch. What're you going to study?"

"I haven't ultimately decided, but probably something holistic. Some of the things Janelli talked about last year have been rumbling in the back of my mind."

His face changed as he assumed a mask of polite interest. "Well, she had some interesting ideas. Why not?"

I slapped him gently on the chest with the flat of my hand. "Mark, you're a terrible liar." I glanced at the two interlocking rings on my left hand that Janelli had made. They were formed in the shape of a branch with semi-precious stone leaves in autumn tones. Meeting her had been fate, I thought.

Janelli was a talented jeweller working in Sydney. When we were there last year for our friend's wedding, Mark had seen a video about her on his plane over and took me to choose a bracelet. She had insisted I feel the energy of each piece rather than only look at the design.

I loved the bracelet, and Mark had secretly commissioned her to make matching engagement and wedding rings for me. Her grandmother had been a healer, where Janelli's ideas about energy flow came from. The concept of energy medicine fascinated me too. I wanted to learn more.

Mark held up both hands and grinned. "Ellie, whatever makes you happy is good with me."

"Right answer!" I mimed applause. "Talking of which, if there is a cold beer in the fridge, you will make me the happiest girl in the world."

He laughed, "Coming up, one cold beer."

I fiddled with my hair for a moment, then added, "I thought working less would tie in with the doctor's advice too. He said to cut back on work a bit because all the stress and being so busy may be part of why we're not getting pregnant."

Mark glanced towards me quickly, and I saw a momentary flick of concern as he assessed how best to answer. "I'd like to see you have a bit more time to yourself anyway, but anything we can do to help is worth a go. I'm sure we'll be fine, though. These things take time sometimes, the doctor said so. In the meantime, we can have lots of fun trying."

Mark linked his arms in the small of my back and pulled me towards him. He rested his forehead against mine and waited until he felt me melt. I raised my head to kiss him, but he pushed me back on my feet. "Not now, though, I'm going to cook," he said, his eyes dancing.

"Tease," I laughed and gave him a push, "I'll remember that."

He winked, "Later…."

Dinner was simple. As Mark griddled salmon, I put together a salad and tossed in toasted sesame seeds and cashews. Torn sourdough for mopping up juices, and we were ready to eat.

We carried our plates outside to the table on our newly finished patio, followed by two dogs with high hopes of salmon skins when we had finished.

The patio was our pride and joy. We'd used our wedding money to buy beautiful stone slabs shot through with flashes of different minerals. With help from Pen, Angus and their farm digger, we'd laid it ourselves over the early summer. It had become my favourite place to relax. To the south was the glitter of the River Crouch, and Pen and Angus' farm fields stretched to the west.

After dinner, we decamped to the swing seat with our glasses to watch the panoramic Essex sky as the sun set in a blaze of colour and the blue sky turned into an inky backdrop for the stars.

The dogs stretched out on their sides, enjoying the residual warmth from the stone, and Mark's arm rested across my shoulders as we rocked gently.

"It's so peaceful here. I love it." I stared up at the midnight blue sky and let my eyes adjust to the darkness. "When you look up at the sky, more and more stars appear, and the sky seems to get deeper. I feel like I'm being drawn into space or hypnotised."

Mark stopped the chair with his long legs on the upswing. "Do I need to add ballast to stop you floating away?"

I laughed and patted my full tummy. "I have my own ballast, thanks. Now the patio's finished, I was thinking, shall we invite Pen and Angus over on Sunday?"

"Yeah, why not? It'd be a nice thank you if they aren't busy. We could see if Dom and Vale can come too."

"Get the gang together? I think we've only all been together twice since the wedding. I'm going to see Pen tomorrow, I'll ask."

I shivered, a cool breeze was coming off the river, and I'd begun to feel chilly. Mark rubbed my shoulders. "Had enough?"

"Yes, let's go in. I'm getting cold."

We pottered about in the kitchen, clearing as an army of crane flies, who'd taken advantage of the open doors, flitted lazily around the opaque glass shade over the light.

As I turned to reach up to the cupboard to put our glasses away, Mark moved in close behind me and circled his arms around my waist. He smoothed my long hair to one side and blew kisses along my neck. I wriggled around to face him, and he leaned in close, bending his head to kiss me slowly, he whispered, "I've finished cooking."

"So I see."

He smiled and held out his hand. I briefly thought about paying him back for earlier, but who was I kidding? He had me at the first trail of kisses.

The following day, I woke as Mark leant over to brush a kiss on my forehead. He smelt of lemons and vetiver, freshly showered, and a crisp cotton shirt contrasted his tanned face. He said, "Early meeting. I'll see you tonight."

Mark ran a business consultancy, helping companies with change and efficiency.

I peered at him owlishly, and he grinned, "Sorry, I shouldn't have woken you. It's early; I'll reset the alarm so you can get more sleep."

I pushed my hair back out of my eyes and watched him fit cufflinks into the sleeves of his shirt and sling a suit jacket over his arm.

Tall and slender, he moved around the room purposefully with a long stride and a slight frown of concentration as he collected bits and pieces. He closed the bedroom door with a quiet click, and I heard him run down the stairs lightly as I snuggled deeper into my pillow, relishing the comfort of our bed.

I had a late list at the clinic, so I intended a leisurely walk across the fields with the dogs to Pen's house for a coffee after this extra snooze. Unfortunately, the low, end of summer sun intruded through chinks in the cream curtains and prodded me awake with teasing fingers.

I gave up the pretence of sleep and followed Mark's lemon scent trail into the shower room, yawning and running sleepy hands through tousled hair. The atmosphere in the room was still steamy, and I rubbed absentmindedly at the long, misted mirror with the sleeve of my pyjamas. I smoothed the baggy jacket over my flat belly and turned sideways. What would it feel like to be pregnant, I wondered? I pushed out my stomach, put my hands in the small of my back, and then rolled my eyes. Time would tell.

As I pulled on the last of my walking clothes, the telephone shrilled, and I skipped downstairs to answer, wondering who would ring this early. To my surprise, it was my mother. "Hi, Mum,"

"Oh, hello darling, I told your dad I must ring you to say I met Amanda Brown's mother. We were chatting, and she said…."

I sighed; I knew before she said it what was coming. Ever since I mentioned we were trying for a baby, my mum told me about every casual acquaintance from school who successfully produced grandchildren for their parents. She also sent every newspaper clip on fertility. I wouldn't mind if her reporting wasn't barbed with regrets that I had left it too late or with the gentle suggestion of her being let down.

Mark thought I overreacted and she was simply concerned, but he hasn't known her for as long as I have.

Her voice rattled on, a background to my thoughts, "Yes, Amanda was having trouble, and her GP told her to wait like yours has, but she insisted on being referred straight away, and she's just had, twins."

From junior school, I could vaguely remember Amanda, with short, shy, brownish hair and a long-toothed smile. Mother similar but with a strident voice and bulging eyes. *Wherever had Mum dredged this story up from*? I wondered. I now had a mental image of two babies with huge teeth and bulging eyes.

"I just thought you'd like to know. Amanda's happy to have a chat about how she got referred."

Oh no! Not one of Mum's engineered 'chats', I suppressed a shudder. "I barely knew Amanda when we were kids, and that was over twenty years ago, Mum. Glad things worked out for her, but I'm happy to stick with what my GP thinks for now."

Mum sniffed, "Amanda's mum said you can't let these things drift when I told her you were waiting,"

"Good for her. Sorry, Mum, you've caught me as I'm off to work. Call you back later."

Mum tutted, "Always rushing about! One of these days, you'll meet yourself coming back. I'll send you Amanda's number, just in case."

I put down the phone and looked at the dogs. They were more than prepared for a stroll and emerged from their beds, looking lithe as they stretched and yawned. A simple shake of their fur, and they were ready to go. If only my morning routine were that efficient.

"Guys, how do you do this? You put me to shame. At least you don't make pushy phone calls to hold me up first thing. Let's see what your Auntie Pen is up to."

They jostled around me as I slipped on a gilet and some trainers. Bird darted in, eyes alight with mischief, to steal my left shoe, then paraded it in front of me while I tried to lace the right.

"Bird, give. Oh, great slobber in my shoe, yuk." I showed her the shoe, wrinkling my nose.

Unabashed, the guilty party joined Jeeves at the door and the two of them bundled outside. They raised their heads to scent the wind, coal-black coats shiny in the sunlight, tan feathers swishing as they ran towards Pen and Angus' land, which marched with our drive.

A narrow track set at right angles led beside three fields towards their house. Bird and Jeeves ran ahead down the path, now and then ducking through the hedge to run free through the grass fields on the other side. I may have to work late this evening, but it was worth it to have these stolen moments at the start of the day. Today the wheat was golden, ready to harvest, and a light breeze flowed like a gentle tune which prompted the whole crop to shimmy and dance.

The walk gave me time to calm down. Maybe Mum meant well. I just couldn't get rid of the feeling that she was having a five-ring circus of her own down in Portsmouth with my failure to get pregnant as the star attraction.

Pen's farmhouse was built on a slight rise, surrounded by a pretty garden flowering in pink, mauve and cream shades. Hectic herbaceous borders burst with colour still, and an arbour of climbing roses made a lovely feature with its blown flowers and carpet of delicate petals scattered on the ground. The old farm reminded me of the house that Jack built. It had character and a certain charm of its own.

The centre section was ancient and constructed of uneven, hand-made bricks, while the more modern Victorian part had a different pitch to its roof.

Pen waved from the kitchen window and beckoned me in. She had gathered her riot of blonde curls into a ponytail from which numerous cork-screw tendrils escaped already, and the ponytail bobbed behind her as she left the window and headed to the door to let me in.

"Hi Pen, shall I stick the dogs into an empty kennel?"

"Hiya, no, bring them in. Mine are still in the kitchen."

Pen's two pointers were great pals with my Gordon Setters, and I suspected it wouldn't be long before all four heaped together on the dog sofa in an apparent tangle of legs and tails.

"Coffee?"

I smiled, "Yes, please."

Lottie, Pen's toddler, was in her highchair, tackling a bowl of porridge with mixed success. Ignoring the paste glued to her face and hands, she waved a plastic spoon, broke into a wide grin and chanted, "Lellie, Lellie, Lellie,"

"If you think I'm cuddling you with that wallpaper glue all over you, you've got another thing coming."

I headed to the sink, grabbed a facecloth from the pile on the side and dunked it. Then applied the flannel vigorously to the offending cheeks and hands. Lottie blew raspberries into the cloth in protest and emerged pink-cheeked but still smiling.

"Up, Lellie," she wriggled against her harness, and as I set her free and lifted her out, I relished her warm, cuddly softness. So trusting as she relaxed in my arms, a well of love for her bubbled up inside me. Her plump thighs just shaved the edge of the highchair table. I kissed them with loud popping noises to make her giggle and set her down to toddle, wide-legged but determined towards the dogs.

"Gently," Pen cautioned and smiled as Lottie dropped to her haunches and smoothed Jeeves' paw with her hand. "Good girl, now leave them alone. They're sleeping."

She scooped Lottie up and popped her into a playpen filled with toys. "You sure you want to exchange your untrammelled existence for this, Ells?" Her gaze swept around the kitchen; washing, dry but unsorted, was heaped in a pile on the side, two dead pot plants graced the window ledge, and I hadn't noticed initially, but last night's washing-up was still stacked on top of the dishwasher.

"Hard to believe after I was in such a mess about it last year, I know, but yes, I do. If it ever happens, that is." A tiny fist of fear momentarily clutched at me, but I pushed it down.

Pen looked across sympathetically. "Nothing doing yet?"

"No, not yet, and Mum's on the warpath constantly rubbing it in. I'm going to take it a bit easier once Maisie gets back. See if that helps."

She squeezed my hand. "Good plan. You do hit it hard, Ellie. Maybe a bit of a break would help."

I shrugged, "You're probably right. Touch is understaffed without Maisie. The doctor said to keep trying for another six months before there was any need to worry."

Pen pulled a face. "Easier said than done?"

"Yes and no. I'm alright at the moment. Not getting too obsessed. It's just disappointing as each month rolls past. I'm sure we'll be fine."

She shot me an appraising glance but must have decided not to pursue things any further. Instead, she pushed a coffee towards me and said, "Cake?"

The crumbling golden cake, jewelled with dried fruits, was delicious. "You should go into business. This is wonderful."

Pen hesitated just too long before she replied and blushed. I pounced, "Pen Drayton, are you holding out on me?"

"No, not exactly, it's just an idea, but I've thought about starting a small business making afternoon teas, either here or delivered to people's houses. The marquee at your wedding set me thinking, we could easily have something like that here, especially as the garden is looking pretty now."

I nodded, and she continued, "Ideally, if it went well, I'd like Angus to repair the little stable to make a proper venue. I love old china, so I'd like to collect vintage tea sets for it. Do you fancy some trips to the local auctions with me?"

"I think that's a great idea, Pen. There's nowhere to go for a posh tea around here. I reckon that would go down a storm."

She shrugged, "Well, it's all pie in the sky, if you'll pardon the pun, but I'm giving it thought. Angus has the farm, Lottie will be starting nursery soon, and I'd like to do something for myself as well as being a Mum. Is that silly?"

I shook my head, "No, of course, it isn't, I love my job, and I doubt I'll give up if we have a family. You'd be great at hospitality; you're a brilliant cook and always make people feel welcome and relaxed."

The mention of cooking made me realise we'd been so busy chatting; that I had almost forgotten why I'd come. "Before I forget, are you guys free on Saturday evening? Thought you might like to come over to enjoy the patio you helped build, and I was going to ask Dom and Vale too."

She looked genuinely delighted. "That'd be fab. Yes, we'd love to come."

I grinned, "Okay, all settled, we'll see you Saturday. We could get all the business heads together for your idea."

Pen laughed and looked a bit embarrassed. "I think they may be a bit highfalutin for this venture. I'm only talking about a few cakes."

I wasn't having her put herself down. "You never know, from little acorns… You could be the next Betty's, plan for success and all that."

She raised her eyebrows and shrugged. “Now you’re scaring me. Something small would be just fine.”

I glanced at the kitchen clock. “Goodness, Pen, better get going, or I’ll be late for work.”

“No worries, good to see you and look forward to the weekend.”

I called to the dogs, who extracted themselves from the heap of bodies on the sofa, and we set off back across the fields to the barn.

I thought about Pen’s idea as I tramped back. She had hit on something that would be popular, I was sure. I had no doubts about her baking or people skills, but how rigorous she’d be with the business side; I was less confident. The piles of paper that often spilt over her kitchen table came to mind, and I smiled. I wasn’t the best administrator myself, so I needed Sarah.

Mark could help her with that side of things if she decided to go ahead, but I laughed about her thinking Mark’s business was too upmarket for her. He had clients from unorthodox one-man bands to corporate entities, so not precisely ‘highfalutin.’ Maybe Dom, Mark’s best friend from school, could be described as a high-flyer. He was a highly successful entrepreneur but not stuffy for all that.

I pushed the getting pregnant issue to the back of my mind, helped by imagining a new business venture for Pen.

Continue reading Bloom, book 3 in the Ellie Rose Series, due for release in Autumn 2022.

A Note to Readers

If you enjoyed ***Dilemma,*** second in the Ellie Rose Series, please consider leaving a review on Amazon and Goodreads.

Perhaps talk about your favourite character, what you liked best about the story, and why you'd recommend someone to read it. Reviews are vital to authors, as they help other readers to find books they may enjoy.

I read and appreciate every review that is written.

For all my latest news, subscribe to my monthly newsletter, "The Windsinger." And claim the novella 'Paradise,' a prequel to Touch and Dilemma, as a gift.
https://angelacairnsauthor.co.uk/sign-up/

Discover new books, meet authors, enjoy a monthly short story and more.

Or get to know me better on my website and social media pages, links below.

Website: https://www.angelacairnsauthor.co.uk/
Facebook: @angelacairnsauthor
Instagram: @angelacairnsauthor

Warm regards,
Angela Cairns

All Books By The Author

Prequel to the Ellie Rose Series.
A summer love story.

Touch – Volume One of the Ellie Rose Series.
A poignant story of lost love and second chances.

Dilemma – Volume Two of the Ellie Rose Series.
Will past trauma derail Ellie's newfound peace?

Bloom — Volume Three of the Ellie Rose Series.
When longing brings heartache…and the waiting seems endless.

A warm-hearted collection of the author's favourite short stories. Here you will find life, love, laughter and tears. Oh, and a few dogs, of course.

Seasonal Produce: An Anthology of Inspired Short Stories about Seasons of Growth

About the Author

Married with two grown-up sons and a clan of Gordon Setter dogs, ANGELA CAIRNS is an author, broadcaster, physiotherapist, and acupuncturist. She directs two multidisciplinary clinics and lectures in physiotherapy. She has broadcast for twenty years with BBC Essex as their Sound Advice Physiotherapist. Writing has always been part of her life; her first published works, Play Pause Unwind 1 & 2, are collections of relaxation stories with original soundtracks by Simon Ramet. She has had numerous articles and stories in national publications and contributed to the short story anthology "Paths Made by Walking."

Her novels, The Ellie Rose Series, have a rich cast of characters from her imagination. However, their authenticity comes from the privilege of working alongside so many different people as a healthcare practitioner.